I0598326

# Dragon(e) Baby Gone

by

Robert Gainey

**Dragon(e) Baby Gone**

COPYRIGHT © 2021 by Robert Gainey

Cover Art by *Debbie Taylor*

The Wild Rose Press, Inc.
PO Box 708
Adams Basin, NY 14410-0708
Visit us at www.thewildrosepress.com

Publishing History
First Edition, 2021
Trade Paperback ISBN 978-1-5092-3658-9
Digital ISBN 978-1-5092-3659-6

Published in the United States of America

In the movies, car chases are neat, clean affairs where the good guy either catches up to or outruns the bad guy. Anybody involved in a car chase knows just how to corner, accelerate, and time their antics to avoid catastrophe for themselves and minimize it for others. Also, the drivers are always shooting at each other and flattening tires or cracking radiators.

Professionals bring gunmen to do the shooting and usually wait for a clear shot before wasting the bullets. Pro drivers know that all they have to do is follow long enough for their prey to make a mistake, get bogged down in traffic or in a wreck, and then they can just roll up and finish their job. The fact that I was dodging bullets going down Hidden Oak Lane in the middle of broad daylight told me that while the driver might have known what he was doing, the lackeys hanging out the windows did not.

"Hang on," I said, which was useless to a man who was handcuffed and shot, and turned my poor little midsized sedan into a sharper turn than any of its engineers had intended, doubling back up a parallel street, headed back to the main road. I needed about thirty cops to show up and shoot these guys, but at the same time, I needed them to also not shoot me.

Bullets stitched their way across a yard as they missed me and sprayed the plate windows of the house into powdered glass before we were gone from the lives of the owner forever. I snarled, shouting profanity out the window.

## Dedication

For Helen, who keeps my feet on the ground and my head in the clouds.

Chapter One

Radios are garbage when you're thirty feet under an industrial park, crawling through hip-deep sewage, and, until somebody decides to build a cell phone relay into the sewage processing center, it meant that my phone was equally useless. This was assuming the waterproof case was also toxic sludge-proof, and the phone would work when I got back topside. Somehow, I had my doubts. I'd already ruined a perfectly good pair of boots, and if it weren't for the steady beeping of the only electronic device designed to work in the endless winding tunnels, I'd already have turned back and reported the mission a failure. Nobody had expected them to go underground. Whoever the buyers were, they had a serious hard-on for secrecy. The gas mask I wore had a chemical filter to keep the noxious fumes from killing me. It also had a heads-up display with all kinds of neat and unnecessary features, like a compass, ambient temperature gauge, and personal heart-rate monitor. Honestly, this is the sort of equipment the Department of Intangible Assets can't really afford. It just goes to show they'll cough up the cash just to throw Senior Field Agent Diane Morris into the sewers every chance they get. The only sensor I actually cared about was a green blinking light, and accompanying sound playing in my ear, that showed I wasn't far now. With a little luck, this recovery mission would be over soon, and the rest of my night would be spent burning these socks. While I had been up above the street, it had given me a ghostly image of a map to help with navigation. It looked like nobody had bothered to map the miles of subterranean tunnels below the city. I would have to bring it up at the next staff meeting.

The tube that I was squeezed in let out into a wide, cavern-like chamber, some great crossroads of filth, with a dozen other similar pipes leading to it. Large channels of poured concrete funneled all of the pollution of a city into a single, massive hole. This dropped into the processing plant proper. I could hear the churning gears below, but the loudest sound was from frothing, garbage-laden water. If people knew where their reclaimed water came from, they might think twice before running through city sprinklers. The chamber was lit by bare light bulbs strung along the edges, keeping it dim and keeping me concealed in the shadows of the sewer I was crouched within.

There were a half dozen men standing near the edge of the pit, on one of the catwalks that kept maintenance workers from having to trudge through too much filth. They had almost certainly come from the stairs at the far end of that catwalk, although where it came out, I had no clue. I barely knew what part of the city I was under now. I tried to focus enough to see if the men were carrying weapons, but in the gloom, I couldn't make out that level of detail. Maybe instead of having the local weather forecast at the edge of my field of vision, my high-tech gas mask could have had night vision. I'd let the tech boys know what was wrong with their latest equipment.

Six of them, one of me, and fifty feet of open ground between us. That wasn't exactly good odds. I watched as one of them lit a cigarette, and a silver gleam showed a large metal case by his side. It was large enough to fit a child, with plenty of elbow room left over. If the thaumometer readout on my screen was accurate, the case held what I was here for. I grimaced. Why weren't professional thieves a little stupider? They could have stashed it in a dark corner before the deal started, and I could have been gone with it before anybody knew.

I pressed the microphone at my throat. It beeped into my ear, telling me I was attempting to transmit.

"Eagle, this is Squid. Are you receiving?" I only needed to let the barest whisper out to be heard. Outside of my mask, it wouldn't be heard more than three feet away. Still, it wouldn't do to be caught because I was desperate for reinforcements. The plan had been that each agent would pick a direction of the sewers and search until they picked up a signal, close in, and call in the coordinates. It had taken me over an hour of crawling, shuffling, and squeezing through the sewers to make it within line of sight of the thieves, and despite my best efforts, nobody in radio control was answering. I cursed silently. Stupid goddamned thieves, ruining my stupid goddamned weekend.

For a moment, I thought that somebody else had lit a cigarette. From one of the far sewage drains, the largest in the chamber, came a glowing orange light. It began to fill the chamber, a miniature sunrise. The six men standing with the case stiffened visibly and then shuffled into a straight line. They put their backs to the case. Perfect. I eased myself down off the lip of the drain and into the surprisingly deep channel full of muck and sank until I could feel it sliding under my shirt. I fought back the gag rising in my throat and assured myself that when this was over, I would burn everything I was wearing, right down to the sports bra and socks.

The slow current of the channel moved me along, and I hoped that my gas mask looked like a discarded football helmet and not like the best technology that could be crammed into the contract of the lowest government bidder. The light in the tunnel was growing, and by the flicker, it looked like somebody was approaching carrying a torch. How strange. What with all the buildup of flammable gases, most people wouldn't be so stupid. Cigarette smoke drifted from one of the thieves' hands. Okay, so some people could be.

I eased the rotting remains of some kind of bird away from me and braced my feet against the bottom of the channel, stopping a few feet away from the drop-off. The grinding of the machine twenty feet down kept any conversation being had a mystery, but based on their fidgeting and the fact that the smoker was lighting up again for the second time in five minutes, they were anxious to get the transaction over with.

Three figures emerged from the pipe, wrapped from head to toe in low-burning fire. They had bodies the size of toddlers, and their atrophied legs dangled below them as they floated smoothly into the chamber, light spreading campfire-like onto the concrete walls, illuminating the thieves, garbage, and inflowing sewage. I froze, hoping nobody would notice a stationary floating head in the constant stream. These creatures looked like horrifying caricatures of children,

4

with gnarled, almost mangled faces and crooked noses. Hairless, but with deep ridged flesh covering the domes of their bloated heads, they resembled naked mole rats in all but their horrible, red eyes. Where they looked, sweeping red light passed, like floodlights off a searching ship. They seemed to take the entire room in at the same time, focusing on the walls and the ceiling before coming to a rest on the thieves.

Elementals. Just my luck. It couldn't have been mundane buyers looking to acquire powerful assets. No, it had to be somebody that could melt off handcuffs and kill with almost certain impunity. And not just any elementals either: I recognized them as mephits, beings of fire who had a reputation for having more than their fair share of malice and greed.

The leading mephit had a bandoleer of gold that glowed almost white with heat, and he raised one clawed hand and gestured at the thieves. He never opened his mouth, but his presence forced its way into my brain.

*I will accept the agreed-upon item at this time.* I shuddered. The thoughts came as if they were my own, but they felt greasy and wrong, like an unwanted memory of some shameful childhood moment. It was like being nine all over again and thinking that invisible ink would take juice stains out of my parents' sitting room rug.

One of the humans broke rank and stepped forward. He was talking, though his words were ground up in the machinery along with the rest of the garbage. I grunted. If I was going to move, now was the time. As he spoke, I let myself drift all the way to the precipice and slipped my gloved hands to the edge of the pit. If I could position myself directly behind them, I might haul myself up enough to grab the case and slip away before anybody noticed.

I slung my weight out over the void and tried not to picture the fact that my feet were maybe fourteen feet off the tops of an industrial grinding machine that was designed to turn organic materials into an easily filtered milkshake material.

*We have brought the agreed-upon price. It will be produced only after you have left our presence, at the agreed-upon location.* More thoughts invading my mind, but I brushed them aside. Extraplanar creatures, that is, creatures from one of our neighboring planes of existence, sometimes choose to broadcast their thoughts in a way that receiving creatures are forced to understand, but that didn't mean they knew I was present. It was more or less a radio transmission, and a radio transmitter has no way of knowing how many radios are tuning in. And just like my useless radio, their thoughts wouldn't project any farther than the stones surrounding us.

I managed to work my way around the lip of the pit by my fingertips alone and crawled up onto the ground below the catwalk. Steel mesh was just inches above my crouched head, and the case would be within arm's reach as soon as I stood up. I took a slow, deep breath.

*There will be no further negotiation. It has been out of courtesy that we do not take the case from you and leave your flesh as ash.* Uh-oh. Looks like somebody thought they could try to squeeze the elementals for more cash.

"All right, all right. Can't blame a guy for trying. Give him the case, Tony." I could finally hear the

Jersey accent of the smoking thief, and I saw feet turn and take a step toward the case.

Tony hadn't been surprised by the appearance of the mephits, but he wasn't expecting a slime-covered monster to jump over the railing and kick him flat in the chest. He let out a shocked cry as he fell into his comrades, and I landed on my soggy boots, dripping still with scum and sludge and who knows what else. Their spokesman half-turned to face me, surprised that his order hadn't already been executed, cigarette dangling on his lower lip. As my hand closed around the case handle, he let out a squealing shriek just before his torso exploded in a flood of steam and gore. I dove to the side, hauling the surprising weight of the metal case with me, hoping the contents were well padded or at least tough enough to handle a little beating. The horror of what was unfolding was something I was desperate to get away from.

The lead mephit already had his mouth open, and once where there were tiny, pursed lips, now a gaping maw of blackened obsidian teeth and fire took up most of the elemental's head. The jet of heat that had erupted would have taken me if it hadn't first needed to cook its way through somebody else. As it was, the thermometer on my gas mask was flashing an ambient temperature that might have been a cold day on the sun, and I could feel the nylon of my shirt shrink against my skin from the heat. My thaumometer buzzed aggressively against the side of my head in the presence of such a display of anomalous power. Slowly, the mouth closed, and the flames that covered the creature's body receded. The other two, however, turned their heads toward me, and now I could see their bodies glowing blue as they prepared to turn me into my own personal Thanksgiving turkey.

"Fuck this noise!" I hauled on the case and hit the steps running. The stairs above me cut a path through solid concrete. Once I was out of line of sight of the death-dealing heat monsters, I could consider a real plan.

I felt the stairwell shudder under me, then lean drunkenly to one side. I wasn't halfway to the top of the first landing, and if I hadn't paused when the ground started shifting, then instead of just watching the metal in front of me turn orange, red, white, and then into liquid, I would have had the novel experience of feeling my guts turn into boiling stew. Unfortunately, while some elementals are dumb as stumps (and in fact, are little more than mobile stumps), mephits are smart enough to think four seconds into the future. They'd neatly cut the stairs from all supporting structures, and I had enough time to catch my breath before it was knocked out of me and I was tossed into one of the channels of sewage.

I didn't even try to surface immediately. I plunged farther down into the muck, sure that nobody could see through what could only loosely be described as water and used the concrete walls to push myself against the current toward the pipe it poured from. A gas mask is not an underwater rebreather, and it wasn't long before my lungs had decided they'd had enough. Thanks to the miracle of modern technology, I could see my heart rate climbing, my oxygen levels dropping, and the temperature of the sewage climbing as pure elemental energy poured into my surroundings.

I popped out of the water and tried to take a breath,

and found all the filters clogged with sludge. My goggles were impossibly smeared with slime. I grabbed under the chin and wrenched it from my head, throwing it aside as I jumped up out of the sludge.

I felt a tug pass under my hair and heard the gunshot. Apparently the other thieves had decided they would rather kill me than take their chances against a supernatural nightmare. The bullets mostly came nowhere near me, spalling the floor, walls, ceiling as they opened up with their pistols. I was happy for them. After all, every time the mephits opened their dickholsters and fired off a blast of heat, they depleted whatever amount of energy they had brought over from the other side. As that occurred to me, a wide trench of concrete blackened and began exploding large chunks like popcorn. I didn't stop running, though, and swept the metal case between me and the onslaught.

*Kill the woman, do not touch the case!* The blast of thought must have shocked the gunmen enough to make them stop, and I threw the case ahead of me into the pipe and dove after it. The world's nastiest slip'n'slide let me skid out of sight, just as the gunfire opened back up again.

"This is bullshit!" I cried, shoving the case ahead of me as I peeled a tear gas grenade off my belt and chucked it toward the drain chamber. The first stinging whiff hit my face, and I coughed it away, adding to my scuttling crabwalk away from the danger. My gas mask would have let me dance my way through that cloud without problems, but wishing for it now was about the same as wishing that I had a unicorn to ride a rainbow out of the hellhole that was my life at the moment.

"Eagle, this is Squid. Eagle, this is Squid. I hope

you can fucking hear me!" The microphone was supposed to be failsafe, but I wouldn't be surprised by my luck if I'd pulled the wires apart in my struggle to keep my ass from bursting into flame.

"She went this way!" came a shout, followed by hacking coughs as the morons ran right into my tear gas. I think that if I was being generous, I'd call them criminals. No, their ringleader had been a criminal. These were the goons. But motivated goons they were, because I could hear their sloshing movement.

I careened off a corner and snatched the case out of the filth, running with high knees to get better movement. Sneaking out was becoming less of an option and more of a sewer pipe dream, so I continued to yammer into my microphone as I alternated taking left and right turns, hoping to confuse my pursuit. If I didn't know where I was going, how could they?

I heard a furious sound, a freight train of burning wind, and dove face down into the muck. I cracked my head on a cinderblock buried inches below the water and felt the heat wash over me, my head aflame. I screamed, mouth filling with the worst thing that could possibly be put in it. So much for throwing off the pursuit. I came up, forced to catch a hot, moist breath of vaporized garbage and atomized concrete, and I saw one of the mephits floating toward me. It bobbed in the air as if riding unseen currents of water and held both arms out for me. Fifty feet away and terrifying, its mouth was closing, and the fire that ran along its body was returning to normal. Maybe there was less of it than there had been initially. I've heard that weak mephits only have enough juice for two or three good blasts. This one looked like it had eaten napalm for breakfast.

I brushed my head, saw blood mixed in with brown sludge, and let out a hysterical laugh. If I managed to get away from the supernatural death about to be dealt my way, I could look forward to some super fungus burrowing into my brains. My legs began churning, trying to push me back away from the oncoming mephit, but the bottom of the concrete pipe was smooth and slick with algae. I hope it was algae.

*Give in.* The voice seemed to caress my brain, and I shuddered. Those long, spindly fingers were closing in, and I knew that if any of the three fingers touched me, it would incinerate me before I could scream for help. All things considered, a pretty fast and clean way to go.

"Fuck you," I growled and shoved the case toward the creature. If it had a moment to consider it, maybe it would have thought that I was offering it as a compromise. It wouldn't have worked. It would have killed me simply for witnessing it. No, for lack of a better weapon, I used the case's widest side as a paddle and shoveled a wall of toxic waste at it. After all, it had to get close enough to grab me since it seemed to be hesitant about overusing its heat beam. It recoiled, but not before its entire lower half was drenched in the contents of a hundred thousand toilets.

The sizzling sound alone would have told you that elementals consisting almost entirely of fire and fire-related products don't like water-based materials. Oh, sure, if I had hit it with a squirt gun, it would have annoyed it the way that pollen annoys most people. Instead, it reacted like a bee sting for a severely allergic fat man.

Its abdomen began to swell at an alarming rate, and the force of the swelling craned its neck up until its chin pointed at the ceiling. Its mouth opened in a silent scream, and the pipes above began to crack with the heat being poured out as the water content of the sewage squeezed every drop of latent elemental energy from the husk that made up the mephit. It was nothing so kind or gentle as forcing the mephit to return home, to the place that had given it life and thought. No, it was being shoved bit by bit through an opening and ground like meat into sausage that my lovely reality would eat up.

The heat cooked my face, and I could feel eyebrows and eyelashes curling back. I forced my feet under me and began my run again, stumbling on the debris that seemed to fill this tunnel, wiping blood from my eyes as I went, hoping to find anything resembling a ladder. There had to be a manhole or something. I'd rather risk being hit by a bus than staying another minute underground.

"Get her!" somebody shouted, from a completely different direction, as soon as I set foot into a four-way intersection. Gunfire erupted, and I just kept right on running, wondering what kind of moron thinks that "Get her" is the way to start an ambush. I reminded myself that crime at their level didn't attract the best and brightest minds available. Thank Christ for that.

Stairs. Stairs leading up. Hell to the yes. I bounded up them, stumbling with uneven concrete steps, and hit the door full-on, bouncing it nearly out of the warped wooden frame and bursting into a storage room. I saw another door on the other side and didn't even pause to slam the door all the way shut before pulling a set of shelves down over it. People that would slow down. Mephits would torch through so fast it wasn't funny.

"This is Squid, Squid to Eagle, come in Eagle!" I shouted, hoping that wherever I was now, it wasn't going to be so lethal for my radio. The storage room was full of shelving units like the one I'd just toppled, and aside from a couple lights on the ceiling and a fire extinguisher mounted next to each door, there was nothing else in the room.

Static fed back, and then, "This is Eagle. We read you loud and clear." Oh man, small miracles are the best miracles. I was at the second door, and this one was sturdier, metal, and locked. I set the case down and pulled out a toolkit from my belt.

"I have the package with me, have encountered hostile natives and even more hostile tourists," I said, trying to keep my gasping breath out of the transmission. Blood fell in fat drops onto my hands as I undid the paneling around the door's push-button lock. "Location, unknown. Out of the sewers, in a storage room." I glanced around for a moment and turned my attention back on my work. Trying to work fast was a good way to get no work done, but it was hard when I knew that the pursuit wasn't going to give up because I'd gone through a mere door. "No indication of location or purpose of storage."

"We copy that. We show you in a junction within the waste treatment plant. Confirm location?"

"Negative. Tracking device was part of inoperable equipment, no longer on person." I eased a lock pick forward, touching one pin after the other as I held them in place using a tension rod. Simple lock. Easy to open under ideal circumstances. It didn't help that now I needed both hands and one of my eyes was effectively glued shut with bloody slime. Just my kind of ideal circumstances.

The goons didn't even have the decency to knock before they slammed into the meager barricade, and I heard one let out a yell as he bounced off. He must have tumbled off the stairs and back down into the cesspool because his yell cut off abruptly. Then the banging continued at a more subdued pace.

"Come on, come on," I muttered, holding a penlight in my mouth like a cigar as another pin slid into place. Triumphantly, I forced the last pin and turned the lock open just as the room filled with smoke and the smell of melting aluminum shelving. I threw the door open and started stepping through. My leading foot hit the spot it thought there would still be floor, only to find empty space. Survival instincts screamed in terror, flinging my arms out mindlessly, heavy case still in one fist. The melted remains of stairs clung to the edge of the concrete, and beneath me, thirty feet of sour air down, was the gaping maw of the industrial grinder.

"Well…shit," I said, turning as two mephits and three men came into the room. The men looked terrified, staring more at the mephits than at me. The mephits floated apart from each other, and if their tiny, scrunched up faces looked furious, well, maybe they'd found the bloated corpse of their buddy before it washed down the drains.

"Take a step, and me and the case gets to find out what it's like to go through a food processor," I said and held the case against my chest.

*Return it to us and live. You have no part of this.*

I decided to try a little reasoning with the mere

mortals, shaking in their boots.

"Do you have any idea what kind of shit you're going to be in? Whether or not you get this case, and whether or not it's me who rains it down on you. Best case, I take you all in, and you're put someplace where you can't find any more trouble. Better still, someplace where trouble can't find you."

"We need to kill her before anybody else finds us," one of the goons suggested and boldly took a step toward me. I leaned my body out the door, grasping the frame in one hand, and dangled one leg and the case out over the pit. It was far enough up that I would be able to take a breath, scream for a bit, and take another breath before I hit. Maybe I'd hit hard enough to knock myself out before the grinder began turning me into mulch. If my luck stayed the same, I'd hit it, get ground up to my knees, and the machine would break. Maybe I'd be eaten alive by rats too.

"My boss doesn't put a huge priority on my well-being." That was a little harsh, I suppose, but I wasn't exactly feeling generous. "See if I don't make this unpleasant for all of us. I'm warning you, I'm a screamer."

"Fucking bitch," Brave Goon snarled and charged at me. I'll bet he thought I was bluffing and that he could get the case out of my hands when I chickened out. What a real critical thinker he must have been. Why on earth he thought to run full tilt at what amounted to a cliff's edge, I'll never know.

I swung the case as he neared and took him under the chin with the corner, driving him off his feet. Unfortunately for him, his forward momentum was too great to overcome, and he hit the floor with his back and slid out of the room and into the empty void. Luckily, he had been going fast enough to arc over the actual grinder and only fell a bone-crunching fifty feet to one of the dry, unforgiving concrete slabs below. Judging by his silence, he had decided to contemplate the mistake he'd just made. Goons. I swear.

I danced back to my perch halfway out of the doorway and stared down the mephits. The room wasn't equipped with a convenient sprinkler with which to rain down a deterrent against them. Not to mention the fact that the other goons had learned from their comrade's mistake, and now they looked more than happy to let the heavier metaphysical/literal firepower handle things.

*This need not end with your death.* One of the mephits moved a few feet closer to me, drifting through the air with almost careless direction, like a balloon on some unseen and weak wind. I stared at its alien and unknowable eyes, trying to anticipate what it might do next. Surely it wouldn't risk damaging something that it had used all kinds of power to try and obtain. Transitioning from another plane was incredibly difficult and time consuming. For tourists like mephits, just being on the Prime Plane was as dangerous as juggling nitroglycerine.

"What the hell is in this case?" I didn't normally care unless it became relevant, but under the circumstances, I thought it had some bearing on the situation. "You're effectively immortal if you stay in the Firelands, so why would you risk a messy end in a place just chock full of water and earth?" Technically, concrete didn't qualify as elemental-grade earth. Too precisely manufactured, too much of mankind's imprint on it. "And why would you use such useless morons to get it and move it for you?" One of the goons sputtered and made an indignant noise.

*You will live without knowing or die trying to find out. It matters very little.*

"All right, you leave me no choice," I said and stepped away from the edge. My heart sank back out of my throat, and I set the case down behind me. I glanced around the room, hoping to see another exit I could exploit, but it looked like my only way out was the same way I entered.

*Surrender is the best option,* the mephit said and floated a little closer. If it got its hand on the case, it could vanish, snapping back to its own version of reality like a rubber band let loose by a schoolyard bully, never to be seen or heard from again. I spread my hands, and the goons relaxed, lowering their firearms. The mephit took its time and approached with caution, but with no visible weapons in my hands, it must have felt pretty safe. If it had been more familiar with human beings, maybe it would have recognized a smirk as opposed to a smile.

I wrapped my hand around the handle of the mounted fire extinguisher beside the door, luckily a required feature for city-operated storage rooms. I clawed the pin from the canister, wrenched loose the nozzle, and shoved it at the mephit. I had one chance, and one chance only. If a cloud of powder came out of the nozzle, I would either die by fire or I would have enough time to throw myself and the case to a slightly more useful end.

It looked like white steam hitting the mephit full in its face. It didn't matter how cold the gas was, really, although it did coat the mephit with a layer of frost. What mattered was that refined carbon dioxide, a natural and abundant gas, was not only one of the best choices for putting out fires, but also an excellent representative of elemental air. Not just because it's on the periodic table, but because of its purity. I've always thought it was a little strange that just plain old breathable air wasn't a better representative, but any refined component was the same as fire, water, or dirt in its application. Air was trickier because purity was important, but it was incredibly effective.

The effect was immediate. The mephit shriveled, its fire going out without any hesitation, and it hit the ground covered in a layer of crystal ice, far more than should have occurred after just a little exposure. I didn't let up on the extinguisher just because one of the mephits was down. I tucked my head and charged forward, blowing out even more extinguisher in as wide an arc as I could. The cold condensation of gas threw up a fog between me, the gunmen, and the last remaining mephit. Gunfire sounded, but I was already on top of them, and as the last of the fire extinguisher sputtered out, I hefted it in one hand and cracked a goon in the chest as hard as I could. I drove a knee hard into the other's crotch, and they both went down. I slid across the last part of the room, grabbed the second extinguisher from its mount beside the destroyed door, and spun to aim at the other mephit.

Its mouth was just beginning to open, and I jerked my hand, squeezing with all my might. All of the air seemed to be pulled from my lungs as two raw elements met each other. Pressure built behind my eyes, and where the opposing forces were meeting, a firestorm of blazing winds swirled, lashing out at the rest of the room, driving fissures into concrete and melting apart metal shelves. The incredible urge to drop the canister in my hand and run was overwhelming, but I knew that my only chance of survival was to stay in the little eye of the storm I had created and pray that the mephit had already used up too much power to overwhelm me now.

The first sputter of the extinguisher before it emptied resulted in a wave of heat washing over me so intense that I could feel sunburn rising on every inch of exposed skin on my head. The extinguisher burped again, and I ducked my head. It felt like my hair had caught fire. I smelled the pungent aroma as it burned. Plastic began to melt on my gear, and I could feel the metal buckles become scalding. For a brief moment, I wondered whether my metal fillings would melt and make identifying me impossible.

Then it was over. My extinguisher had nothing left to give, and I stood there in a room scoured clean of anything combustible, heaving to breathe air that would have been too hot for desert nomads. The extinguisher slipped from my boneless hand. I barely held myself up as the steaming air cleared of the nascent energies. Of the last mephit there was no trace, though there was a perfect circle on both floor and ceiling above it that was free from scorch marks or other damage. It must have been where it had been protecting itself.

Two vaguely human piles of ash and bone were curled on the floor, and I stepped over them, staggering toward the case, still sitting without damage at the entrance. That's the nice thing about these kinds of events: they have a sphere of influence, and even though the amount of energy being used was impressive for such a small scale, it hadn't gone farther than ten feet from the epicenter. I counted myself lucky, grabbed the case, and went looking for an exit.

Chapter Two

It was four in the morning by the time I made it back, and the only person I saw after I got off the elevator was the wizard who works in the basement copy room. If Rubin the Pontiferous thought that my appearance was strange, he said nothing. Maybe the sight of me with my burnt, frizzing hair, almost complete lack of eyebrows, and full-body coating of now-dry filth was what kept him from saying good morning, or, like was often the case, maybe he was too busy pondering whatever it is that wizards ponder to notice. I limped along, carrying the case as my ruined boots ground dirt into the freshly cleaned carpets. I think on Thursdays the cleaning crew comes in sometime after midnight, so everybody would have all day to wonder about the conspicuous trail of what would at best be dirt and ash.

I'd come up a couple blocks away from where I'd gone into the sewers, and since my headset was only receiving static and my microphone cord had melted through entirely, I had flagged down a cab, paid generously in advance for the cleaning, and hoped no further surprises came at me during the ride. Somewhere, a collection crew would be trying to get in contact with me. Search parties would be combing the sewers. Until I talked to my boss, nobody would know that I was even alive. Except for Rubin, but I doubted he knew how to operate a phone, and I knew he didn't care enough to report my whereabouts.

The lights were off in most of the offices, but not mine where I'd been working only a few hours before. If I had it my way, I would only do paperwork. Leave the fieldwork to the stupid and crazy. It had been nice, coordinating with local law enforcement to track down those thieves, and even if I was commissioned as a field agent, it didn't take long for the veneer to wear off, exposing what a pile of shit fieldwork was.

The Director of Field Operations had a corner office, large enough to reflect his status, though perhaps not large enough to accommodate his stature. A modest brass plate on a wooden door of unspecified grain proclaimed his title and name: Director Jermaine LaFleur. LaFleur, known by his employees as Flowers, or sometimes Flower Power when nobody important was nearby, always kept his door shut. Even as I marched up to it as if about to storm Normandy, I knew better than to barge in. I stopped at the threshold and took a deep breath to compose myself and tighten the strip of cloth across my head wound. I figured it would undermine my whole intimidating approach if I had to wipe blood from my eyes every few seconds. I glanced at the doorjamb, anonymous wood of the same kind as the door itself, and engraved skillfully with Latin script and esoteric symbols. I stood there for a moment and knocked twice.

"Come in," the director's baritone voice called from inside. The door swung open. I stepped through and approached the huge slab of mahogany my boss called a desk, ignoring the two fat leather chairs there. I felt some satisfaction in knowing that he was going to have to be disturbed by the cleaning crew if he wanted his beige carpet to be clean ever again.

"Good morning, Agent Morris. I see you've had an eventful night." He sounded amused, if only a little. The director was a massive man, and under his giant, folded hands, even his huge desk looked like nothing more than a child's writing table. Huge and bald, he kept his ebony skin clean shaven at all hours. A creeping tattoo swirled up and around his left ear, and on the opposite side he wore a simple silver loop. As always he wore a dark suit with a dark tie, and it showed no signs that it was anything but freshly pressed. If he had been up all night, he gave no indication.

"That's one way of putting it," I said and slammed the case onto his desk, throwing a stack of papers to the floor and knocking over his little cup full of pens. I'd have gotten more than a little satisfaction if I had startled him, but he simply moved his hands before the case would have hit him.

"Would you like to submit a report in writing?"

"Not yet. I thought I'd just come in here and shout at you for a little while." I was grinding my teeth to keep from raising my voice. "I thought you said that this was a simple heist. A powerful object. Nothing higher than a three-two, three-three yellow severity. Being dealt between two *native* parties. Maybe Russian occultists, maybe Mayan witch doctors, that's what you said. I remember, because it was ten goddamned hours ago."

"We had no information about any local planar travel. Things can be missed, even by us. You know that."

"Well if I didn't before, I do now! Three mephits don't just appear out of nowhere, and goons don't accidentally contact them to sell whatever the hell is in this case. We're lucky the cops saw them duck into that access shaft, otherwise we'd never have gotten there in time." I laughed a little and shook my head. "Oops, did I say we'd never have gotten there? I meant that *I* would never have gotten there. Six agents underground, and I don't have any equipment that can contact them until I'm practically on the surface?"

"I have great faith in all of my agents to make the best of bad situations. Would you prefer that I send the police down to search?"

"Of course not. They'd have shot first and been incinerated second. Oh, by the way." I drew my still-damp pistol and set it on the case. "There's a reason that I didn't fire a shot down there. Logistics won't appropriate cold iron, silver, or ironwood bullets without approval from a senior administrator or a signed DS-408. Oh, but wait, you won't let me transfer to Logistics! And what was that on my desk when I walked past it just now? A report that I did two weeks ago, requesting standard essential equipment be issued to all active field agents, covering basic needs. And guess what?"

"What?"

"It was denied because apparently a field agent can't request their own goddamned specialty ammunition. Not even ironwood rounds, which, by the way, actually *do* grow on trees!"

"Ironwood rounds wouldn't have helped you against the mephits. They might have dealt with the thieves themselves, but your standard rounds are more than enough to deal with them."

"But not the mephits. One cold iron round apiece, all I have to do is get a solid hit. I could have gotten them from fifty feet away before they pinpointed my location, and then I promise I'd have switched to hollow points and taken down the rest. I got lucky with the elementals, and if any of the human operators had been smart, I'd be talking to you through a séance."

"How did you deal with the mephits?" I paused before answering. It was one thing for him to let me vent at him. It was another thing entirely when he asked me a direct, official question.

"I managed to soak one with sewage. There was enough water to wring out the elemental's power. The other two I hit with a fire extinguisher, crystallizing one and maybe evaporating the other, but I doubt it. I think he rebounded back home before he ran out of juice. It was lucky he did, because I was about two seconds from being charcoal."

"And the thieves?"

"The mephits got one trying to get to me in the initial confusion. One fell from the storage room, maybe dead, maybe alive. Two cooked after I knocked them down while engaging the mephits, and I'm not very sorry to say that the collateral damage couldn't be avoided. There was a fifth, but I don't know where he went. Maybe he got lost in the sewers, maybe he ran after seeing his boss get turned into an overcooked Hot Pocket." The director nodded and wrote something on a pad at the edge of his desk. I had a feeling that the missing fifth man wouldn't be missing for long. "Whatever's in the case, they must have been crazy to get their scaly little hands on it, because the only thing that stopped them from vaporizing me was the fact that I was dangling myself with the case over an industrial grinder."

"I'd like your report on my desk by the end of the day." He straightened the case on his desk and inspected the lock.

"I'll have it for you when I have it for you," I snarled. "I need to get my goddamned head examined first, start antibiotics for whatever infection is about to eat my brains, and get changed into some real clothes."

"I'm sure I'll be hearing about it from the custodial staff," the director mused and lifted the lid to the case just barely enough to see inside. Warm, amber light oozed out, illuminating his face, and his hard features compressed into a frown.

"This was the only case present?"

"The only one I saw. Tell me it isn't the wrong one." I could handle dangerous missions that ended successfully, as long as the success was real and not a false flag operation.

"There's still an object in the field to recover." He sounded like he'd rather be chewing up roofing nails than seeing the contents of the case.

"Well? What is it?" I asked. He glanced at me for a moment, as if to tell me that I knew better than to ask. I crossed my arms stubbornly. "No, not this time, boss. If it's a diamond the size of a grapefruit or some ancient occult artifact, I need to know the difference when I go back out. It's not like it's just going to be in an identical case being carried by the same idiots."

"How long have you been in this department?" he asked. That amber glow emanating from the case seemed to change in intensity, slowly growing and fading every few moments. Like a very soothing night light.

"It'll be seven years in August." Saying that felt weird. It felt like twice as long, and I had the scars to support the theory. Then again, thinking about it, all the memories didn't seem to fill the space quite right. Time's a weird thing.

"I've never known you to ask questions above your pay grade. You've always known where you stood. Where the line was."

"If you tell me that this is beyond me, that's fine, but I don't want to find myself hip deep in wizards, warlocks, or witches who might come climbing out of the woodwork for this case. Especially not because I didn't ask what I was getting myself into."

Director LaFleur nodded and stood. He ran one massive hand over his bald head. Was he wiping sweat away? I'd never seen him sweat. Not even when I was twenty-two years old, in the middle of a Texas summer, and he'd pulled me out of a burning barn. No sweat then. Sweat now? I suddenly wished I'd kept my mouth shut. I wanted to stop him from turning the case to face me.

The burnished, brassy light washed over me. A crawling cold tingle started at my feet, chewed its way up my spine, and settled into my scalp.

"Tell me that's not real." A scarlet, almost blood-red orb sat on a custom-fit cushion. Light emanated from its semi-translucent surface. I could see the vaguest shape of something within, something that might have been just barely moving.

"You've seen one?" he asked.

"I read a description, with a picture," I said. It

hadn't been a polaroid, but a very old hand-drawn sketch, probably from memory. The description that had gone alongside it had described the surface as "pebbled, as if embedded with hundreds of river-worn rocks." Maybe his experience had been different from mine, but I didn't see that. It just looked like asphalt. Fresh asphalt, with the tar showing light through a thin surface, but the heavier particles on the surface like armor.

"One of Merlin's accounts?"

"No. Sigurd." Why were we having this conversation? He had to know how bad this was, how dangerous this case was to even have been near. I felt sick. I had been about to drop this into a grinder pump to be processed into the city's outgoing waste. It would have left a smoldering crater where Jacksonville used to sit, slowly being filled by the river.

"I didn't know you read Old Norse runestones."

"I don't. I had access to one of the translations for a while." I realized that I had backed away from the case, from the desk, and was nearing the door. Well, if I was going to turn to run and move to the remotest part of Mongolia I could find, it was time to do it. Either that or stand and see if LaFleur had a plan. Christ, I hoped he had one. I could see something shift within the orb. A tiny form, stirring in its sleep, still small and harmless, contained in the shell of an egg.

"Very fortunate, indeed, that you read Sigurd's accounts. He had firsthand experience with just this situation."

"I'm not Sigurd." I paused and looked more closely at the egg in the box. I stared hard, trying to see if I'd cracked it while I'd used it to bludgeon my way through the sewers. "Did you know what it was before you sent me?" The surface showed no signs of damage. It was, after all, very durable.

"No. I had my suspicions on what it could be, but this was the last thing I feared. Something to consider: anybody stupid and capable enough to steal from the clutch would have taken both eggs." I sucked air through my teeth. He was right. Taking one would have the same reaction as taking both of them. Even knowing where the nest was could bring a quick end to a mortal's life.

"Whose are they?" I asked. He cleared his throat and brought out a piece of paper from his desk and wrote nine letters in his perfect, block print.

*Ziraxariz.*

Brood Mother of the Black Dragons.

"Well...shit." No wonder he hadn't said her name aloud. There was the chance, just the barest chance, that it would draw her attention. To the room, outside her lair, where one of her eggs was being held by two filthy mortals. "I guess I'd better get after that last thief then."

"We should consider ourselves fortunate that he survived, because it's possible that they had the other hidden away and were going to release the information following the deal. If nobody is left alive who knows the other egg's whereabouts, we have no chance of finding it before she stirs from her slumber and finds them missing."

"When was the last time she opened an eye?" I asked. "Please tell me it was a month ago and everything was fine then." Slumbering dragons didn't really wake up, not all the way, but a reflex made them open an eye and take stock of their lair every now and then. Sigurd indicated that this happened roughly every twelve months or so. Less, if something disturbed them.

"Given her extraordinary tendency to be unpleasant to mortals, there can be no actual confirmation. Nobody willingly enters her lair, let alone explores all the way to her sleeping form. The histories suggest that she only stirs once every year, sometime near the summer solstice. Something about being restless in the season she despises."

"Oh good. Any time now." I shook my head. "She's going to wakey wakey, shake and bakey, and then we've got a pissed-off mother of dragons on our hands."

"This is going to become our only priority until this situation is resolved." The director closed the case and very gingerly set it on the floor beside his chair. His forehead was beaded now with tiny droplets of moisture, and I felt bile rising in my throat. There was a reason that dragons held a permanent, terrifying fascination in culture, despite having been out of sight for all of modern history. The last time they'd roamed the earth, they'd left a deep, scarred imprint on our collective memory. It's actually the reason so many people have phobias of snakes. A striking resemblance, or so I read.

"I'm dead on my feet, sir. I need a few hours of sleep, a shower, stitches." I dabbed at my forehead. At least it had stopped bleeding. The thick, crusty scab that had formed was still full of muck and grime.

"I'll put every agent I can on finding this thief. Agent Rowlings will see what his contact in the Plane of Fire can find out about the deal, and in the morning, I'll let you know where you'll be heading."

"Yes, sir," I said.

"Try to get some rest. I have the feeling that the next few days are going to be very busy." Yeah. Get some rest. It's easy to sleep when all you can imagine is being melted in dragonfire.

I'd spent my night hip-deep in human waste, and it still wasn't going to be the shittiest day of my week.

Chapter Three

I guess there's always been a Department of Intangible Assets, in some way or another, since humanity first banded together against the dark. Ancient orders of knights, sects of religions, monasteries and their like had been the first real organizations determined to hold off the things that bled into our world from other realities. Great and epic individuals did a lot of work in the past, though more often than not mere pawns as one ultra-powerful being played against another. Gilgamesh. Solomon. Miyamoto Musashi for a while even worked as a kind of Japanese defender against the supernatural. Things must have been easier back then. If somebody had a problem with a corpse rising from the ground and eating people, or with creatures slinking out of the mountains and taking children, they could talk openly about it, and people would fit it neatly into whatever cultural narrative they had. No press releases concerning carbon monoxide leaks, no awkward local police trying to stutter their way through an ogre rampage by blaming gang violence and drugs. If you were a seventeenth-century farmer in the Tajima Province of Japan and tengu started picking off your village one by one, Musashi would come by one day, cut down all those dark spirits, and then leave. You'd replant your fields, mourn your losses, and tell warning stories about warding off evil. And, probably, pay him whatever he wanted.

Modern times gave way to a general idea that reason and logic were enough to stop something from dragging you into the sewers and wearing your skin to protect itself from daylight. It's easy to see why: it doesn't happen to a lot of people, therefore it must not happen. I see it all the time, people who say things like "I've never seen a ghost, so they must not exist."

Oh yeah? Because if spirits did exist, they'd all be tripping over their ghost dicks to haunt you? Do you understand the preternatural forces that conspire, the circumstances that line up, to create any kind of ghost? Let alone one that shows up in your room at night and moans about revenge or betrayal or rattles some chains and teaches you a valuable lesson about being selfish?

"Well, there's no such thing as Bigfoot. All those pictures are super blurry and grainy," they say, their voices nasally and snobby, like all the knowledge of the world is pumped directly into their tiny brains through their tiny phones. I don't care to get into whether or not any of the literally thousands of kinds of entities that flit in and out of forests would like to be called "Bigfoot," but just because you haven't left your couch in twenty years doesn't mean there's not something out there you don't understand. Go stand out in a remote Colorado forest one night. Turn off your phone, open your eyes and ears, and wait. When you feel those eyes watching, and when you know, deep in that primitive monkey brain, way, way down inside, that there's more than just the animals you have names for sharing that clearing with you, then you can call me to tell me that there's no such thing as Bigfoot.

That is, if you live to turn your phone back on again.

I've got a badge that says that I work for the FBI, and that I'm a special agent. I'm not Scully, and I don't hang out with Mulder. I don't look for aliens in the sky or anywhere among us. The visitors that I look for aren't from other worlds—they're from other places. The other Planes of Existence, some of which are elemental in nature and some of which are representative of other fundamental parts of reality. Light and dark. Order and chaos. Positive and negative. There may be an infinite number of these Planes of Existence, and some are so close to our own, with a balance of all the energies bleeding over from the rest, that if you put a gas station and a burger joint on one, some people would never know the difference. The rest…well, not so much.

I've never been to the Plane of Fire, just like I've never been to the center of the Sun. Not many humans have. It's hard to survive a trip to a place where every atom is in the process of being combusted and reformed to be combusted again. Not like the other planes are a picnic either. The Plane of Air sounds like a great place, until you consider what an infinite realm of different air pressures, gases, and temperatures turns into: storms the size of Jupiter, raging and churning, with tiny, tiny pockets of calm that come and go as fast as a breeze.

But just because I've never left my own reality doesn't mean that I don't know the others exist. Just like the mephits, every other plane has their own denizens. Some are intelligent and can communicate, and some are even friendly in their own way. Others are violent, cruel, and conniving. And then there are just predators that leak through, taking easy victims when pickings get too slim where they're from.

And that's why I have my badge. As a senior field agent in the Department of Intangible Assets of the FBI, I'm a lot like the Senior Rodeo Clown. My job is to distract the bulls long enough to wear them down and to get them back to their pens before they hurt somebody. There's a lot of code words and slang, mostly because if you spend your entire life talking about mermaids and goblins, you'd stop taking it seriously because those things have been so trivialized that nobody in the modern age can really separate them from the fairy tales. Anything from another reality is a tourist. Anything from good old Prime Plane is a native. I'm a native. Then again, so is Ziraxariz. Native doesn't mean nice.

****

About the time I got down the hall to my office, I'd managed to force the little queasy ball of panic into the back of my throat and swallow it. A quick tap on my keypad unlocked my office, and the little whoosh of wind as I opened it told me that the room's positive pressure seal, meant to keep all sorts of things out, hadn't been broken since the last time I'd gone in. I locked the door behind me and headed right into my bathroom. No measly half-bath, with an overshared toilet and a cheap, plastic sink. Being senior field agent has its perks. A full shower with frosted glass windows was waiting to embrace my filthy form, and I resisted the urge to simply walk into it and let the hot water clean my equipment as well. I unfolded a little table I kept in the corner for just such an occasion and began putting all the equipment I carried onto it.

Most of it was practical. My phone, still wrapped in a plastic bag, had come through unscathed, and with it went my house keys and wallet, in which my badge and ID card were probably just as muddy as everything else. Wasn't the first time, though, and I'd long since laminated everything important. Two large coins with pitted, ancient faces went onto the table as well, followed by a pocket knife that would need a deep, deep soak. The little flashlight I kept in my pocket was probably ruined, but I'd try to clean it later. I just tossed my disposable lighter into the garbage and rolled my eyes. Getting a new one would be as easy as getting my morning coffee.

I off-loaded all of the work-related equipment I had as well, and it's tedious to list them all in detail, so the abbreviated version goes something like this: Shoulder-sling with pistol and spare magazines, hip holster with pistol and spare magazine, ankle holster with small pistol, large belt knife, small belt knife, silver belt knife, silver boot knife, belt containing several pouches of various materials and tools, steel handcuffs, iron handcuffs, wooden handcuffs (now soaked and warped), and all of the electronics that had gone with my high-tech mask to monitor my heart rate, respirations, and surroundings. It all amounted to a stinking pile, which I set in the sink and let the faucet flush clean. Anything that didn't like the water was already destroyed, I supposed. Speed things up a little.

Finally, I stumbled into the shower, and even the cold water's initial burst felt divine. I could feel my poor pores dislodging sludge joyously. When the steam began to rise, I just lowered my head into the wide spray and held on to the wall as an intense wave of relief washed through me. Hot water is the cure for so many ailments of the mind and body, and after a twenty-hour day and the fight in the sewers, I needed this more than anything.

The black-brown of the runoff was disgustingly refreshing, the same way that a particularly large pimple popping is satisfying. Usually, a shower is just rinse, lather, rinse, done, but this time I lathered, rinsed, lathered, rinsed, lathered in some places that I was hoping had been unaffected, rinsed, and then lathered there some more. I wished that I had some steel wool to really get at all the dirt, but the shower poof I kept was doing a fine job, even if I was using it so hard that it left my skin red and frayed the little fabric to pieces.

A thirty minute shower washed more than just filth down the drain. Tension and headache went with it, and even though I opened up the head wound yet again to scrub it clean, it didn't hurt like it had before. Fatigue didn't vanish. I could still feel the dawn approaching, and my body was aching for sleep, but that ache faded a little, and by the time I was toweling off my hair and putting what was left back into a bun, I felt almost human again.

"I swear, if I never see the inside of a sewage treatment plant again, it'll be too soon," I muttered, giving the pile of dirty clothes a grimace before turning to grab a toothbrush. I had a choice to make: head home and try to get a few hours of sleep before LaFleur pinned something else onto my agenda, or power through the day, start looking into the thieves, or one of the dozen or so other things I had piled on my desk.

"Screw it," I muttered, slipping a plastic bag around all the filthy essentials. "Had enough overtime for today." My body was making it pretty clear that if I wanted to try my luck with staying awake, it was more than willing to let me crash and burn without warning.

****

Home was a small house in a nice, normal neighborhood, with a lawn overrun by crabgrass, shaded by one haggard magnolia tree, and was probably in need of new paint around the eaves. I'd bought it while the housing market had been crazy expensive, and since that had shit the bed, I was so far under water I was surprised it didn't count as riverfront property.

My neighbors were nice enough geriatrics who had moved into their houses when they'd been built in the early fifties, starter homes for young people. They'd grown old together and didn't like a lot of fuss, noise, or questions, which suited me just fine. If they didn't like the fact that I was a woman living alone, or that my lawn maintenance schedule was often one day a month of looking witheringly at the grass, they never gave me any grief about it. The Joneses always handed me a Christmas card in person, while Mrs. Murdoch on the left somehow managed to remember a cake for my birthday every year. The third year in a row, I'd had her investigated for possible anomalous abilities, but the results had been conclusively negative. She was just genuinely kind, I suppose.

Mr. Murdoch was sitting on his front porch in a bathrobe, freshly captured newspaper in his hand, pipe perched on his lip. Dawn was barely a thought on the horizon, but he read by the ever-burning light bulb on the porch, absently shooing the morning bugs away. He folded the edge of the paper down to peer at me as I locked my car and staggered toward the door.

38

"Ms. Morris, good morning," he called out. Our tiny yards were so close together he could have probably whispered and I'd have heard him. I stopped, swaying in place, and turned with a beleaguered smile.

"Mr. Murdoch, good morning to you too." These people looked after my cats when I was out of town. I could spare five minutes of politeness.

"Long night, eh?" he said, sounding delighted.

"You know it. Office had to have me there all night," I said.

"It ain't tax season. You tell your boss that if he can't get it from you from nine to five, he doesn't need it." Oh, and my neighbors naturally had no idea that my work was anything but a boring accounting position. I even took care of both houses come April. And by "I," I actually mean the department's tax guy took care of it to help keep my cover. As retirees, they were absurdly easy to help, though.

"Maybe I'll give you his number, let you tell him for me." I laughed it off, taking a small step toward my door. Sometimes he'd just go back to whatever he was doing. He folded the paper and set it on his lap. Damn it.

"Young lady, you have to stand up for yourself a little more," he said, his tone grandfatherly and stern. "These government folk'll walk all over you if you let them. Young gal like you ought to be cutting throats, jumping up that ladder!"

"Believe me, it's cutthroat enough some days." The coppery tang of boiled blood hit the back of my brain, and I smiled through the unpleasantness. "How's the missus?"

"Still alive," he grumped. "Won't let me smoke in

the house. Gotta lose a pint to the mosquitoes if I want my pipe and paper. She never cared before we got that damn yappy dog. She's worried it'll hurt the dog's nose."

"Maybe she's got a point."

"Bah." He waved his pipe at me. "Speaking of animals, you leaving your television on for your cats again?" I frowned. "Seen it through the curtains when I got up to take a piss. One of them must've walked on the remote then. May want to keep it in a drawer. Electricity ain't cheap, you know?"

"I'll do that, Mr. Murdoch." I gestured at the house. "I'm going to go ahead and make sure they've got food. Expected back at the office later." He made a loud, indignant sound.

"It's Saturday, woman! Don't tell me they've got you working nights and weekends to boot!"

"Afraid so," I said. "Someone lit a fire under the department's feet, gotta scramble."

"Well, if you need anything you let me know. Don't mind watching the cats. You have better cable than we do."

"Yeah, well, at least somebody gets a chance to watch it," I said. "Say hi to your wife for me. Talk to you later." He grunted in reply, already unfolding his paper. Secretly, I thought it was all a cover. He didn't read the paper. He just stared at it until his wife dragged him off to a farmers market.

Four deadbolts and an electronic keypad later and I was in my house, bolting the door closed behind me again. I peeled off my sneakers, dropped my bag of filthy gear on the floor, and made a beeline directly for the fridge. Along the way, I stopped to turn the blaring

TV off.

By the time I turned from the fridge, yogurt in one hand and cold pizza in the other (an excellent breakfast for the health conscious yet famished), I had a pair of cats on the counter staring at me expectantly. The calico, Babylon, with her notched ears and tiny, kitten-like features, was trying her best to appear even tinier and more pathetic than usual, knowing that begging almost always worked. I sighed and tossed her a pepperoni. The other, a black cat with a white star on his chest, just looked at me sullenly and expectantly, long tail twitching across the counter. I squeezed yogurt into my mouth and stared back. The black cat licked its chops. I took a bite of pizza. Babylon, catching the mood, decided that she'd gotten all there was to get and pounced into the living room to harass some floating lint.

"I hope you don't think you're getting any of this," I said through a mouth full of cold leftovers. "Pizza is for cats that don't make the neighbors start peeking through my blinds." The cat cocked his head quizzically to the side and started licking a paw. I pointed the crust at the cat. "Don't you act that way with me. I said no more TV while I was gone. I'm sorry I didn't get back in time for your show, but it was going to be recorded anyway."

He sank onto his belly, front paws crossed, and just looked at me.

"Don't look at me like that, Jericho. You know that I do everything I can to accommodate you, and that includes letting you use the tablet whenever you want, and don't think I don't see what you're looking at on there! You should be ashamed, by the way, for some of those searches." The cat looked at the fridge, then back to me. "No, I'm eating the last piece. You can have cat food."

"You know I hate cat food," Jericho said, sounding on the verge of grinding his teeth. I set the yogurt cup to the side and crossed my arms. "And you knew that I wanted to see that season finale before somebody had a chance to spoil it for me. There were so many zombies being killed in it, you should have—"

"Hey, man, you just talked about spoilers!" I said, making a face. "Have some courtesy."

"Oh, I'm sorry. Did you think the last episode of a show about a zombie apocalypse wouldn't have a thousand zombies being killed? I'd assumed you'd seen it already. Maybe you were off on some kind of date."

"Yeah, I had a date with cholera and botulism," I said. "Anyway, that's not the point! You can't watch the TV if I left it off. The neighbors noticed!"

"So? Tell them that your cats get lonely. God already knows that they think you're a crazy cat lady anyway."

"Shut up. I only have one cat. Most days it feels like you've got me."

"I prefer to think of it as having a roommate who pays for everything," Jericho said. "Now, about that pizza?"

Faerie is a broad term for a kind of native supernatural creature that mainly originates in Europe. There's a certain kind of power that spawns them, and that power is found in Old World forests, meadows, streams, and the like. It's almost nature made manifest, really, and from that strange kind of energy comes all kinds of the more popular, well-known, and recognized supernatural beasties. In this case, it also included *cait sith*, a breed of intelligent, magical, and pain-in-my-ass cats. Luckily, only one had managed to implant itself into my life, although one time I'd come home to nine of them meeting in my living room, all with identical black coats, white marks, and unnaturally long tails. They'd been playing poker.

"Fine, you can have the last slice, but only because I'm so tired I'm feeling sick to my stomach." I opened the fridge door, and he pounced across the gap, seizing the piece from the plate and retreating to the counter again. He ate in tiny rapid bites, like any other cat, but picked the olives off one at a time and put them to the side. I got another yogurt. It was a two-yogurt kind of morning. "You ever run into any mephits back in the day?"

"Oh, sure, loads," Jericho said between itty bites. "All over the Firelands, and they live in a bunch of volcanoes here in our world. Usually pretty reasonable, but they can get greedy." He glanced up at me. "I take it the eyebrows aren't just a new fashion craze?"

"You're not wrong," I said. "How would a bunch of mephits find criminals to do mortal dirty work?"

"What, like kill somebody? Usually they'd take care of it themselves. Most cases of spontaneous human combustion are thanks to a mephit. Used to call them fire imps, but they're technically not demons, so it's kind of a misnomer."

"No, like steal something."

"Something they can't just take themselves? Well, if it's officially sanctioned, they do what all elementals do and go through their emissary."

"And if it's not?"

"They'd need a wizard. Or at least, somebody who can send and receive messages between planes." Satisfied he'd picked his pizza clean of all meats and sauces, Jericho sauntered away from the remains to clean his face and paws. I tossed the rest in the trash and rinsed the plate. "Mortal wizards usually get into all kinds of debt with the elementals early on, so it's not hard for them to get that kind of message across."

"Only wizard I know is Rubin at the office." I rubbed my face, shaking my head. "The Cabal of Wizards isn't going to let the department just ask for their roster and go down the list looking for suspects."

"What'd they take?" Jericho asked.

"Nothing, in the end, and you don't want to know what they were going after," I said. He shrugged his little shoulders. "There anybody you can name, by chance, cozy with the Firelands and the local criminal element?"

"I've been out of the world for a few years, lady, chilling at your place and enjoying all the free Internet I can use."

"Yeah, I noticed. Some of these things I've never seen and wish I hadn't."

"You're welcome. You could use a little more art in your life."

"It's porn, not art, little guy." I drummed my fingers along the counter, and his head followed the movements. Despite his intelligence, Jericho couldn't help but have some baser instincts. We'd agreed that I'd lose the laser pointer as long as he agreed to stop shitting in my work boots. It was hard to find harmony.

"So did you kill the mephits?"

"Pretty sure one got away," I muttered.

"Bummer. He'll be back." Jericho raised a foreboding paw. "None of the firefolk like to lose, but a mephit that gets sent scurrying by a mortal isn't going to keep his standing for very long once his buddies find out about it."

"Speaking of standing, he was wearing a bandoleer made of gold. Mean anything to you?"

"Depends. Could be the payment for the goods, whatever they were, or it could be a sign of rank. Gold's pretty rare as far as resources on that plane go, so it's hard to say."

"Any idea how long it would take for a banished mephit to find a way back?"

"You know the answer to that," Jericho said. I sighed.

"Listen, blessedly it's been a while since I had to deal with tourists like these. The last five cases across my desk dealt with natives, two of which turned out to be hoaxes that I got to arrest and let the local police deal with. If I've forgotten a detail or two about the intricate workings of planar travel, you'll have to let it slide, okay?"

"All right, all right, geez, lady." Jericho dropped his head a little. "Okay, well, you know that any extraplanar creature can only exist in this world if it manifests a body for itself, right? I mean, a powerful wizard can create a body for them, but most of the time, they coalesce a form out of their own essence. Time spent in this world saps that, and they eventually return back unless they find a source of energy to keep them going. It's why vampires drink blood, it's why most mephits live in volcanoes, and it's why if you force them to go full strength in a brawl, those fights tend to last minutes, not hours. Rebounding tires them out, so unless they get pulled back through by something on this side, we're talking days, if not weeks, of this mephit being out of the game."

"Any way to force this specific one to appear? I'd love to ask it some questions."

"You get a name?"

"No."

"Then just go out back and scream 'Mephit! Come here, mephit!' and whistle very loudly. They'll know which one you mean." Jericho rolled his eyes.

"I get it, I get it," I muttered. "As usual, you've been very helpful."

"Hey, don't look at me. I'm not the one who let the thing get away." Jericho swished his tail. "You can summon elementals with the right ritual, or if you have a friendly wizard, they can do it if they have the right name. Outside of that, until he comes looking for you, you can count on not seeing him for a while."

"Great," I said. I glanced at the stove clock and sighed. "Doesn't seem worth it to just get a few hours of sleep. I just know I'll wake up more tired than before."

"We could watch some golf. I know that puts me right to sleep," Jericho said.

"Surprising. You're from the land that invented golf. I'd have thought you'd love it."

"When you don't have thumbs, it's hard to get excited about sports," he said. "You mind telling me the new password for your computer? I want to do some research. For your work."

"No. I don't have time to get all the viruses off this week, and I still haven't paid off my credit cards from last time." I trudged into the living room and fell onto the couch. "You could try tidying the place up a bit while you're here."

"I don't hear you telling Babylon to grab a broom. I'd remind you about the thumbs again, but I can see you're too sleepy to be reasonable." Jericho jumped into the armchair and pawed at the remote until the TV turned on. Some history channel thing about one of the World Wars.

****

Patton was giving a rousing speech on TV when I finally opened my eyes to the doorbell ringing over and over again. My face felt numb from being pressed so hard into the couch, and drool had soaked into the cushion. I propped my head up, brushing hair out of my mouth and face, and looked around.

"Whozzat?" I grumbled, regretting the soreness in all my muscles and bones. My head was throbbing again along the line of the gash, and I felt very warm until I realized that I'd never turned the AC on. The doorbell continued its chiming. The little four note tune must have been easier to bear back in the eighties when it had been installed.

"I'm coming, I'm coming!" I yelled, rolling onto the floor and barely finding the balance to stand. Less than an hour of sleep had turned me into a useless pile of garbage, but I managed to slouch my way to the door and start undoing deadbolts. Despite me clearly answering the door, the ringing continued.

"I swear, if you're with the government or the church, you're going to regret being on my property," I growled, swinging the door open. Somebody shoved hard against the other side and sent me sprawling flat on my back, my head bouncing off the carpet hard enough to send stars shooting through my vision.

That woke me up. I rolled back and got my hands and feet under me and threw myself forward. The man was through the door already, throwing it shut behind himself, his hands raised and ready to grab me, but I wasn't aiming for him so much as the umbrella stand beside the door. I hit it crouched down, sweeping a long bamboo cane out of it and throwing the rest between him and me.

"Wait!" he said, batting umbrellas away before I rammed the bottom of the cane right into the bridge of his nose with the satisfying crack only breaking bones can afford. He went down with a startled yelp, blood squirting down his chest. I grabbed the top of the cane and slung it to the side, throwing the bottom away and revealing three feet of naked steel in the form of a slender sword. A novelty gift from an old friend, but practical enough when push came to shove. The man on the floor went very still when I pressed it hard against his inner thigh.

"That's your femoral artery," I said. "If the next words out of your mouth aren't really fucking good, I'll have my day ruined by having to mop you up for the next hour."

"Please, I'm sorry. I had nowhere else to go!" he rushed, hands in the air despite his bleeding face. I was surprised myself. I never thought I'd actually get a chance to use a sword cane against a home intruder. Nobody in the past had been dumb enough to come at me in the safety of my own home. This guy didn't look like a random burglar, and besides, what burglar breaks into a clearly lower middle-class house in the middle of the day? His face looked somewhat familiar, though.

"What's your name?" I asked.

"Tomas. Tomas Gabriel," he whimpered. He smelled familiar too. Like garbage. It dawned on me.

"You were in the sewers!" I said, nearly shoving the sword through his leg as I tensed up. I slapped my free hand over the deadbolts and secured the door in a hurry. "How'd you find me? How'd you know where I lived?"

"Followed you from your office. Followed you there first. Thought I could get the case back, but I didn't know you were FBI." He was starting to bleed onto the floor.

"Well, I wasn't dumb enough to bring it home. Did you think you could use me to get it back?" I laughed. "You're worse at this than you are at stealing."

"Considering what we stole, I'd say I'm actually very good at that," he said, eyes narrowing. So he still had some professional pride. Neat.

"So you know what was in the case," I said. "How surprising. Are you insane?"

"Please, I didn't come here to hurt you. I wouldn't have rung your doorbell if I was trying to get at you. I came to turn myself in," Tomas said.

Oh. Well, that actually *was* surprising.

"Why?"

"What do you think my chances are of surviving another day out there?" Tomas asked. "Frank was the one with the contacts. Even if I wanted to negotiate a deal with the buyer, after the colossal fumblefuck in the sewers, it's probably not going to go too good for me, is it?"

"I wouldn't bet it would, personally," I said.

49

"Didn't like seeing what happened to your buddies, did you?"

"Fuck no. I knew it was too good to be true, but once Frank blew up like he did and I heard the others die, I had to get out of there. If I thought I could run, I'd have blown town already, but I get the feeling that if these people want to find me, they're going to."

"That's actually a smart move," I said. I relaxed the sword a little. "You make a move on me and I'm going to put you down, do you understand me?"

"Yes, ma'am," he said. I took a step back, keeping the sword ready as he sat up and held his nose shut. "Broke it, I think."

"You're lucky I just got up from a nap, otherwise I'd have shot your dumb ass."

"Sorry. I got jumpy, thought somebody had followed me." I pulled one of the side curtains and looked at the street. No signs of anything out of place. The neighborhood was pretty quiet.

"I need to take you to headquarters. You're under arrest." I held him at sword point and walked him into the kitchen until I could slap handcuffs on him.

"Aren't you going to read me my rights?" he asked.

"Are you human?"

"Yes." I sighed. Miranda only applied to humans. It would have been nice if he'd have turned out to be extraplanar as well. I read him his rights, which he claimed to understand in full.

"I'm cooperating. Can we at least cuff me in the front?" he asked. I shook my head and went to the house phone, punching in the direct line to the director. I put my finger over my lips. Flowers answered on the third ring.

"LaFleur." He didn't sound like he'd been up all night or that a catastrophe was waiting to happen. He sounded just as boringly professional as always.

"Morris here," I said. "I've got the thief with me."

"Which thief?" he asked. I rolled my eyes.

"The one who stole the Declaration of Independence. Which one do you think?"

"A little early for sarcasm," he replied dryly. "I told you that I would have other agents looking for him. Where'd you find him?"

"He found me," I said. "I've got him in custody. He says he wants protection, knows what he took, all that." There was a silent sort of surprise on the other side of the line.

"Amazing," LaFleur said. "All right, bring him in."

"How about sending somebody to come get him?" I asked. "I've got knives in my eyes from having my head bounced around, and I only got like an hour of sleep."

"Agent Morris, I have five field agents in my department, and four of them are currently three hours or more away looking for the man you have in your house. Bring him in for a full interrogation. We need the location of the other egg."

"Understood, sir." I rubbed my forehead. "Headed that way now." I hung up the phone a little more forcefully than was probably polite. I looked at Tomas. "Where's that other egg, pal?"

"Which one?" he asked. I stared at him with my best dead-eyed hatred. It wasn't hard to muster the sincerity. If not for this man and his buddies, I could be enjoying a nice, boring report about the increase in cursed household plants because of a spiteful druid running amok.

"It's going to be a bad day to be your testicles when I get done with you," I said, cane sword dipping back toward his groin. He shook his head.

"Immunity first. After this is over, I walk away. I get to lay low at a safe house until you get the package back, then you help me get out of the country, and we never need to bother each other ever again." Cheeky bastard. Of course that was what he wanted. It would be what I would ask for, in his position.

"Not up to me, but I'm sure my boss will go for it. After all, you're small potatoes compared to what you were selling."

"My thoughts exactly," Tomas said, with a sure smile. He nodded his head to the door. "The sooner we get out of here, the sooner both of our problems are solved."

"You have any weapons on you I should know about before I go through your pockets?"

"Thief, not a hitman. Is this really necessary?" I twirled my finger. He rolled his eyes, facing the wall. Cell phone, wallet, some receipts from restaurants, and a mossy brass coin were all he had on him. Nothing in his socks, nothing strapped to his legs or chest.

"All right, buddy, let's go," I said, taking his arm and leading him toward the door. Locking it behind me with one hand was more annoying than difficult, and it just served to prove that even the little things were going to be a pain in my ass. I got him into the passenger seat, buckled him in, and climbed behind the wheel. I reached into the door's little side pocket and slid the revolver there free from its holster and aimed it across my lap at him. I smiled reassuringly.

"It's not to say that I'm not trusting you, but your buddies were thieves too, and I remember them shooting an awful lot of bullets my way just a few short hours ago. If you move funny, I'm going to shoot you right in your kidney."

"Noted. Could you at least put my hands to the front?" I shook my head and started the car with my free hand. Luckily, Mr. Murdoch's morning coffee had kicked in, and he'd retreated to the safety of his commode, giving me privacy with my new friend. Tomas grumbled, resting his head against the seat, and I pulled out of my driveway.

The little neighborhood I lived in was at the ass end of a series of ever-narrowing streets, designed to have an aesthetically pleasing set of curves matched with the most available land space for houses. On a humid but sunny morning such as this, plenty of people were out, mowing lawns, planting flowers, pruning bushes. You know, mundane, boring suburban kind of stuff. This is why I was taken entirely off guard at the stop sign when the white van coming from the opposite direction pulled up beside me, slid open its door, and began vomiting bullets.

## Chapter Four

If I were a more law-abiding driver, my insurance company would have had a fit. After all, a few broken windows were cheap compared to paying out life insurance, reupholstering the entire interior, and cleaning my brains out of the center console. My rolling stop, which consisted of my foot leaving the gas, considering contact with the brake, and reapplying the gas, turned out to be the most responsible irresponsible thing of my life.

Every piece of glass found a bullet in the span of a heartbeat. I slammed my foot down hard, turning abruptly to put as much of my vehicle between myself and the shooters as possible, and smelled rubber burning as my tires fought to bite the asphalt for enough traction to get me the hell out of there.

"What the fuck, man?" I yelled, head down to where I could barely see over the steering wheel. Tomas was shrieking beside me, and I glanced long enough to see blood streaming out of his arm. I jerked the car hard to come around a red convertible and heard the popping sound of automatic weapons behind me as a few more rounds hammered into my trunk. I looked up as I sailed through a solid red light, across an intersection that couldn't have been busier if the Pope was in town, and into another web of residential neighborhoods. "Are these friends of yours?"

"No!" Tomas yelled, wheezing in pain. "Everyone I worked with is dead already. *Mon Dieu,* I've been hit!"

"It's fine, you'll live. Keep your head down," I said, looking behind me as quickly as I could. The van had passed through the intersection seconds behind me, and I saw a wreck go down in its wake. I had other more pressing issues.

In the movies, car chases are neat, clean affairs where the good guy either catches up to or outruns the bad guy. Anybody involved in a car chase knows just how to corner, accelerate, and time their antics to avoid catastrophe for themselves and minimize it for others. Also, the drivers are always shooting at each other and flattening tires or cracking radiators.

Professionals bring gunmen to do the shooting and usually wait for a clear shot before wasting the bullets. Pro drivers know that all they have to do is follow long enough for their prey to make a mistake, get bogged down in traffic or in a wreck, and then they can just roll up and finish their job. The fact that I was dodging bullets going down Hidden Oak Lane in the middle of broad daylight told me that while the driver might have known what he was doing, the lackeys hanging out the windows did not.

"Hang on," I said, which is useless to a man who is handcuffed and shot, and turned my poor little mid-sized sedan into a sharper turn than any of its engineers had intended, doubling back up a parallel street, headed back to the main road. I needed about thirty cops to show up and shoot these guys, but at the same time, I needed them to also not shoot me.

Bullets stitched their way across a yard as they

missed me and sprayed the plate windows of the house into powdered glass before we were gone from the lives of the owner forever. I snarled, shouting profanity out the window. Nobody sane came after anybody in public like this. Their little van of hitmen might have worked if they'd gotten us in the first shot, but now they were just begging to run into a barricade and die resisting arrest.

It was terrifying, by the way. Never before had I been in a car chase, and I'd always imagined it the other way around. I kept picturing some kid following a soccer ball into the street ahead of me, or a baby carriage and attached mother slowly crossing an intersection, something classic like that. Instead, a bullet turned my front windshield into a mess of spiderweb cracks, popped off my rearview mirror, and a cloud of glass powder swirled through the car, stinging my eyes and burning my throat.

"Shit!" I leaned my head out the window, turning down a long, straight stretch of road. I had to be able to outrun the van. It looked like a rental only the homeless could afford.

Tomas grunted, lifting his feet over the dash, and I reached for the gun before he slammed both feet into the ruined windshield, sending it flying up and over the car, landing in the road behind us.

"Thanks," I said, pulling my head back into the moderate safety of the interior.

"Do you know where you're going?" he yelled at me over the wind. I assume he would have been yelling anyway.

"Trying to get back to the main road. If I keep going back here, I'm either going to drive through a house or end up at a dead end." I shoved the wheel hard to the left, blowing right through a stop sign and again disappointed that no red and blue lights lit up behind me. Forget to signal a turn one time on the freeway and I get pulled over, but the second lunatics are trying to fill me full of holes and fill those holes full of lead, well, the donut shop must have just gotten a fresh batch out of the fryer.

"Tell me where that egg is!" I shouted.

"Not a chance! Get me the hell out of here!"

"If you die and nobody finds them, do you know what's going to happen?"

"The same thing that'll happen if I die now anyway! The rest of the world isn't my problem! You better keep me alive!"

I had a moment where I heard the revving of the big engine behind me, and I half-turned in my seat to aim the pistol out the shattered rear window before the van rear-ended me going much faster than I'd thought possible. The pistol went off, punching a hole into the front grill of the van, but it didn't even do me the courtesy of burping out billowing smoke, let alone exploding in a rain of bad guys.

"Hey! HEY!" Tomas shouted, turning me back forward again. Well, at least I'd found the main road again. The bad news was that traffic was at a standstill. Even the space between the lights was a parking lot.

"Son of a bitch!" I snarled, hauling on the brakes and turning the wheel hard, trying to make it into a parking lot, maybe fast enough to turn around and try my luck shooting it out with the fools behind a gas station.

The van hit my rear left panel hard enough to start

tipping me onto my side before both of us slammed hard into the stationary traffic. The van flipped, throwing bodies across four lanes of stopped traffic, and immediately a heavy whoosh of igniting fuel billowed up. I had enough time to see and smell and feel that heat before we hit, bounced into a roll that sent both of us jittering in our seatbelts as the frame bent and warped around us.

My mouth was full of dirt from the median when my senses finally came together, and I could feel every bone in my body barely holding my mortal form in place. I was upside down, hanging inches above the caved in roof of my poor car, still in my seatbelt. Saves lives, kids.

"Tomas! You alive?" I coughed, spitting out sprigs of grass thrown into the vehicle by the wreck. I could hear the roaring fire at the wrecks outside. This was going to be some paperwork, for sure.

Groaning on my right reassured me that at least Tomas had a pulse. I thumbed the release of the seatbelt and hit the ground hard. I wasn't pinned, and all my limbs were at least still working.

"Come on, let's get out of here," I said, pulling him out of his seat as gently as I could. His arm was bleeding pretty badly. Probably needed a tourniquet. He feebly wailed as I shoved him out his window and crawled after him.

Loud popping drew my gun across the bottom, now the top side, of my car, aiming at the fire. Blood was in one eye, but the other pulled its weight searching for the threat. More bangs, and I realized it was just ammunition cooking off in the blaze. Four cars were fully involved now, and people were shouting to each other, screaming for help, trying to figure out what the hell happened. None were coming our way quite yet, but it was only a matter of time.

"Oh man, I think my other arm's broken," Tomas groaned, standing beside me. It really didn't look good, honestly. The handcuffs had bent his forearm into a very awkward angle.

"Yeah, well, let's go get that taken care of, little guy," I said, staggering toward a sidewalk. I needed to make a call, get help to move us out of the area, back to safety.

I felt the wave of heat wash over me as a car erupted into staggering flames. I shielded my face from the burning.

A humanoid figure rose from the burning wreckage of the van, atrophied and covered in scarlet flames. Slowly in the air it turned, its red, beady eyes focused on me. A bandolier of gold gleamed across its chest, heat waves rippling from its entire form. I only stared in horror for a moment. My mind did an accelerated form of *No, impossible, it can't be!* Just to cover the clichés. Then survival instincts took over.

"Run!" I yelled, grabbing Tomas by the less broken arm and pulling him after me, going for an abandoned SUV, and throwing both of us behind it. I popped up over the hood and unloaded what was left in my pistol. You could actually see the impacts on its body, like angry welts appearing and being smoothed over in seconds. It focused its red gaze on me with a grim satisfaction. The flames across its body swelled and turned blue, and the lips parted.

The engine block turned into a puddle of aluminum and steel, and the asphalt itself caught fire, but I was skittering away like a water bug and dragging Tomas by the arms, headed for a retention pond a hundred feet away.

"Move your ass!" I screamed at him. He was kicking his legs and yelling back at me, but I kept my eyes forward. If we got into the water, we had a chance to just submerge until the mephit was forced to disappear. It wouldn't be able to boil the whole lake, and if it came too close, I might be able to snuff it out like the others.

Tomas must have gotten his feet back under him, since he was coming along easier now as we scrabbled forward, and just in time. I could feel the hairs curling up on the back of my neck as I hauled him with me over a railing and fell down the embankment into the cattails.

*Foolish girl.* Oh great, now the mephit wanted to talk.

"Come get some, Sparkles!" I yelled, kicking back into the water. "Come on, Tomas, need you to help a little more, getting tired just dragging…you…around." As I kicked clear of the vegetation and pulled, I realized why Tomas was so light now. He hadn't been running with me. He'd lost, like, a hundred and thirty pounds.

It looked like he'd taken the mephit's heat ray straight to the chest, and it had burned off his torso from the armpits down. All that was left was a seared and cauterized pair of arms, shoulders, and head, locked now in a twisted scream of final pain. I jerked my hands away from those arms, only now realizing why they'd been gripping me so tightly.

*I would end you now, but your cowardly retreat has cost me precious time. There will be fire to come, for you and your kind.* I looked up and saw the mephit staring at me, and I prepared to dive into the water. Instead, it just watched for a moment and in a flash of blazing smoke, vanished. It had snapped back to its native plane.

Bystanders probably had never seen a grown woman screaming at the sky in a rage, but hey, it was a first for me too.

\*\*\*\*

Like a disappointed father, LaFleur stood and watched the firemen rolling their hoses up, and I tried not to think of the monumental ass-chewing I was in for when the medics finally finished mummifying my arms. I hadn't even noticed the glass as I'd dragged myself free, but my arms were just juicy with tiny cuts.

"The same mephit, you say..." He wasn't quite talking to me. He had a habit of just talking out loud when the rest of his head was full of anger. It was rare, but I'd seen it before. The last time had been when two field agents had gotten themselves caught smuggling forbidden elixirs out of our secure room.

"Looked that way," I said, fidgeting away from the stinging peroxide being dumped unceremoniously on my arm. The paramedics knew the scoop. Whatever was said around them fell on deaf ears. They didn't know anything, and if at the end of the month they had a little extra discretionary cash in their account, well, that's why they were on call every day of the week. "And as much as he had a hard-on against me, he was aiming for Mr. Head and Shoulders over here." I jerked a thumb to the body bag containing what was left of our illustrious thief.

"If they were looking to kill him, it means they

don't need what he knows about the last egg," LaFleur said, rubbing the top of his smooth head vigorously. Normally, I'd remind him that it wouldn't help grow the hair back, but right now, he was liable to break my arms to ease his frustration.

"Maybe they've got some way to locate it. Objects that rare and powerful? Must be some way to find 'em."

"The mother herself wouldn't be able to sniff them out, and that's if the other egg is even on this plane of existence to begin with. Anybody with the resources this group had probably had a pocket dimension to store it in until the deal was done."

"If the mephit's back so soon, it means somebody on this side is summoning it and pouring power into the spell. Enough power where it didn't worry about cooking its way through all these cars."

"This puts us in a very tough situation, Agent Morris," LaFleur said. I could tell by the way he wasn't looking at me that he was angry. Not that it was personal, but I was the closest place to direct that anger. Lucky for me.

"I know, sir, but honestly, how could I have anticipated a van full of machine guns to be driving into my neighborhood?" I felt a little sick. "If I'd left two minutes later, they'd have caught me in the driveway, or in the house, and that's not going to look good when I try to sell the place."

"This puts us dead in the water," LaFleur said. "Our options have dwindled drastically."

"Yes, sir, they have," I said. The medic tied off my bandage, and I shrugged into one of the FBI jackets LaFleur brought with him. "I'll start shaking the trees and seeing if I can get anybody to bite. These guys had to have contacts somewhere. Maybe they stashed the egg with them."

"Other agents will handle that," LaFleur said. "You're on a plane to Nevada as soon as I can get one chartered."

"I am?"

"There will be a helicopter waiting for you there. I believe you know Agent Braeburn?"

"Yeah, we were at the academy together. I thought he was working Cyber Crimes."

"No, he works for us now. Has for the last two years. He'll fill you in on all the details. I need you back here as soon as humanly possible, with the package he'll give you."

"What package?" LaFleur shook his head, tapping his ear.

"You'll find out once you're in Nevada." Ah. Too many people nearby, too many ears that might hear the specifics. Once I was in Nevada, I'd probably be ferried into one of the surrounding states. The department didn't have any outposts in Nevada. It was a wasteland, at least as far as the anomalous world of assets was concerned. It was strange only insofar as nothing strange happened in Nevada. Magic didn't function well there. Nothing could enter our plane from another inside the borders of that state. Even summoned creatures were at a huge disadvantage. LaFleur must have been afraid I'd be followed, so a stop there made sense.

"Understood, sir," I said, hopping up from the back of the ambulance. "Can I stop by the office for my weapons?"

"No, there's no time for that," LaFleur said. "I'll

have a plane at Cecil Airport by the time you get out there. It'll take you the rest of the way. And don't forget your friend. Tomas." I raised a confused eyebrow, glancing at the body bag laid out on the asphalt.

"Excuse me?"

"You'll need to bring him with you."

"I know you must have noticed that he's dead, sir," I replied. "What's left of him could fit into an overhead compartment."

"Well, that's lucky for you, isn't it?" I frowned. "Don't ask why, just bring him with you." He handed me the keys to the company sedan parked nearby. "If there are any changes, I'll let you know, but I need you to hurry back here. I'm counting on you to do whatever it takes to safeguard this city." He pulled a cell phone out, punched in numbers, and turned to ignore me. He could get like that after giving orders. Often it seemed like he was indifferent to his people and their progress, but I'd learned a long time ago that the agents that he ignored were the ones that he trusted to get the job done right.

With a weary, aching groan, I got in the sedan and headed to the tiny rural airport way outside the city, with my grisly luggage in tow.

****

The Department of Intangible Assets isn't some off the record government agency, operating in the shadows without oversight or control. The CIA runs some of their operations like that, I'm told, but we report to the director of the FBI, and we have finance committees that constantly cut our funding and question our existence. Granted, to everybody except the director of the FBI, the phrase "Intangible Assets" refers to things like personnel management, certain types of finances, and agency goods that aren't measured in pounds or gallons. Officially, we're tasked with assisting the IRS with investigations and enforcement. It's about as boring as you can get without actually being painted beige. That's probably why we're so forgotten, along with our budget needs.

Of the five divisions of the DIA, the Southeast Division is by far the least liked and most poorly funded. Oh, sure, if we were the Southwest, with their sexy death cults that always pop up and threaten major population centers, or the Midwest with their hordes of mythological creatures running amok, we'd probably be able to afford things like individual vehicles, better and unlimited weapons, or two-ply toilet tissue. Instead, it often got to the point where I was using the fake tax records' blank sides to print official reports because my salary doesn't afford such luxuries as paper or pens.

All of this is to say that when I arrived at the little airstrip in the pine forests and found a G5 luxury jet waiting for me, I was less impressed and more angry about the fact that we were rinsing out and reusing coffee filters in the break room. There was a stewardess standing by the little stairs waiting for me as I walked up, the half-corpse over my shoulder in its black rubber bag, and her picturesque smile faltered as she saw my burnt, bloodied stagger. More likely they were used to suits and ball gowns.

"Can I take your luggage?" she asked, carefully pronouncing luggage when she clearly meant garbage. It was a shame. Under other circumstances, her bobbed brown hair and hazel color eyes would have been cute.

"No, thanks," I said, clambering up the steps. White leather interior. Very posh. "Is this all that was available?"

"A Mr. LaFleur scheduled this pickup. Is there, uh, something I can get you?" she asked.

"A towel? I'll lay one on the seats so I don't mark them up." I'm just nice like that. I dropped Tomas onto the little table, hoping that he wouldn't start leaking anywhere. I bet they'd make us buy the plane, and then I could kiss my hope for a replacement high-tech gas mask goodbye. I wondered briefly if they'd recovered the one I'd left in the sewers. Man, that felt like it had happened weeks ago. The stewardess put out a thick robe over the seat, and I fell into it, buckling up and looking out the window. Tomas "sat" across from me on the table, and though the thick bag prevented anybody from actually seeing anything, I could imagine an outline of the face staring at me.

"We will be leaving soon," the woman said. She actually was cute, with her pristine powder-blue skirt, practical but nice shoes, and hair framing her striking, professional smile. "If we don't have any delays, we should arrive at just before noon local time."

"That'll be fine," I said. "Can I get some water? Soda?"

"Sure," she said, glancing at the body bag once more before going to the back of the plane behind a screen. The kind of day I was having, I half expected her to pop out with a machine gun and make sure I didn't enjoy my flight. I was virtually unarmed, which was really a bizarre experience for me, but Nevada was a safe place. Relatively speaking. Then again, home was supposed to be pretty safe as well.

Seven years I'd been chasing ghouls, goblins, and mad mages across the Southeast, and in all that time, I'd never been in a car chase. I'd been shot at plenty, although I'd avoided getting myself ventilated. A few big bumps, bruises, and close calls hadn't left me broken, but every time it took me a little closer to the edge. As the plane taxied and took off, I closed my eyes and felt my stomach drop as we pulled into the sky. I could picture a great precipice before me, stretching to the infinite void, and I shuddered. I'd come too close for comfort. Seven years of field work, with the last twelve months as the senior field agent. My predecessor had died in the line of duty, his predecessor had gone mad after being exposed to eldritch horrors beyond mortal reckoning, his predecessor had been butchered after retiring (probably because of a grudge following a long and storied career), and the one before that had simply vanished one day without a trace. That accounted for the past ten years of senior field agents. My odds of surviving to the end of my mortgage weren't exactly great. Most of the time, I didn't think about it. I thought about filling out paperwork, hanging out by a water cooler, watching the clock for the end of the day. You know, the kinds of things that normal workers do. Hell, even the agents at the FBI headquarters a few miles from our rented space had boring lives.

I sipped the water she brought me, watching the clouds fall below us, stifling a yawn. Maybe after this case was over I'd get to transfer to Logistics. They almost never found themselves in the field, and I couldn't remember the last time one of them was eaten by a lycanthrope. Being denied the transfer on the basis that we were short-staffed with able agents had been frustrating up until this morning, but now it was too much. I did have a duty, but damned if I was going to die after all the hard work I'd put in. Surely LaFleur would understand that.

I could always quit.

They'd have to let me. Hell, I could demand reassignment to a normal branch of the FBI, take a decrease in rank for it, and never have to worry again about whether or not my last moments would be spent knowing what my vaporizing flesh smelled like. The only problem with that was I didn't have the luxury of ignorance anymore. Every day, I'd drive home looking for telltale signs of weird, scary shit, until my paranoia drove me crazy or forced me back into the DIA. More than one agent had come back because tapping phones and listening to white supremacists rant about the cultural meltdown of the nation was teeth-grindingly boring. More often, we'd hear about ex-Agent Such and Such being found in his garage with the doors closed and an empty tank of gas in his car. Then there were those who simply vanished without a trace. Any agent worth their salt made a lot of enemies in their time at the DIA, and a certain safety net existed while on active duty.

I rubbed my face and leaned my head back. It was best not to think about it right now. Transfer or not, resigning or not, I was committed to this case, and I'd be damned if I let a preoccupation with what might happen get in the way of what was happening. Needed to keep my head in the game, at least until this was over.

\*\*\*\*

When you think about how the FBI gets around by helicopter, you probably think of Black Hawks or at least heavy, coal-colored aircraft bristling with instruments and/or weapons. Something very spy-movie, or at least crime drama. Hell, it's what I imagine, and actually, what I was used to. So when we landed at a small airstrip a couple miles south of Las Vegas and the only helicopter in sight had a large yellow smiley face painted onto the side with a logo for "Big Bob's Canyon Tours," I figured I was in for a wait until my actual transport arrived. The stewardess thanked me for flying and closed up behind me as Tomas and I staggered down the stairs. I was rubbing sleep out of my eyes as two large men in khakis and flowered shirts came over from the chopper.

Now these were some violent men. The way they walked, the way they held themselves, and the way they carried very large pistols under those loose clothes made me immediately think they were professional, but still violent. I paused where I was, and they stood, arms clasped in front of them, easy expressions on their faces and an almost lazy posture. We all waited until the private jet taxied away toward the little fuel shack at the other end of the runway.

"What's your name?" Oh boy, that's not a polite first question.

"Who's asking?" I replied. They glanced at each other. Thing One was six-foot-gigantic, bald, and wore a red shirt with white flowers all over it. Thing Two was a couple inches taller than his counterpart, with short-cropped red hair, and if I had to put an identifying feature into a report, it would have been the fact that his left ear was little more than scraps of long-healed scar flapping in the breeze.

"Ma'am, we're here to meet somebody, and if you aren't her, we're going to have to ask you to leave."

"You're here for me guys, relax," I said. "Special Agent Diane Morris, DIA. Want the badge?"

"Please." I sighed, pulled the badge holder out of my back pocket, and tossed it over. Thing One caught it and looked it over. He pulled out a small monocle, like the one a jeweler would appraise diamonds with, and gave it a look. I nodded. FBI badges could be faked. A DIA badge had more distinct layers of security for trained eyes. A portable thaumometer was just the thing. Thing One nodded to his partner, though with that tree trunk of a neck, it was hard to tell.

"Agent Morris, I have to ask you some standard questions. Please cooperate with them, answer truthfully, and it'll be over in a minute."

"Nobody told me anything about any questions. I'm here to receive some kind of package, right?"

"This is standard security for this meeting." Thing Two took a small booklet from his pocket and flipped through it.

"The following sentence is the truth. The previous sentence is a lie." And then they just stared at me. I blinked a few times and frowned.

"O…okay. That's not really a question. What, uh, what is it you're looking for in response?"

"Twenty-two minus ten is thirteen." Again, a silent stare followed. Underneath their calm, though, I could sense a tension. If I moved wrong, they'd pull their pieces and leave me bleeding in the sand.

"You'd better check your math there, buddy." This was a new sensation. I'd seen a lot of strange procedures over the years, been asked and answered a lot of strange questions, but this was the first time I'd been given something like this. A test, for sure, but a test for what?

"Several silver slivers of savory slick salmon shivered sensually subverting sadistic shipments." The best part of this whole thing was their serious, stern expressions as they watched my face for what I assumed was treacherous tells.

"Alliteration aside, that makes no sense." The novelty was really wearing off. "Look, guys, can we just wrap this up? I've got shit I need to take care of."

"Just a little longer, Agent Morris," Thing One said. Thing Two just kept right on with whatever was written down.

"What color panties are you wearing?" If he hadn't said it with the most dull, disinterested tone, or if his pal had chuckled, it would have been time to start beating ass, but instead, they managed to make it sound like some kind of frequently asked interview question.

"Blue," I said, rolling my eyes.

"I'm going to need to see them," Thing Two said.

"Absolutely not," I said, heat rising to my face. "I don't know who the fuck you two are. Let's see your ID for a change." What had I even been thinking? I must have been even more zonked out of my mind than I thought. For all I knew, this was Bob and his brother waiting for clients, who were having a go at me.

"Agent Morris, please don't prolong this. We need to confirm your answer."

"Oh yeah?" I asked. "By having me strip here, in front of God and everybody?"

"We don't need you to take your pants off. Just

show us the edge." I felt hotter than the sun would give credit for and ground my teeth. Whatever. If they were having fun with me, I'd see them skinned alive. I knew entities that would do it too. I thumbed out one of the edges of my underwear and held it for them to see.

"There you go, fuckers, blue, as promised." And with that, they relaxed.

"Sorry about that, Agent Morris," Thing One said as his counterpart tucked the booklet away. "If you'd been replaced by a tourist trying to get to the Observatory, we needed to stop you before we got in the air."

"So that's what that was about?" I asked. "Why the hell did you need to see my underwear?"

"Doppelgangers can appear to wear anything, but they can't do layers. Not everybody wears a bra or undershirt, but our experience is that most everybody wears underwear."

"That's a pretty big assumption. You're lucky I'm not late on laundry," I said. "And the rest?"

"Inevitables won't let the math question slide, they have to correct such a simple error. We would have continued with four more to confirm, but you didn't bother giving the correct answer. Any fey creature would reply in alliteration of equal length, no matter how hard they tried to stop themselves."

"And the first one?"

"It's a paradox, and any artificial intelligence would have noticeable malfunctions following that. It also weeds out creatures of pure logic and consistency."

"So it's all a test." Made sense, I guess. Was nice of them to explain. "You have a lot of imposters trying to visit?"

"No," Thing Two said. "We don't have many visitors to begin with, and those that come almost never know what they're coming for. And almost all of them are administered class one amnestics once we return them to the airfield."

"Wait, what?"

"Not you. Most others," Thing One said. "Our orders are to take you to the Observatory, where you'll be briefed on the package and handling instructions. Can I take the corpse, or would you like to carry it?"

"Be my guest," I said, holding the bag out. "What're your names?"

Thing One turned out to be Ronald, and his opposite was Donald. No shit. Normally I'd assume that whatever names they gave were pseudonyms, but nobody would have been dumb enough to use those two. Ronald carried Tomas to the chopper and got into the back with me, while Donald got up front and dusted off as quickly as possible.

"So what's the Observatory you mentioned?"

"It's a department facility a ways into the desert. The package you've been sent to utilize is stored on site, and you have to take custody of it there before it can be used," Ronald said through the headphones. Even the inside of the helicopter smelled like civilian use. I was pretty sure it had been used to transport animal feed at some point. The smell of oats and something else really brought back old memories of home.

"The DIA doesn't have any operations in Nevada," I said, confused. "You guys do work for the DIA, right?"

"Oh, yeah, for years," Donald said from up front.

"I've been picking up people for the Observatory for most of my career."

"It's kept off the books. It's secret enough that it's not often we get special agents. Mostly just SAC or ASAC, some of the directors from time to time."

"A repository for relics?" I asked.

"Something like that. You'll get all the details when we arrive."

They refused to go into any further detail, so I just sat back in my seat, folded my arms, and watched the desert roll out from under me. One long tan swathe of land, with the occasional rocky outcropping. A stark, beautiful country, but not one I'd like for very long. I already missed the forests of Florida.

A butte rose out of the desert ahead of us, towering over the rest of the horizon like something out of a magazine. It was large enough to fit a white domed observatory on top, looking like a giant golf ball on a rust-colored tee. The telescope was hidden behind the shielded doors, but the whole building gleamed clean in the sun, and a number of smaller attached buildings looked intact and well-maintained.

"I guess I understand the name now," I commented as the helicopter swept around the side of the buildings and settled in toward a concrete landing pad. It must have been a huge pain in the ass to get all those building materials up the cliff face. I couldn't see a road access at all.

"Actually, it's fully functional, although the tech hasn't been updated since the late eighties," Ronald said. "To avoid suspicion, we put out new astronomical data every few months."

"I named a nebula after my mother," Donald said,

sounding absolutely tickled. A cloud of dust swirled up around the landing pad, thick and red, and the engines shut off with a tired whine.

I hadn't seen Jeremy Braeburn since Quantico, and even then, we'd only been passing acquaintances. Unlike most of my fellow classmates, I'd known where I was headed after graduating and didn't have the patience or time to be making friends. I remembered him as a beanpole with perfectly parted brown hair and a baby-innocent face. He'd been well-liked by both peers and instructors and never made snide comments about women training beside men. The last time I'd seen him, he'd been wearing a suit and tie and had been all smiles showing his mother around the campus.

The man standing in front of me looked like somebody had dragged his alcoholic, cancer-ridden brother out of a cave to see sunlight for the first time in a decade.

"Braeburn?" I asked, stepping out of the helicopter with the corpse slung over my back.

"Welcome to the Observatory, Morris," he said, and it was clear that he was tired. He was still tall, but now instead of being slim, he was tortuously skinny. Bent. Warped. Heavy, dark circles hung under his eyes, and his previously perfectly parted hair now hung past his ears. The most shocking difference was that the color had changed drastically over the years. No longer chestnut, he had a mop full of gray hair verging on straight white. He looked like he'd aged forty years.

"You, uh, you're looking good," I lied, smiling. "I brought you a corpse."

"It's not for me," he said. "You been enjoying your time down in Florida?"

"Hot, muggy, buggy," I said, shrugging. "Could be worse. What is this place?"

"This is the department's deep dark secret," Braeburn said. "Beyond top secret, of course, but you've already been told that, right?"

"I kind of figured it out on my own," I said. "Can you fill me in yet?"

"In a little bit. We have to go inside first. This way." He gestured to one of the small square buildings away from the main complex. I trudged up alongside him, and Ronald/Donald took up the rear.

"What happened to your Cyber Crimes gig?" I asked. He blinked at me for a moment and then chuckled a little.

"Oh, right. Yeah, I was there for a while, but I ran into something kind of horrific in some recovered files. I was offered a choice between an amnestic reversion or a change in jobs, and since I was worried what the long-term effects of drug-induced amnesia might be, I chose this one." He laughed again, this time without any real humor. "Good choice."

He unlocked a heavy metal door, and it slid open smoothly, revealing a plain elevator with a row of buttons on it. A second key slid above the buttons, and he turned it with a click while jamming his thumb on one marked seven. The floor lurched, and we began to descend.

"There." He turned to me, pocketing the keys. "Are you familiar with numerology?"

"Sure. Numbers have powers. They can predict things. There are codes in everything. That sort of thing."

"That's about right," Braeburn said. "I did a lot of

analytic work at Cyber Crimes. Looking for codes, writing algorithms, that sort of thing. Probably why I'm here. A lot of the assets we acquire can be safely held in things like lead, or wax, or ice, or whatever, but some of them, specifically entities with intelligence, require a little more precision."

"I don't follow."

"This facility is an international effort by various foundations, societies, and governments to house entities and creatures that pose a significant threat, categorized as severity level five-plus, and can't otherwise be contained," Braeburn said. The elevator dinged, and the doors slid open. Braeburn stepped out, and the rest of us followed. I heard rustling and turned to see my escorts both putting heavy foam earplugs into place.

"What's that for?" I asked.

"Standard precaution," Braeburn said. "Some of our tenants, while safely held, can still have negative effects outside of their cells."

"Cells," I repeated. "Like prison cells?"

"Pretty much," Braeburn said, gesturing around. We stood at the center of a room with seven walls, each built out of white granite inlaid with runes and warding symbols. I recognized some of them, but there were hundreds more that I'd never seen before. The floor was the same white, and it was tiled with interlocking stars, each with seven points, and each with gold inlaid words and scripts. There was a desk surrounding the elevator's shaft, which made up the center of the whole shape, and on that desk were seven sets of ink blotters, lamps, papers, staplers—essentially everything found in an office before computers were commonplace. None of that really concerned me. What did concern me was the fact that all seven doors were wrought out of steel, reinforced with more steel, gilded with precious metals in intricate patterns, and barred from the outside with heavy beams of metal.

"A prison for the anomalous threats..." I muttered. I could recognize religious symbols carved into one door and images of hieroglyphics on another. Another was emblazed with a single eye within a triangle, but when I looked at it for more than a few seconds, I felt the creep of nausea climb through my guts.

"I don't recommend looking too hard," Braeburn said dryly. "These powers are contained, but that doesn't make them safe."

"Department policy is to force the return of hostile tourists to their home plane," I said. "I...we don't hold anything for more than a day or two, tops."

"That's what the DIA wants its own people to think," Braeburn said. "But some of these threats are too great to simply 'send home.' In time, they would return, possibly many generations from now, and their return would bring terrible calamity." He pointed at the door directly ahead of the elevator. It alone bore no carvings or decorations. "If I had any say in the matter, you would never have come here. I don't really care what else might happen out there. It's not worth this."

The doors each had a smaller, shielded window that was latched closed, but as I looked, I could see this one vibrating against its clasp.

"It wants out," Donald muttered. "Always wants out."

"They all want out," Ronald said. He had his hands clasped in front of him, knuckles white with grip.

"Are you going to give me details on who or what are held here?"

"No," Braeburn said. "My instructions are to yield custody of ADN1974008 to you, but I have no reason or desire to give information on anything else held on the premises. Part of that's security. If you were ever caught by outside forces, and they discovered some of the beings here, we would be under threat of assault. Our greatest defense is that nobody, absolutely nobody, knows all of the things here."

"And what is that asset you mentioned?" Braeburn pressed his lips together and cleared his throat.

"Asset Designation Number 1974008. Refers to itself as…Archades."

I set Tomas down and folded my arms across my chest. It helped with the shaking. I licked my lips, trying to counter the rapid-drying mouth that was having a hard time forming words. I could actually feel my heartbeat in my ears, and I'd been hit with a flop sweat bad enough that I had to blink my eyes free to see the look of deepest resignation on Braeburn's face.

"I'm sorry, I didn't hear you. It sounded like you said Archimedes. You know, the mathematician?"

"You know what I said." He reached into his pocket and withdrew a small silver key on a long leather loop. He held it out, but my hands didn't move.

"Archades can't be in your containment facility because it's been permanently banished from the world for forty years."

"That's what the official explanation was. The truth is that Archades can't be sent away permanently. It was captured and secured here, where it can't do any more damage." He shook the key at me. "You have to take it. I may not agree with this plan, but it's not my choice. And if you don't do it, they'll just send somebody else."

He had a point there. LaFleur was one of the highest ranking people in the DIA, and he didn't get there by being stupid. I had to remind myself that he'd gotten me out of some pretty shitty positions, sometimes at great personal risk. He wasn't just putting me into a meat grinder for no reason. And by the looks of Donald and Ronald, if I declined to do my job, I was going to have to spend a little time having my memories erased. Maybe they'd be able to erase my embarrassing break-up from the previous week.

"How much is true?" I asked. "I mean, what they say about it?"

"It's hard to tell. It doesn't do much talking, and when it does speak, it's my personal policy to let somebody else listen." Braeburn unconsciously tugged at his left earlobe. "I, uh, listened too much one day, and I haven't slept well since."

"But the department has to know something about it. Allegiances, plane of origin, weaknesses?" This was just naive hope. The department knew precious little about all sorts of things. We had catalogues of anomalous materials with incomplete information, where any information was available.

"All I know is that a lot of good agents died trying to bring it down, and the best that any of them could do was...contain it. At great cost." Braeburn shook his head. "In this country, it's hard to tie Archades to anything in particular, but if you look at the past, the previous times it was conjured and given form, well...if half of the stories are true, it is by far the most dangerous asset we have in containment anywhere in the world."

"And I'm here to take it with me," I whispered. Braeburn opened his mouth but was cut off by the rising sound of chuckling emanating through the steel door. There was no earthly way that a gently amused sound like that should so clearly penetrate the steel, but all the same, it sounded like somebody peering through a closet door. It was so ordinary that, under any other circumstances, it might have been contagious, but surrounded by ancient symbols of power meant to isolate and suppress the power of malign demi-gods, it felt sinister.

"I am releasing it to your custody. There are specific rules to how this entity operates, and right now, you are designated Warden of the entity known as Archades. You act with the authority of the Department of Intangible Assets with respect to this entity's treatment, conditions, terms, and agreements." Braeburn cleared his throat. "Please. Take the key." I looked at it for a long moment before finally picking it up. It was heavier than it looked.

"What the hell am I supposed to do?"

"You have to make that decision. Do what you think is right. Keep it contained, however you can," Braeburn said, stepping back, closing ranks with the - Onalds.

I strode up to the door, and the chuckling cut short when I reached arms' length. I wiped my forehead across my sleeve, trying to take deep breaths and shake the nausea. My fingertips were tingling. My lips felt numb. I knew I'd been hyperventilating.

Archades. At orientation, my first day in DIA, I'd

been told the name. The closest thing to it was hearing about the Unabomber, or the Zodiac Killer. It was a boogeyman, except our instructors, grizzled and seasoned as they were, barely used the name and spoke with hushed tones. Archades the Hungry. Archades the Bloodied.

In the mid-1970s, death cults were all the rage. At a time when Jim Jones was charming his way into a mass suicide, following Manson's little family of terror, and while slasher films were being spawned by gruesome reality and reality mimicked that kind of fiction, the DIA was working behind the scenes to counter one evil spirit after another. Most of the tragedy that reached the mainstream news was a hundred percent human. People don't need a supernatural puppeteer to do terrible things. But some of them, including a string of low-profile murders in the southeast, were a part of something more inhuman.

Somehow, a group of amateur occultists came into a book of power. They weren't the first to stumble across esoteric and dangerous knowledge, but unlike their counterparts who only dabbled, this bunch went whole hog. Calling themselves the Sons of Salvation and led by a man who was only known as Father Solomon, they recruited anybody with even a marginal talent for magic and set them to work conducting the rituals outlined in the Codex Archades. Fifty murders later, they had nearly completed all the ritual, but with special agents of the DIA closing in on one side, paladins of the Vatican's Knights Templar coming down like the righteous hand of God, and a number of rival diabolists trying to steal the power out from under them, Father Solomon finished the ritual hastily and brought the entity forth.

Archades, in the ensuing battle, killed a hundred and eight cultists, including those from rival and friendly sects, four of the five paladins, and thirty-nine agents of the DIA. Three agents survived with the last paladin, and they retreated to regroup. One of my predecessors, Special Agent Nathan Tullman, had managed to retrieve the Codex Archades from the cultists and devised a plan to exorcise Archades from the world. As it was always described to me, "Long story short, the plan worked, but Special Agent Tullman was killed as he completed the task." Details of the Codex, Tullman's exact method of banishment, and the names of the rest of the agents involved were never released, not even to the senior field agents that succeeded Tullman. I'd read the official reports, and there was more redacted information than actual text. The rest of Tullman's service record was impressive enough that the thought that Archades had been his end was enough to leave us respectful of the memory of Archades.

More respectful now that I knew I was one key turn away from being face-to-face with it. I wondered for a moment, right before I twisted my wrist and heard the metallic click of the lock disengaging, if I would feel it killing me or if I'd just wake up dead.

The door swung toward me, slowly, and I braced myself for an impact that never came. The darkness beyond the door was stifling. It seemed that the light of the antechamber was swallowed by something at the threshold, and I was staring into a void. Strangely, warmth wafted at me, a soft scent of cinnamon touched my nose, and I blinked a few times. The mashing of the dreadful vision and homey smells took me a little off balance.

I squared my shoulders and huffed out my nose. Being on guard was the only way I'd make it through the day.

"Let's see what all those stories were really about," I declared, trying to sound strong and surprising myself when my voice sounded angry rather than terrified.

A pair of eyes opened in the distance, small and blue, and something laughed in all that dark. It wasn't the laugh of a human being or anything that had evolved in a reality that I understood. It was almost metallic, ringing like music dropped too many octaves. Those eyes stared at me, almond shaped and jagged, burning with blue fire that emanated around the edges and circled black pits in the center. It stared through the dark at me, and though no mouth was visible, I could sense a smile.

"Come on in," that deep, hair-raising voice beckoned. "You haven't got all day."

I glanced over my shoulder, and while the three men who'd shown me this place were still there, they might as well have been looking at me through prison bars. Thanks a lot, fellas.

"We'll speak like this," I said. A deep sigh from within the room was followed by the tutting of an old man.

"It's too early for you to be stating the terms with such certainty. You're here to make a deal of some kind. I'm not going to eat the first visitor I've had in almost forty years. I simply would like you to step into my humble abode so we might speak more…privately."

Standard Operating Procedure 204.11 Paragraph B

specifically states that no agent shall enter into a one-on-one conversation with any asset deemed "Hostile," or any asset categorized as Severity Level 4 or Greater on the Humphrey-Moreau Power Scale. So in all honesty, I should remember to put myself on report for violating the rules by stepping across that threshold.

## Chapter Five

For the briefest moment, I thought I was back in college, in my old loft apartment, crammed between other undergrad students trying to scrape a living in budget housing. Wedge shaped and only one room, it served the purpose of kitchen, bedroom, and a combination bathroom/shower. Classical piano drifted from a small stereo on the counter of the kitchen, and the smell of cinnamon grew stronger as a tray of steaming buns rested on the stove. The bed was a crisply made affair of lavender, with a single pillow, and a small television sat on a box opposite the nightstand.

It stood at the counter of the kitchen, taking oven mitts off slowly and hanging them on little hooks just over the toaster. Tall and lanky, it looked more like a retired gym teacher than the nightmare monster whispered about by terrified DIA recruits. Perfectly parted, tastefully graying hair sat on the head of a tanned, leathery face, from which brown eyes were watching me step into the strange prison cell. It wore khakis and a Hawaiian shirt that would have matched the Ronald/Donald set.

"Hello, Diane. Lovely to meet you in the flesh," it said, and I flinched at the sound of its voice. No alien, demonic voice. That I was prepared for. This was just a normal old man, genuine and polite. It sounded...fatherly, almost.

"Are you Archades?"

"I am he." He reached out to take a cinnamon bun and jerked his hand back, wincing. "Ooh, I sure did think you'd take longer to work up the nerve. I was hoping they'd be ready."

"This is an illusion, isn't it?" I asked. I tried to focus hard on little details. The subway tiles behind the stove looked uniform, but grimy with oil. Intricate details for a fabricated image. The floor was the same stone as the antechamber, but without the carved runes. Purposeful, or a forgotten aspect of the illusion?

"Certainly not," Archades said, sounding taken aback. He clutched his chest in feigned horror. "I haven't got nearly enough strength to do something like that. A little darkness and fire illusion, sure, but this?" He gestured around. "This is the hole they put me in four decades ago and mostly forgot about." He glanced at his surroundings and scratched his head. "Well, I *would* offer you a seat, but unfortunately they never did give me one. I can make some tea, if you like?"

"No, thank you."

"More polite than I expected. The last agent I talked to who was not assigned here was not so polite." Archades sighed. "No matter how bad things are, it's not an excuse to be rude. Wouldn't you agree?"

"I haven't met many tourists who were polite."

"Ah, 'tourists.' A funny little aphorism for anything that doesn't fit neatly into your government's understanding of the world." Archades slid a drawer open and took out a butter knife. He began doling out icing from a small tin. "I've lived in this world now as long as most of your kind, and if you count my time in other forms, I've been here much longer than any human that ever lived. Few trees have lived longer, I think."

"You're from another plane of existence. Extraplanar creatures are commonly—"

"Yes, yes." He waved a hand impatiently, icing dripping sweetly over the floor. "It's fine. I concede the point that I am not from your world and that I meet all those qualifications." He ran the knife under the faucet, wiped it with a sponge, rinsed it again, and set it on a drying rack. He turned, drying his hands. "Why don't you tell me what brought you all the way here?"

"I was sent to talk to you," I said, unsure of my actual instructions here. Take custody? What was that supposed to mean with something like him?

"To what end?" Archades asked, eyebrows raising. "My initial assumption was that you were here to plead with me for either power or knowledge, but you don't strike me as the pleading type." As he dragged the towel back over a knob, I caught a glimpse of a brass band under his left sleeve. A quick glance told me that he had a matching bracelet on the other wrist as well. He bore no other signs of ornaments that I could see.

"Just following orders," I said. "I was told to bring a body with me. My guess is that you're supposed to help me extract some information from it."

"Oh?" Archades said, testing the buns again with a careful prod from his finger. "Information from a dead man, is it?" He gingerly picked one up and held it out. I crossed my arms. "Please, I made them especially for you." He waggled it in the air.

"Is it poisoned? Enchanted? Otherwise rigged or set up to harm me?" I asked.

"I would be a terrible host to do that without warning you," Archades replied. "Besides, so far you've been a delight. I don't exactly relish the thought of never having another visitor. This place is so tediously boring. You have no idea." He smiled and held out the bun. A big drop of icing drooped on one side and threatened to let gravity take it away.

I took a cinnamon bun from a demon, and God help me, it was delicious. It had a homemade quality that reminded me of my grandmother's baking. Archades took one himself and plunged it wholesale into his mouth. Nothing supernatural, only stuffing it until the whole thing fit. Smacking loudly, he chewed and chewed and chewed until it was clear he was being obnoxious on purpose.

"Mr. Archades, I'd like your cooperation in this matter," I said. He blinked a few times at me and swallowed the whole bun at once. I could physically see the motion as it went down his gullet, strangely inhuman in its transit.

" '*Mister* Archades,' " he scoffed. "I could get used to that. Usually they call me 'it' or 'that thing' or 'He Who Devours,' but Mister Archades has such a nice, normal ring to it."

"I'll call you whatever you want if it gets me through this," I said. He took another bun and peeled a piece off, chewing it thoughtfully.

"I'm more than able to take a dead man and make his thoughts available, but nothing is free in this world. Or, for that matter, any other." He flashed perfectly white, even teeth in a wide smile. "If they sent you to me for help, it means that something terrible is threatening the safety of your people. The dead man must be critical, and somebody let him die before they could get that information."

"Something like that."

"Was it you?"

"Does it matter?"

"It sure does," Archades said. "I've got to know what kind of woman I'm dealing with. After all, you've heard stories about me, but I don't know you from Eve."

I considered this. Anything I told this creature was surely going to be filed away to be used against me in the future. If he wanted to negotiate a price, then knowing more about what happened would just give him the edge. Then again, straight up lying to a demon was a good way to not see another birthday.

"He came to me for asylum, but we were attacked by a third party before we could debrief him," I said. "The rest of the details don't matter." Archades smiled wider.

"Truth. What a rare currency here. I personally love the truth. It's so easy to keep straight, and let's not forget that nothing turns friends into foes faster than lies. I like you, Diane. Let's make a deal."

"What kind of deal?" I asked.

"Well, it's not much," Archades said, waving a bit of doughy bun in my direction. "It will benefit you immensely, help thousands of people who are at risk from whatever schemes are being laid, and make your superiors look good in the process."

"What do you want?"

"What you would want in my place," Archades said with a smile. "Freedom."

I laughed before I could stop myself. I stood in the

kitchen of an extraplanar being so powerful that a secret facility had been built to house him, and I laughed in his face. He took it well, but the smile faded from his lips.

"First, I don't have the authority to free you. Second, I know what you are and the things that you've done. If I let you free, you would be the first priority of every agent on the continent. As it stands, we're struggling to get additional resources on my case." I shook my head, still reeling.

"Miss Morris, you don't understand. I've been in here longer than you've been alive. Forty years is a short period of time for an immortal being such as myself, until you spend it trapped in a physical form such as this one. I didn't have a television until five years ago, and in that time, I've only had two local broadcast channels, one of which consists entirely of evangelicals preaching nonsense. I had a VCR until I destroyed the thing for eating my only movie, which was the first half of *Titanic*." Archades had his hands by his sides, but I could see the fists clenching and his jaw stiffening. "By the standards of your country, this is cruel and unusual punishment for certain."

"Those rights don't apply to you. Only native residents of Earth. Sorry," I said.

"It's been a long time since I saw sunlight. Or smelled fresh flowers." He waved a hand around the room. "This place has been my prison for long enough. I deserve to be let out."

"Set loose is more like it. There's not a chance," I replied. "I can see about getting you better entertainment. Books, magazines, maybe a DVD player or Netflix."

"I have no idea what those things are," Archades said. "And I don't want to watch movies. I'm feeling very cooperative these days. I will promise to cause no trouble to this world for as long as I am its guest."

"No," I said. He sighed and hung his head.

"Well, that's disappointing. If that's the case, you can show yourself out. You're on your own." He began taking the buns one by one and setting them on a plate, carefully ignoring me.

"You never expected me to agree to that, did you?" I asked. "I'm a field agent, not even a special agent in charge. I don't have the authority to free you."

"Oh, come now. That can't be true," Archades said, turning back to me. "I can sense your power over me, even now. The bindings forced on me do not support the hierarchy of your system. Whoever held the mantle of responsibility passed it to you, and now you can tell me to be free, and it will be so." He wagged a finger. "I believe you were given a key?"

Holy shit. I had no doubt that he was telling the truth. He was too excited at the prospect of freedom to be pulling a fast one on me. Besides, why would he lie? If I agreed to free him and had no power, he gained nothing. It felt like having the codes to a nuclear weapon. The key, still in my hand, felt like a hundred pounds of lead.

"What else can I do for you, if I'm not going to just set you loose on the world?"

"Not much, I'm afraid," Archades said. "All the riches in the world would do little to brighten this cell of mine." I considered him for a moment.

"You're a demon, right?"

"Not exactly in the classical sense, but it's close

enough for your kind," he said, eyes flicking over me. He was trying to figure out where I was headed with this line of thought. So not all-knowing.

"Demons are bound to their words, without exception. If a demon agrees to something, they have to follow that agreement, right?"

"That's true for many kinds of beings," Archades said. "Unfortunately, that includes me." A quick grin crept onto his face. "Are you looking to bargain with me, mortal woman?"

"That all depends. How reasonable are you going to be?" I asked. He licked his lips, and for a moment, his calm veneer faded and showed excitement underneath. No. Not excitement. Hunger.

"I can be extremely reasonable."

"If I'm going to give you any concessions, I'm going to need more than just information. I'm going to require your help."

"Go on."

"I'm currently involved with an investigation that my superiors have deemed the utmost importance. If you agree to help me with my case, to accompany me, I agree to take you from this prison for the duration. After my case concludes, you'll return here with as many new amenities as I can arrange."

"Ah, but I see a problem with your request. Say that I leave this place and provide you with whatever information you came for. Within a single day, the problem could be solved. Then I'd be back here having barely seen the outside world." Archades drummed his fingers on the counters. "I want a guaranteed year. Unsupervised in the world, with my word that I will not seek to harm any living soul, and with my word that I will willingly return here a year from the end of the investigation."

"No. Never unsupervised," I said. "And no guaranteed time. You could draw the investigation out for several months, and then where would I be?" Dead by dragon attack long before then, I thought, but no point giving him that advantage.

"You have to give me something," Archades said. "I'm trying to be reasonable."

"You want reasonable?" I asked. "All right. You agree to help me, and for as long as you remain cooperative, you can remain with me in the outside world."

"Define cooperative."

"You stay honest with me, don't try to cause trouble, and don't go running off on your own. The first time you try to impede my progress or refuse to give answers to questions I need answered, or start behaving in a manner that I find unacceptable, I'll have you back here so fast it'll make your head spin."

He paused, fingers still tapping out a pattern on his cheap countertops. He looked like he was muttering silently to himself. His face scrunched up with concern, and he shrugged up his shoulders as if wincing out an old ache.

"Serving a mortal in such a manner would seriously damage my reputation." Archades sounded like he was chewing on rocks for all the joy he had in his tone. "I'm obligated to keep my word if I agree. However..." His face tightened up, and his eyes locked on mine. "Oath-breaking humans always find themselves at the mercy of powers greater than they can imagine, with no protection."

"I haven't got all day," I replied. I know for a fact that Standard Operating Procedure 212.4 Paragraph A begins by saying "At no point and under no circumstances should bargains be forged with any extraplanar creature without consulting three (3) or more senior agents and at least one (1) administrator." I also knew that my best, maybe only, chance of getting a deal with Archades was here and now. Besides...if he helped and continued to help, he could be an asset. A true asset, not simply a euphemism for "anomalous event" as our nomenclature preferred. If Archades got out of hand, well, I could simply force him to return under the auspices of our agreement. That was if I had as much control over him as he and my superiors seemed to believe. Big if, but these were "big if" times.

"I will agree, in no uncertain terms, to serve you and your interests while you conduct your investigations. I will not attempt to harm you in any way, including physically, mentally, and spiritually, and I will make my best efforts to prevent others from doing the same. I agree to remain honest with you, to stay with you or in positions you are aware of, and I agree to cause no trouble you do not request of me. I do not agree to obey every command, but I do agree to aid you however I can," Archades said. I stood silently for a moment. It wasn't just that I heard what he said. I could feel the gravity...the power behind those words. It was as if he had bundled up part of the universe and laid it out before me. There was no reality besides this one.

"Then I agree to take you from this place, as long as you continue to abide by our agreement." I paused for a breath, mind racing to consider the agreement's final terms. "It is my sole discretion to determine if you've broken faith with me, and at such a time, you will return to this cell. Should I die before this agreement is fulfilled completely, you will return to this place and be given previously mentioned amenities, so long as your oath remains otherwise fulfilled."

His smile was unnaturally wide, and his teeth, though human indeed, were offset just enough to appear sinister. He took a quick step forward and thrust out a hand. Every inch of me tensed up, but I held my ground. I could now see clearly the thick brass bracelet hanging loosely on his wrist. I took his hand.

"Oh, Diane, you and I are going to have a hell of a time." He sniffed the air for a moment, and I pulled my hand away. It felt greasy, though whether it was from the baking or something else, I didn't know. "I believe you brought me something."

"Yeah, sort of," I said, turning back to the door. I hadn't noticed that it had closed behind me, and for a terrifying moment, I was sure that I'd just been locked inside. I put a hand against it, and it swung open easily. I breathed a sigh of relief. "Last night, we tracked down a ring of thieves who had made off with some…something powerful. We recovered one of the items, but the other is still at large. The last living thief came for amnesty and…"

"And he got *got*," Archades laughed. "Oh, that's rich. I was wondering why you'd need me to get information from a corpse. His spirit probably wouldn't cooperate with a séance."

Braeburn and his buddies were still as statues when we walked out. Archades closed the door behind him with a crisp click.

"Morning, gentlemen," he said. "Been a while

since we actually saw each other." His eyes drifted to the black body bag on the desk. "I take it that's our guy?"

"Yeah. Tomas."

"He's not half the man I thought he'd be. Where's the rest?" Archades asked, walking up to the bag and unzipping it. Donald looked like he was about to have a stroke, and Ronald hadn't blinked since the door opened. I wondered how much contact with Archades they'd had over the years.

"Vaporized by a mephit," I said.

"Crispy little bastards," Archades murmured. By now, Tomas was stiff and hard to move, but Archades lifted the body and looked at its head. A gentle stink wafted from the bag, reminding everybody that nature was about to make things very messy for these remains. "Fresh enough for me. All I need you to do is relax my restraints a bit, and I'll get everything you want to know."

"Relax your restraints?" I asked.

"Will you explain this to her?" Archades asked, glancing over at Braeburn. He just glared back. "No? Not accepting requests today? That's fine." Archades held his hands up and jangled his matching bracelets. "I'm sure you've asked yourself, 'Diane, did my boss just make me set free a demon with no ways to ensure he behaves?' And to that question, I direct your attention to my jewelry. It does a number of things to keep me in check, but one of the most irritating is that it prevents me from accessing any of the real power I'd normally have. You, being my capital W Warden, have the authority to remove the restraints from me."

"Some of the restraints," Braeburn said. "It's not

an all-or-nothing thing." Archades' face clouded with irritation.

"I thought audience participation was over." He shrugged and went back to smiling. "My previous warden is correct. You can choose to loosen the chains that bind me in increments." He touched the bracelets with opposite fingers. "If you were kind enough to release me from the full containment, these would fall from my arms, and I'd be free. I really would be eternally grateful."

"What it's not saying is that the more power it can draw, the more it can direct against the remaining restraints," Braeburn said. "Nobody really knows how they work except their creator and..." He lowered his eyes. "It's the one resource we can't use."

"How touching," Archades said. "Honestly, I've never been beyond the one percent I'm currently allowed, but at three-quarters my natural ability, I expect I'd make quick work of any problem you'd have."

"And you'd probably chew through the rest of the magic holding you back pretty quick," Braeburn said. Archades shrugged.

"Yes, well, that, but at ten percent I'm more than capable of performing this menial task." He rubbed his hands together, the dry leathery scraping of old calluses punctuating his words. "Even dear Braeburn can't argue that there's much of a threat of me breaking out at that level of release." I met Braeburn's eyes, and his frown deepened.

"No. From what we gleaned from the schematics recovered, it would give it access only to the most basic of its abilities."

"Most basic, he says." Archades groaned, acting wounded as he clutched his chest. "Even fully bound, I'm far from basic." He winked at me. "After all, I foresaw your arrival and knew your name without being told."

"It's not the first time I've run into some creepy tourist who could do that. It wasn't much of a surprise," I said. "All right, fine. How do I do this?"

"I'd begin by giving me your command," Archades said. "Then I'll tell you what I need, and you can simply give me permission."

"Fine," I said. "Archades. Will you please find the location of the item this person was involved in stealing?"

"I would be overwhelmed with joy to do that, but I will need permission to release myself from the first ten percent of restraints."

"You have my permission," I said.

When magic is afoot, mortals feel it in peculiar ways. Each type of magic has a distinct flavor to it. Magic that affects the mind gives off a strong sense of déjà vu, while evocation manifests as a smell, usually unpleasant, like that of burning hair or released natural gas. If you're ever around someone and suddenly feel terribly nauseous, there's good odds that they're looking into the future, and if that's the case, you should remind them that divination magic is strictly controlled, and that if they're not licensed, they're likely to have somebody from the Cabal of Wizards show up.

In this case, I could feel the air being drawn from my lungs ever so slightly, as I watched the featureless surface of the brass around his wrists shine with molten light. Geometric patterns ran across the surface, covering it in a honeycomb of lines and sigils. Archades flexed his hands and took a giant breath. His chest swelled, and he held the air until finally letting it out in one whoosh that dispelled the gathering energies in the room. He turned to look at me. His eyes had changed from the boring muddy brown of an older man into a crisp, clear blue of a summer morning sky.

"Would you like to see a magic trick?" he asked, his voice giddy but otherwise unchanged. Without waiting for a response, he reached out and grabbed Tomas by the neck and lifted the half-corpse off the table. He held his right hand out and extended his forefinger.

Shadow crept out from under his sleeve and engulfed the finger in wispy strands that coagulated into something hard and shiny, some weird shadowstuff, until the finger had turned from a human digit into a single, inflexible hook more than ten inches long. He slid it around Tomas' head in a light caress. I grimaced, revolted at the idea of being touched by this thing. It wasn't until he'd turned the head completely around that I saw that the very end of the claw had been plunged through the skull. With a horrifying sucking sound, Archades tugged on the scalp and pulled the entire top of the skull clean off, revealing a gray brain covered in black ropes of coagulated blood.

"Such a funny thing, you humans," Archades said. "Every single thing in your body is devoted to supporting this one organ, and yet its only protection is a few layers of bone and tissue." He tossed the detached bone to the side, and it clicked against the stone floor. "Maybe with more protection, your secrets wouldn't be so simple to retrieve." He gave a small apologetic look my way. "You might not want to watch this part."

I should have listened. With both hands, he plunged fingers into the sides of the brain and took great scoops into his mouth. It would have been easier to watch if his jaw had distended like a snake and he'd taken it whole. Instead, he looked like a baby trying to eat a handful of oatmeal. Ropes of gray matter fell back to the table and down his front as he greedily smashed more and more and chewed frantically. A deep groan resonated from his chest, primal and sexual, and he nodded as a man enjoying a fine steak might. His whole hand disappeared into the skull and retrieved the last bits. He sucked his fingers clean one at a time.

I threw up as politely as I could, trying to aim for a spot on the floor that looked easy to clean. Braeburn and his buddies looked on stoically, though my old classmate was clearly more furious than sickened. I wondered if they'd ever seen him do this before. Had we been forced to resort to this monster in the past?

"Oh," Archades said, standing up from his hunched meal. "Oh my. You should have told me what they stole." He grinned, ribbons of brain still between his teeth. He let go of Tomas, who fell limply off the counter. His hollow head hitting the ground was too musical for me to be able to forget without the help of chemicals.

"Was all of that completely necessary?" I asked. Archades wiped his mouth with one hand and leaned down to clean himself on the remains of Tomas' shirt.

"Oh my, yes." His eyes were wide, and his pupils filled them almost completely. He looked stoned. I wondered if it was a normal effect for his kind after eating brains. "The pair of them...from Old Miss Z herself." He shook his head. "What a bold plan."

"You know where the other is?" I asked.

"I know where it was at least." Archades tapped his fingers on the table a few times. "I've got to hand it to you, Diane. Had I known that you were going after dragons' eggs, I would have negotiated a better deal. Your superiors knew that you couldn't possibly do this without me, and they sent you to physically bring me back to help, not just retrieve this information from a corpse."

"Where is it?"

"Back from whence you came," Archades said. That long, wicked claw retracted, the shadowy substance of it retreating beyond the brass cuff. "It seems there are players you're not aware of out there."

"Fill me in on the way," I said. I turned to Braeburn. "I need that flight back right now."

"I wish you'd reconsider letting it loose," he replied, voice low. "I know you're the *wunderkind* and all, but this thing you're dealing with, it's not a man."

"I know that," I snapped. "But lives are at stake, and I'm not going back without answers."

"So get your answers. Leave it locked up," Braeburn said.

"That wasn't the deal," I said. "Besides, I can take care of this."

"Look at that face," Braeburn said. "You're not the first person who thought they could outsmart Archades. The last person who did? He's still paying the price."

**\*\*\*\***

Archades stretched his long legs out into the aisle of the luxury plane. He'd ordered a gratuitous amount of alcohol and was sipping a daiquiri out of a hollowed pineapple. I, on the other hand, was still reading some of the paperwork that Braeburn had given me. A thick manila envelope stamped Top Secret wasn't anything new to me, and as I riffled through stacks of incident reports and conversation logs, I got a better sense for the thing sitting across from me.

"You...you're possessing that body right now, aren't you?" I asked. Archades paused mid-drink. "It was a person before, right?"

"That's kind of a personal question," he said. "Now, Diane, if you want to get to know me better, then I expect a little reciprocation on your behalf. Where are you from, originally? Do I detect a little Midwestern drawl?"

"Minnesota," I said. "I haven't been home in a couple years."

"And why's that?"

"You first," I said. He slurped noisily through his straw and kept his eyes fixed on mine. Eyes the color of deer hide searched mine, and I refused to look away. He looked entirely human now, without the tricks or the shadows. The more I looked, the more familiar he seemed.

"I am indeed possessing this body. Unfortunately, those children who stumbled upon my Codex failed to manifest a proper form for me to inhabit, and I've been forced to find host after host." He chuckled. "This was before you were even born, by the way, not that it makes a huge difference. I'm sure there are still a few left back in the department who would recognize this face."

"It's Nathan Tullman, isn't it?" It suddenly struck

me, clear as a bell.

"Tut-tut, it's my turn for the question," Archades said. "Why haven't you been home? Don't Mommy and Daddy miss their little girl?"

"There's nothing interesting about why I haven't gone home. Work keeps me too busy, and most of the time I can't risk something tracking me back to them. A lot of petty people are lurking in the shadows that would like to make short work of someone like me. I talk with them all the time. They think I quit being a cop and got into the tax business." My father had been delighted when he'd learned he'd never have to file his own taxes ever again. Momma was just relieved I wasn't giving out speeding tickets in Texas anymore.

He considered me for a while and then nodded.

"Yes, this is the body of Nathan Tullman. He was nearly fifty when we faced off, but luckily, I keep enough power to hold back time."

"How did you end up possessing him?"

"That's a very long story, and one I'm not interested in relaying at this moment." Archades narrowed his eyes. "You said you were a cop. Tell me about that."

"That's a very long story," I said dryly. "One I'm not interested in relaying at this moment." He chuckled, setting his empty drink down.

"You haven't asked about the eggs again," he said.

"I trust you'll let me know in good time." Strictly speaking, that wasn't a lie. Most beings like him were incapable of going back on a deal. The elementals could do whatever they wanted, but sane, rational powers of his ilk relied on order and rules to continue their existence. It was the only thing that made dealing with him even remotely sane.

"How about you tell me what you know so far?"

I shrugged. "Not much. There were two eggs stolen, the entirety of the brood, and we've recovered one of them. As long as any egg is missing from the nest, we're in danger of having a rampaging dragon on our hands."

"And ol' Ziraxariz can be a bitch to deal with." He must have seen me grit my teeth and freeze, as if the dragon were going to climb over the clouds and swallow us up. "What? Worried about the whole 'naming the beast to draw its attention' thing?" He rolled his eyes. "I'm not too worried about that. Besides, me and Z, we've known each other for a few minutes. You better hope returning the eggs is enough. If she smells humans in her lair, she's liable to be apoplectic regardless."

"No doubt, but we'll cross that bridge when we get to it," I said. "Regardless, I recovered one egg when a group of mortal thieves were trying to sell it to some mephits in Jacksonville, but the other was nowhere to be seen."

"They didn't have the other anymore," Archades said, swishing his champagne around in its glass. He was enjoying drawing this out. "Gave it to someone for safekeeping."

"To whom?" I asked.

"Nobody I recognize," Archades said. "A lot of the players have changed since the last time I was really in power. Some kind of middleman, Chinaman by the name of Lee Arnold."

"I know him," I said. "Works out of a flea market on the west side of Jacksonville. He's gotten warnings about peddling minor magical artifacts but never been caught with anything this big. Doesn't make much sense."

"Well, either he's been sandbagging you, or it's his lucky break. Dragon eggs have so many uses. You can sell them to just about anybody for a ridiculous fortune."

"What do the mephits want it for?" I asked.

"Either they're working for the Firelord, in which case he'll hatch the egg and convert it into a steed for his eternal wars, or they're working for a rival, in which case it'll be consumed to great effect and probably spark a civil war on the Plane of Fire." Archades scratched his head. "Your buddy Tomas didn't know, so that's just my guess."

"What did he know?"

"Not much," Archades said. "Worked for that thieving outfit, called themselves the Magpies. Pretentious shits. What else do you expect from the French? Had some very strange habits. Quite the pornographic film enthusiast."

"That's not helpful."

"No, I didn't think it would be." Archades set aside his drink and folded his hands on the table. "To be honest, I wouldn't be so worried about finding the egg. One rampaging dragon isn't the end of the world. Depending on where the nest is, she'll at most wipe out one big city or a few small towns. Eat enough to go back into hibernation for another thousand years or so."

"What should I worry about, in that case?"

"There's a powerful wizard out there who orchestrated the whole thing," Archades said. "It's how Tomas and his gang even got into the nest in the first place. I think there's a gateway, looks built into an armoire. The thieves had some nice techniques to keep the dragon from noticing them. I guess the deal was that the mage was going to get an egg and the mephits would get the other."

"So the one the mage is expecting?"

"Must be the one they kept with this Lee fellow. Tomas took it to him the same day as the heist…I suppose it could be called an egg-napping?" Archades chuckled. "This Mr. Arnold gave them a respectable sum as collateral. The other egg they had, but it was being delivered to the elementals when some woman with karate jumped them and…oh. That was you."

"You knew that." I struggled to keep my voice level. "So the elementals were paying for an egg?"

"Well, not much," Archades said. "Couple dozen pounds of gold is all. I guess after Mr. Arnold's collateral, they felt they were being cheated a little."

"Who brokered that deal, then?"

"Hmmm, didn't know." Archades took an individually wrapped toothpick from the tray in front of him. He pulled something gray and slimy from his teeth and regarded it fondly before flicking it down his throat. "Must have been somebody else in his group."

"Any of them left alive?"

"No. He seemed to hold you responsible. He was just as surprised to be shot at as you were, so it's a mystery where that lot came from. All that's left is the mage and Mr. Arnold, I'm afraid. Oh, and the mephits, of course. Working with the mage, I assume."

"I'll get our liaison with the Cabal of Wizards to see if he can find anything. In the meantime, we'll go pay the flea market a visit." Archades grinned widely, shaking his brass bindings and rubbing them with the tips of his fingers. I could see my reflection in them. I looked tired.

Chapter Six

I'd made a slight miscalculation on my itinerary. Our return flight parked us right where I'd left, fewer than nine hours later. Evening was heavy in the air, and I missed the dry heat of the desert when the soggy night rolled across my face on the walk to the company car. Archades strolled beside me, his long stride almost a dance as he looked around at the pine trees in the distance and the heavy clouds overhead. It looked like we might end up with rain before the night was through.

"Somehow I'd hoped that my first car ride as a free man would be a little nicer than a...what's this? Toyota?"

"First off, you're neither free nor a man, so I wouldn't worry about it. Second, my car blew up this morning, so I'm in this until I find time to wrangle with my insurance company." I unlocked the doors and got in. Archades made a disgusted sound and clambered into the other seat.

"It smells like a pet groomer used this to transport wet animals," he said, nose wrinkled.

"Yeah, well, I took a bath in a retention pond before coming to get you," I snapped. "Do you eat?"

"What?" He seemed surprised.

"I guess I'm stuttering without hearing it. Do you need to put food into your body?"

"I heard you. I just didn't think you would care very much. Yes, I need to eat. I may be immortal, but this body still requires all of its old comforts."

I cranked the engine and pulled out of the parking lot, trying not to think about how better I could have used the money spent on the private jet for the day.

Archades continued, "I even need to sleep from time to time. Oh, I can keep this body from dying regardless, but eventually the hunger, thirst, exhaustion…well, they add up. When first I was taken captive, they thought that if they managed to kill the body, they might kill me, as I'm tethered to it."

This was surprising.

"Wouldn't you just wind up banished to your native plane, whichever one that is?"

"Well, no. Normally, if my mortal host is killed, I leave the body at its death and find a new host. It takes a binding ritual and then a banishment ritual to remove me. However, I'm spiritually incapable of leaving this body. Apparently Nathaniel was far too crafty in his technique to allow that loophole. Even with my limited reserves right now, I can keep it alive. Otherwise, I suspect I'd simply inhabit a corpse."

Archades popped open the glove compartment and began rifling through it. I snapped it shut, almost catching his fingers in it. He frowned at me.

"Don't distract the driver," I said, pulling onto the highway. "You have a preference for food?"

"My rations at the prison weren't terribly varied. Baking ingredients were a reward for not attempting to kill any of the staff for a whole month, but normally I had to settle for freeze-dried and canned meals." He shuddered. "I'll eat whatever you consider good, as long as it's not meat out of a can."

I drove for a ways until I saw something I thought I could keep down, ordered through the drive-thru, and ate on our way to the office. As much as I wanted to go straight to the flea market, I needed to let my boss know that I'd made a deal with a demon to keep the case alive. Much to my surprise, Archades didn't order an outrageous amount of food, or a strange combination of flavors and textures. Just a normal combo meal and a milkshake, which he ate with a spoon as we drove.

"You know, I'm surprised you haven't tried to convince me that everything I know about you is a misunderstanding," I said. He glanced over at me, licking the spoon, acting confused. "Oh, come on. It's not the first time I've come across a tourist from an outer plane. Normally I get the same canned speech about my limited perspective on morality, and about how things are 'just shades of gray' as a vampire once tried to convince me."

"Yes, well, vampires would say that. They don't see color at all," Archades said. "Would spinning a story about how I'm not a terribly bad guy get you to remove my shackles?"

"No."

"Then why would I lie to you about my past?"

"Guess I expected you to trick me into letting you free or something," I said. He chuckled, licking the inside of his cup clean. I could hear his tongue scraping the bottom free of ice cream, and I shuddered. He blinked and withdrew his head, wiping his lips.

"Apologies. I know that can be unnerving," he said, putting the empty into the greasy paper bag the food had come in. "I have no intention of tricking you into anything. I've made an agreement with you, which I intend to honor."

"You'd better," I grumbled. "A lot of people are going to die if you don't."

"I don't particularly care." Archades laid his seat back a little, crossing his arms over his chest. "Keeping you alive is my highest priority, anyway. I'm sure you'll throw yourself at this dragon, if the time comes, and then I'll likely be destroyed alongside you, but until then, I imagine I'll manage." My ears perked up at that. Ziraxariz could "destroy" something like Archades? Fascinating. "Besides," he continued, "there will be a time when nobody's going to have to trick you into releasing me. You're going to do that all on your own. With all that human free will."

"And why would I do that?"

"It'll just happen. You'll do it at the right place, at the right time, for all the wrong reasons," Archades said. His head was listing to the side, and he sounded sleepy. Probably an act.

I couldn't help but wonder where Archades was from. Most of my experience came from dealing with elementals, but I had a lot of contact with the denizens of the Plane of Shadow and the Plane of Light, both of which could be real assholes at times. Beyond those, though…contact with the demi-planes was limited to religious orders and emergencies only. Angels, demons, devils, archons…I'd read about them, but unless one was wreaking havoc in the middle of the public view, there were other channels that dealt with them. Bringing down Archades originally had been an unprecedented act of cooperation between the Vatican and the DIA. That made me believe he was from one of the Underworlds, planes of existence beyond the Plane of Shadow that housed mortal souls not deemed worthy of eternal grace or glory. I thought briefly of asking him, but I doubted I'd get a straight answer out of him. So instead, I just let his breathing get deeper and deeper until it sounded like someone was running a chainsaw. At high idle.

*For now, it doesn't matter*, I thought as I turned down the road leading to the office. He'd agreed to some pretty explicit terms in our contract, and while, yes, making a deal with the devil is classically a bad idea, it was far better than having no clue what to do or where to go. So I parked the company car in the back of the lot with the rest of our secondhand government vehicles and shook Archades awake.

"Already?" He sounded just like a grumpy old man, blinking his eyes.

"You were asleep for, like, three minutes," I said. "I told you it wasn't far. Come on. I've still got to call my insurance company and tell them they're going to have to shell out for another car."

We crossed the blacktop of the parking lot, still warm from the day's sunbake, and Archades yipped a short, barking laugh before covering his mouth. I glared at him.

"What?"

"Oh, it's nothing. I just expected the dreaded DIA to have a much nicer headquarters," Archades said. "I guess I should count myself lucky that I didn't have accountants hunt me down in '74."

"Shut up," I muttered. "There's four other divisions that need funding, and ours is bottom of the pile. Maybe if Northwest could handle their shit a little better, we could afford more agents and wouldn't need to have you here." Archades rolled his eyes.

"Poor thing." He shoved his hands in his pockets. "Does anybody else know who I am?"

"I doubt it, considering I didn't even know," I said. "Just keep your mouth shut and try not to attract any attention." I swiped my access card on the front door and pulled it open. The IRS guys actually got to go home at five, like normal people, so I wasn't surprised to find the lobby empty. I had to flash a badge again to get our dedicated elevator to work, but once in, I settled myself a little, straightening out my hair and trying to contain some of the stray frizz that had gotten loose. Damned humidity. Damned mephits.

I tried to walk straight down the hall to the director's office, but *she* got to me first.

"He needs a visitor's badge." A high, nasally whine pierced the otherwise quiet of the office. Ah, fuck. I plastered a smile across my face as best I could and turned to the front desk, just outside the elevators.

"Yancy. Hello. You're looking great today." Archades coughed a little, and I wondered if he could actually tell when I was lying. Yancy O'Reilly looked like all the worst stereotypes of the British Isles mashed into a burlap sack, which had then been subsequently drowned. A short, not overly large woman in her late thirties, she always had lipstick on her giant teeth and never looked like she was happy to actually be alive. She was sitting in her tall-backed chair, looking over her computer at us.

"Agent Morris, you know you can't have people here without a visitor's badge," Yancy said and even tapped her little plastic sign that read in big, bold pink letters: *Visitors MUST Sign In!*

"I know that if Director LaFleur has to wait thirty more seconds to talk to me, the world could end," I muttered. Archades put a hand on my shoulder and laughed.

"Oh, what a kidder. Yancy, isn't it?" He strode forward confidently. "I knew a Yancy once when I was in Denmark. Beautiful woman, charming conversation. Are you related, by any chance?" Yancy blinked a few times at him, half a frown on her face while she tried to figure out if he was having a laugh at her.

"My family's from Boston," she finally said.

"Oh, well, I'm just lucky then. Must be the luck of the Irish." He winked. He actually fucking winked at her and picked up a pen, scribbling something on the paper pad she kept out for just such an occasion. I rolled my neck in frustration and rejoiced at the snapping sounds of my vertebrae realigning.

"I can't read this," Yancy said, squinting at the sheet he handed to her. "Muscle? Does this say muscle?"

"No, my dear," Archades said, leaning over the counter. "Mussalem. Mortimer Mussalem." God bless her heart, she actually typed that in, and the printer pushed out a tiny little badge that he peeled and stuck onto his chest.

"Any messages for me?" I asked, feeling exhausted all of the sudden. Yancy huffed and didn't even look up from her computer at me.

"I'm not your secretary. I'm the receptionist for the whole floor. Check your email. You've got your own voicemail too. Try using it."

"Gee, thanks, Yancy," I said, silently counting to

ten. "What would we ever do without you?" I gestured to Archades. "Come on…Morty. Let's go see the boss."

"We're already with the boss," Archades said and smiled at Yancy. "Hope to see you soon. You know how it is. Busy, busy, busy."

"Well, I…" Yancy seemed a little pink in the face. "Have a good day, Mortimer."

"Please, Morty is just fine," he said. I glowered at him as we went down the hall. He seemed to sense my subtle displeasure. "What?"

"Stop trying to make good with people. She's not going to get you anywhere you want to go. Leave her out of this."

"I've always thought that you can tell a great deal about a person based on how they treat people they don't need to treat kindly," Archades said. He stopped short of LaFleur's door. "Are those Aramaic wards in the frame?" I glanced at the carvings.

"There's a lot of wards in the frame. It won't be a problem once you're invited in," I said.

"Who put them there?"

"Wizards. Living saints. Who knows? Before my time."

"Ah." Archades extended a probing finger, and a hot spark jumped from the wooden frame to the tip of his fingernail. He jerked his hand back, grinning. "It's nice to see proper craftsmanship in the modern age."

The door opened unbidden, swinging wide, and Director LaFleur sat behind his desk, as unruffled as ever, leaning with folded hands on the desk. His eyes were locked on Archades the moment a line of sight was clear. I half expected him to have every agent bearing weapons in defense, but if we had that many to spare, they'd be out looking for the egg.

"Director LaFleur," I said, and he gave a bare twitch of his head. Permission to enter, I dared to assume. I stepped across the threshold, and when my molecules remained attached to one another, I breathed a sigh of relief. The door shut behind us, and as we approached the desk, LaFleur stayed in the same exact position. "Sir, this is Archades."

"Jermaine," Archades said, voice tight. "I didn't know I'd have the pleasure of seeing you here. I would have thought you'd gotten yourself heroically killed somewhere exotic by now." A sharp, brief glimpse of electric blue light overwhelmed Archades' mortal eyes for a moment, and then it was gone, as fast as the flash on a camera.

The director shifted his attention to me. It was like being pinned to an autopsy table.

"Special Agent Morris, I had hoped for a different solution." I almost laughed, a knee-jerk reaction to so much pressure and anxiety building up. Instead, I schooled my face to be still and held myself professionally.

"Sir, given the circumstances and the urgency, I have acted with the greatest care possible." I stepped forward and set a neatly written paper on the desk. "I have recorded the agreement made between myself and this asset, whom I assume you are familiar with."

"We have a long history together." Archades' eyes flashed again, like distant lightning striking a mountain of sapphires. "How did it feel to close the door on my cell? Did you see me, or could you only see your partner?" Director LaFleur was reading the words on the paper, the thin line of his lip growing ever tighter into a frown.

"There is a line about 'aforementioned amenities,' " he said. "What does that entail?"

"There is an addendum on the bottom, sir," I said. "I wanted to have the quote of the agreement as I said it verbatim." He glanced down, then back up, and put the paper down.

"And it agreed to these conditions, using these exact words?"

"That's right," I said. "Already, I have good information about where to begin searching. I'll head directly there, dig up any leads, hopefully get this taken care of."

LaFleur turned his gaze back to Archades. "Wait outside."

"I don't take orders from you." Arms folded, Archades rocked back on his heels as if he had all the time in the world. I grimaced.

"Archades, stand outside. Please." A moment later, the door shut again, and I was left to bear the brunt of those brutal eyes.

"Sit." Like a trained dog, I did as I was told. "Special Agent Morris, I cannot express how vital it is that the creature you've struck a deal with does not go free." I narrowed my eyes.

"Sir, with respect, no shit." I was too tired and cranky for this kind of lecture. I wasn't some first-year rookie out of recruitment; I was the senior goddamned field agent. "Nothing's going to happen under my watch."

"Let me make this clear," LaFleur said, standing. It was a move to make himself look more imposing, threatening, and serious. It worked. It was like looking up at a national monument made flesh and angry at the nearby tourists. "If the choice falls between freeing that creature or stopping the destruction of this city, state, or nation, you cannot give it freedom. The world may mourn a country in ashes, but nobody will mourn what happens to humanity should it be let loose."

"I got it, I got it." I sounded a lot more flippant than I felt. Somebody had turned gravity up inside the office, and I felt crushed into my seat. I didn't need this shit. I could have been a park ranger. Should have been, by the looks of things.

"It will do or say anything it thinks might persuade you," LaFleur said. "It will be harder than you want to believe. I know. I still see the face of an old friend. But it is only a monster."

"I'll bear that in mind," I said, standing. "In the meantime, I need papers for him, some ID, and I'll need to draw on petty cash if I'm going to keep him fed and happy." He nodded, filling out a slip of paper.

"I'll have Logistics prepare a packet. In the meantime, do you intend that he stay at your residence?"

"I don't expect to be going back there until this has all blown over." Not only did I not want Archades knowing where I lived, but I also didn't want to risk drawing my neighbors into a rapidly escalating conflict. "We'll arrange that sort of thing as we go."

"That's fine." LaFleur nodded. "Any details on the remaining egg?"

"I'm following up on some leads. I'll let you know when I have something more concrete."

"Try and get some sleep, Agent Morris," LaFleur said, fingers rapping against the desk in a procession of tiny mortar strikes. "You'll need all your wits about you."

"Yeah." I turned to leave and paused. As I opened the door, I shot him a smile. "He's going by Mortimer Mussalem now, so that's something you'll need on the paperwork." The flat stare he gave me as I pulled the door shut was almost worth the headache that was already building.

**\*\*\*\***

"Would you like me to help?" Archades asked, his feet kicked up on my desk, watching through the open bathroom door as I peeled the bandage off the cut on my forehead and dabbed at it with iodine. The skin around it was red and inflamed, and the actual cut was a soggy scab that looked like a ravine of green and brown.

"Unless you've got a bottle of amoxicillin in your pocket, not really," I muttered, dancing in place as I swabbed out as much of the scab as I could in one pass. Mother had always insisted that iodine was far better than, say, peroxide, despite the fact that the latter simply foamed and barely stung at all.

"Looks infected." He had his arms folded behind his head and was leaning back on my one guest chair until the front legs were off the ground.

"It's not," I lied, pressing a fresh pad of gauze against it and taping it securely. "As clean as a whistle."

"Indeed." I slumped into my office chair, powering the computer on and pouring a cup of coffee out of the pot I'd started brewing the second I walked into my office. "I take mine with two sugars, please." I rolled my legs under the desk, sipping on mine without any such frivolities.

"Pot's there, cups in the drawer under it, along with whatever you need," I said, enjoying the warm caffeine seeping into my bones. Despite the sweaty summer evening outside, I needed something hot to keep me going. It was going to be a long night. I busied myself with some research online, gathering basic information that was publicly available. We could just make the flea market before it closed. It was open late Saturday nights.

"Did Tomas know where the other egg was going? I mean, ultimately?" I asked.

"They gave it up to Lee when they left Old Lady Z's lair," Archades said, shaking out a couple single-serving sugar bags. "My guess? The mage who got them access into the lair was going to get it."

"Does this mage have a name?" I asked.

"I'm certain he does, but Tomas didn't know it. Never even saw the mage in person. They only referred to him as Mr. Wizard. A reference to something pop-cultural, I believe." Archades returned to his chair and clomped his feet back up on the desk. "Oh, this is terrible coffee, Diane." He smacked his lips and took another sip. "Even in my day, we had better than this."

"I like it. Keeps people from coming in here asking for some." I didn't enjoy any flavor of coffee, to be honest, but it did its job. "I need to consult our wizard about the mage, then we can go see Lee about his involvement."

"Oh, you have a court wizard?" Archades asked, arching an eyebrow. "A Merlin to your Arthur?"

"Only if you're counting the cartoon version," I muttered, reaching for my phone. I punched in an extension, and as always, it went straight to voicemail.

"I am Rubin. If I am here, I am listening. Speak your business, and I shall fulfill my duty." There had been a long, drawn out battle to even get him to set this up, and after three years of him lurking in the office, it had become clear that he was never going to learn how to answer a phone. More than likely, he was within arms' reach of his answering machine, staring intently at the infernal machine as if demons would leap hither and thither if he took his eyes off it.

"Rubin, Diane Morris here. I need a consultation on a possible rogue element of your persuasion." On the phone, even in the office, it was important to keep things vague. Once, there had been a freedom of information act used to acquire some tapes, and I'd actually had to go to a deposition to explain that all the conversation about a unicorn had been code for some rare tax loophole we never saw. "Now would be a good time for me, if you're available. Call me back if you're not coming now. I've got pressing issues to deal with." I hung up and realized that the odds of him actually calling me back were slim indeed.

"I've known a number of wizards in my time," Archades said. "Mages, warlocks, druids, whatever you want to call them. Different names for the same thing: mortals out of their depth."

"Yeah, well, if you're a better resource than Rubin, I'm all ears." I pulled out a new, unlabeled folder from my cabinet and wrote a big capital "Z" in the header. I gathered some of the notes I'd taken, all written in the mandatory code the department used, and slid them in. "The Cabal of Wizards loves their secrets, and they won't let any of us close enough to get real information about their members. Still, in cases like this, they've agreed to help the DIA in exchange for certain…considerations."

"Such as?"

"Wizards like to do a lot of weird, technically illegal but not really harmful things. Between ingesting substances on a number of banned lists, importing exotic and illegal items, and practicing magic which is strictly against the nation's anti-witchcraft laws, Uncle Sam could make life for them pretty hard. Just look at Germany. Almost no German wizards, because they'll kick your ass out if they find you manipulating the universe to suit your needs."

"I had no idea," Archades said dryly. "Life must be so difficult for them."

"We get along." I began filling out a requisition form while I waited. "Every branch of the DIA has a full-time liaison, and Rubin has been here longer than any of the others since I got here. Before him there was Jervis, and before that Gavin, and before that—"

"I got it," Archades said, holding up a hand. "To be clear, I don't trust wizards. They all have one thing in common."

After a long, expectant pause, I finally gave in. "Which is?" Archades grinned and started to say something when my office door flew open.

"I have arrived!" Rubin intoned, loud and solemn as he strode into my office. He was every inch a wizard, so long as those inches were from the neck up. A long white beard met with long white hair, both flowing down over his chest and shoulders. White eyebrows heavy enough to act as speed bumps shaded his gray eyes, and the entire magnificently magical appearance was thrown off by the fact that he wore a tweed jacket, khakis, and loafers. He looked like a homeless man applying for a job in a suit donated by another homeless man.

"Rubin, thanks for coming so quickly," I said, rising and offering a hand. He walked right past me and stood to look out the window.

"Why, woman, have you summoned me to your presence? Do you wish to consult with the power of earth and sky? Do I, and I alone, have the knowledge you require?" I'd almost forgotten what it was like to be this close to him. He smelled very strongly of horseradish and cloves. There was a large patch of fresh char on the elbow of his jacket.

"I certainly hope so," I said, sitting back down and glaring at his back. This was why he wasn't on my Christmas card list. That, and I didn't know where he actually lived. Maybe he slept in the basement, where his little magical laboratory was housed. "Is there any possibility that you could make a list of the best wizards you know for teleportation? Or portals, or whatever it is they do."

"Do you plan to make a trip?" Rubin asked, still keeping his eyes out the window. He probably thought it made him look pensive, but all it really did was make it hard to make his words out. Between the odd accent, the beard, and the fact that he sometimes forgot to actually move his lips, it was a wonder anybody ever got any information out of him.

"No, I've got a case I'm working on," I said. "Anybody who could teleport around eight people into an obscure stronghold and get them back out?" Rubin hummed for a moment.

"Hrmmm, yes, that would require a magus of

immense power indeed. I understand why you came to me now." Rubin swept around the room until he was looming over my desk. All five feet of him. "Perhaps if you could provide me with more details, I would be capable of assisting you better."

"Let's start with assisting me at all, and then see how we can do better," I muttered, coffee cup in clenched fist. This was the trouble with Rubin, or his predecessors, or any other Cabal member that I'd had the misfortune of working with. It was actually better to be at odds with a wizard because at least then you didn't have to play any funky little games with them. Kicking down the door to an illegal alchemist lab was way more straightforward than finagling Rubin to actually do his job without scratching his back. My administrators would deny it, but I was sure that the Cabal wanted information about the department just as badly as we wanted information on magical happenings.

"Who do you know that would be able to summon a strong elemental twice in as many days?" Archades asked. Rubin swiveled his head to stare at him reproachfully, his yards of beard slowly catching up with the sudden movement.

"And who might you be?" Rubin asked.

"Morty," Archades said, shaking several packets of sugar together and tearing their tops off. "I'm a private consultant."

"May I see your credentials? Agent Morris"—his head turned back to me, dragging its encumbrances with it—"I must object to the uninitiated being allowed to ask questions like this. It is Cabal business who *might* be capable of any feats."

"I operate with Special Agent Morris' full confidence. Isn't that right?" Archades grinned around a sip of coffee.

"That's right," I said, gritting my teeth. I actually did have confidence in Archades. At least, as long as the question was whether or not he would use any opportunity to make my life more difficult. "Answer his question. Who might be around that could pull off that sort of thing?"

Rubin sighed. This was not the simple, everyday sigh of a vexed teenager rolling her eyes at a mother demanding she go put on a more modest skirt. No, this was the professional expression of disdain. It said, "You are wasting my time, and every second of my time is more valuable than the rest of your life."

"Let me assume that you believe it to be the same exact elemental," he said, stretching the word *assume* so that it only made an ass of me. "The esoteric and demanding rituals required to produce a specific desired elemental are, shall I say, difficult at best. Without cooperation from the target, sequential summonings are nigh on impossible."

"Let's assume that there is cooperation," I said.

"I see. In that case, it isn't a matter of focus but rather one of materials and power." Rubin shrugged. "An experienced wizard, with the proper knowledge and items of power, could summon the same elemental once per week, if necessary. Once a day? I hardly think it's likely."

"Let's say it happened," I said. "Same elemental being brought back within twelve hours of returning to…wherever it came from."

"Both parties to the summoning would need to be

very motivated." Rubin scratched his bearded chin. "I suppose it's not impossible. It would require a great amount of energy to allow the elemental to coalesce, which means it would need to be in a remote location to avoid notice."

"Can you give me anything more specific than that?" I asked. "Like, should I be looking for lights in the sky, dead animals on the ground, fish floating in the river?"

"Will you tell me what elemental is being summoned?" Rubin asked. I paused. Wizards were funny. Even with the Cabal to keep them in check, you never really knew who their friends were. If Rubin had contacts in the Firelands, he might mention it to them and escalate the problem there. Especially if the mephits were on officially sanctioned business, and not just rogue elementals.

"Let's say it was an air elemental. A djinn, or something like it."

"In that case, I'd say that unless there's been a hurricane parked over the city the past few days, which I have failed to notice somehow, there is no source likely to allow such a thing to happen."

"What about using an artifact?" Archades asked from Rubin's other side. Again, the head turned like an owl's.

"There are untold numbers of artifacts, many forgotten in form and function to modern man." Rubin shook his head. "There may even be an artifact crafted in years long passed that simply pulls an elemental into this world at a whim. I have never seen such a thing." I finally got up from my desk and walked to where he could talk to the two of us together. If that damn beard swayed any more, I was afraid it would unscrew his head.

"Rubin, what could somebody do in order to fuel a ritual without waiting for a natural disaster?"

"It would not be a subtle thing. There are no dams to break to unleash floods, no mountains to collapse, and the summer has been too damp for a forest fire. I say to you, it is more likely that you have mistaken two different elementals for the same one."

"All right," I said, seeing no reason to belabor the point any further. "I don't suppose the Cabal would be willing to submit a report of all planar travel within five hundred miles?"

"I will pass this request along as is appropriate for our working relationship," Rubin said primly, in the tone of somebody who would pass it right alongside his next bowel movement. "Now, is there anything else, madam?"

"No, that'll be all."

"Thanks for all the help, buddy," Archades added cheerfully. Rubin didn't even look at him, turning away as he held his nose high and strode out of the room with all the pomp and circumstance he'd entered with.

"That was useless," I grumbled, going to the wall behind my desk and putting my hands on the large painting of a grassy Minnesota farm. My father, in his retirement, had painted it in the amateurish yet enthusiastic way he always took up new hobbies. Beneath the canvas, as I took the whole thing down carefully, was a large wall safe with a mechanical lock dating from the early sixties or so. Wards embossed deeply in the steel had been filled with silver, gold, and other metals that were less identifiable.

"Wizards are all like that, if you haven't met many." Archades came up to the desk and peered over my shoulder. "What's this, then?"

"I don't like leaving certain things lying around the office. You met the secretary. She can have...sticky fingers." I finished spinning the combination and turned the large brass handle to unlock. It always gave a hearty click before swinging open. I withdrew my spare service pistol to be displayed on my hip, a smaller belly gun that went into my pocket, and briefly considered the arrangement of coins sitting on their little solemn plinths. I selected, after due consideration, one with a trio of stylized monkeys spiraling outward from the center. Sanzaru Amulets were hard enough to come by that I kept the few I still had locked up. This was the sort of time for using all available resources.

"Do you think you have enough weapons?" Archades asked as I locked the safe and sat to break the pistols down, inspect them, and reassemble them.

"My good stuff is currently sitting in a trash bag at my house, waiting to be cleaned," I said, setting a box of ammunition on the desk and loading magazines.

"I couldn't help but notice the silver dagger. Surely that's not standard issue?"

"They barely issue us a badge, let alone specialty equipment like that. I had it made." I slipped the dagger from its belt sheath and set it on the desk. He picked it up by the handle and inspected it.

"True inherited silver?"

"Yes. Very inherited," I said. In actuality, it had been a whole dining set, with enough for ten places and four courses, but he didn't need to know that. He also didn't need to know that it was one of four knives, which had been half of the actual metal I'd inherited. The rest were cast as bullets, some of which were in the safe behind me, and some of which were at the house.

"Somebody's paranoid," Archades tutted, flipping the knife over and grasping the blade to proffer the handle to me. His skin didn't sizzle or burst into flame, and his grin never faltered. Looked like he wasn't going to have that sort of weakness for me to exploit.

"Somebody's prepared," I corrected, putting the knife back. I clipped the badge to the front of my belt and tidied my hair up into a tight bun. Most of the ends were scorched from the heat, but it was manageable. "How about we go see a man about an egg?"

## Chapter Seven

Pecan Park Flea Market. The name should pretty much tell you anything you want to know. I suppose in places more refined and civilized than North Florida, it's possible not to be exposed to quite that level of bumpkin. It could be romanticized as a place where the pure, unfettered capitalist spirit was free to trade and buy without the pesky interference of regulation. More accurately, it was a place that the law avoided when it could. It took more than bootleg DVDs, stolen appliances, and food prepared to questionable health standards to get the police on the property. The whole place was a sprawling array of huts and kiosks, spreading like mold from the central buildings. Originally it had been a self-storage facility, until somebody had started selling cheap tools out of one and everybody had seen the appeal.

Most large cities probably have a place like it. Sometimes, it's more circumspect, a true anomalous market requiring a secret knock, an introduction, and cash money to find. Other times, it's pretty small, maybe one or two shops in the whole place that can provide the specialty services of a wizard or witch. In Jacksonville, they just shoved these things right next to the bogus palm reader and the guy who would put a new stereo in your car for fifty bucks, no questions asked.

Lee Arnold had been in the business longer than I'd been alive. Hell, he'd been in the business longer than there's been a Pecan Park Flea Market. Some of my contacts told me that Lee had shown up sometime in the seventies, on the run from some powerful people in China, and accidentally fallen into dealing with the occult. That's right, Lee was nothing more than your average, everyday human being, complete with all the faults and weaknesses inherent in man. Luckily, I knew some of those weaknesses.

"Lee!" I said, forcing cheer through the fatigue in my voice. "How've you been?" I almost had to shout over the general din in his shop, which looked like a culmination of all Asian stereotypes crammed into the largest space the flea market had to offer. It must have once been the main office of the original building, and if it had ever been empty, it probably would be described as spacious. Instead, it was chock full of tchotchke. Of the worst kind. Cheap stuffed pandas, oriental dragons, and samurai filled a whole wall, with shelves of waving Japanese cats that doubled as coin banks. Undying plastic bamboo plants sat under their thick layers of dust, the plastic rocks around their base in desperate need of either painting or recycling. Under the yard-deep counter, visible through grimy plastic and about a thousand promotional stickers for various quick heating noodles and candies, were racks of samurai swords that probably would crumble to rust the moment they were exposed to humid air. The auditory nightmare came in the form of K-Pop on the radio and Chinese string ballads over the speakers above.

It was behind this deep counter that Lee sat, staring into a small television set and slurping noodles from a wooden bowl in one hand. He gave us no notice. He did his best, in all circumstances, to not move a muscle unless he had to. It was probably how he'd managed to get so old. There were mummified Buddhist monks entombed in Tibet who had nicer-looking skin than Lee, and if it weren't for the crystal-clear eyes set back in his withered skull, he'd look like just another cheap piece of merchandise that had been neglected too long.

I was prepared for this deliberate blindness to our presence. I waited to see if he was going to play nice today, and when he failed to even register that I'd spoken, I brought out the big guns.

The clink of glass on glass drew his eyes toward me. Somewhere in his brain, he'd learned what a bottle of Johnny Walker Blue being placed on his counter sounded like. Once, I'd tried cheaper stuff, but he'd known without looking. This time, I didn't want to give the impression that I wasn't serious, so I even had the label where he could read it. Those eyes turned up to look at my face, and he cracked a smile. He had as many teeth left as a jack-o-lantern.

"Good to see you, Lee," I said, hand still on the bottle. "How's business?"

"Business is good," Lee said. Now his whole body turned to face me, swiveling on the stool at the behest of the long ivory cane he was fond of. "It's been a while. Thought you forgot about me." Rumor had his cane carved out of a single elephant tusk, but I happened to be pretty sure it was just knock-off acrylic. He'd never have let something that valuable go to waste.

"That would be pretty hard to do, Lee," I said. You'd think he'd be nearly unintelligible. After all, if he looked ninety now, he must have been fifty or so when he came over from China. He should have had an accent so thick it would be racist to even attempt to transcribe it. Instead, he spoke slowly but surely, enunciating around his gums and remaining teeth, and carefully picking his words. There was still that accent, but it was one carefully curated. I'd heard him when he didn't want to be understood, and even though it was technically English, you'd have needed a team of FBI linguistics experts to decipher it. We were well past that between us now, though.

"I see they gave you a partner," Lee observed, casting his gaze to Archades, who was looking at a cheap mass-produced wood carving. It showed some kind of Chinese general fending off what might have been Mongolians.

"Consultant," Archades said, from the other side of the shop. "Is this Matsumoto?"

"Matsumoto was Japanese," Lee said. "That is Su Dingfang putting down a rebellion."

"Terrible likeness," Archades said. "They got the eyebrows all wrong." Lee glared at him, and I could see the retort forming.

"Move any interesting merchandise lately?" I asked, tapping my nail on the bottle to get his attention back. He glanced at me for a moment and eased back on his stool.

"I sometimes do a little business on the side, Miss Morris. You are aware of this."

"Yes, I am. In fact, the Bureau is very understanding of your side hustle, Lee, because more often than not the DIA is your best customer."

"So true, so true," Lee said, nodding. You could

hear the bones in his neck creak with the movement. Maybe it was the leathered skin. "Ironwood saplings are difficult to come by, yes? Arnold's Imports keeps you safe."

"And I appreciate that," I said. "You're pretty crackerjack when it comes to finding rare and exotic materials."

"So true, so true," Lee repeated. His attention was drifting back toward his television.

"We're looking for something that might have passed through your store this last week," I said. I reached to my belt and brought my badge up. I tapped the metal edge on the bottle to bring those eyes back my way. "You know what I'm looking for?"

"Just got a new supply of black widow webs. Very fresh. Very few spiders."

"Oh, that's very neat," Archades said, sauntering over to the counter. "Wild gathered?"

"Naturally," Lee said.

"Under what light?"

"The light of the new moon. What do you take me for?" Lee asked. Archades nodded to me.

"That's the right stuff there," he said. "It's nice to know a professional."

"Everybody knows Lee. He's the best," I said.

"It's going to be a shame when his shop burns down because he's holding out on us." Lee let out a tetchy cough, glowering at us.

"You can't come in here and threaten me," he said. "I've done nothing wrong."

"So you say," Archades said. He drummed his fingertips on the counter, looking through the glass at the baubles and trinkets below. Junk, the lot of it. The real good stuff was in the back, of course. Away from the less discerning eyes. "Don't like it when people waste our time."

"He's not wasting our time, Morty," I said soothingly. "Lee's been a friend to the DIA, and he'll keep being a friend." It was the first time I'd ever done good cop, bad cop with somebody who was actually straight-up evil cop, but it was an old routine. For somebody as experienced as Lee, it didn't have much of an effect.

"I don't know what you mean," Lee said. "I have new talismans. Scandinavian runes this time, good in a pinch."

"I was hoping for something with a little more…heat." I floated the word out there, waiting for a reaction.

"I sold the Staff of Ra. It was nearly depleted anyway. I may find another if you need one. Good price, for you."

"I'm talking about something special. An egg. Very valuable." Still, nothing to indicate that I was anywhere near my mark. Instead, he bobbed his head in a nod and got off the stool. He slid the glass display open and rummaged for a moment. He came up with a speckled black chicken's egg that looked like it was carved from wood.

"Authentic century egg. No magic, but delicious and good for heart." He offered it to me, showing all four of his teeth in a crooked smile. It was all I could do to not smack it out of his hand.

"Why don't you go ahead and push the little charity collection box aside and show us the private collection?" Archades asked. Lee's eyes finally betrayed some surprise, freezing in their languid journey from face to face. It's a good thing he looked at Archades' shit-eating grin, because it wouldn't have helped our case to see my startled expression. Lee was always on the up and up. His specialty merchandise wasn't for general perusal, but he'd never held anything back. He'd even had a number of dangerous objects confiscated by the DIA over the years and still hadn't tried hiding his wares.

"I don't know what you're talking about," he said.

"Oh? Maybe I'm badly informed. Tomas told me that he saw you open it before he and his buddies were sent out by Pierre." Lee looked at me, eyes narrowed.

"What is this, Miss Morris?" he asked. "Years I help you out, and now I have this man slander me in my own store?"

"Do you know what you have, Lee?" I asked. There were a lot of ways to go around doing things. In other places, with other people, I might have simply drawn down on the old man, checked to see if Archades was right, and gone from there. This was Lee Arnold, though. When I'd needed real Dead Sea salt, he'd dealt with me honestly and for a fair price. I'd bought my first warding charms from him, and I hadn't seen a single ghost come through the wall of my bathroom since. Lee knew more tourists than everybody in the department put together and had legitimate contacts all over the world with all kinds of people and not-people. Leaning on him was necessary, and he probably knew that, but it always paid to give somebody the opportunity to save face. It's hard to save face with a gun stuck up your nose.

"These guys, they were probably in a hurry. Maybe

they didn't tell you exactly what they were asking you to hold, so maybe you took something in escrow. Something without looking too closely. I also know that you don't always look too closely at things that are in escrow. After all…it's not your business, right?" I leaned on the counter, folding my hands peacefully. I nudged the bottle toward him. He licked his lips, a sandpapery sound, and glanced at Archades.

"Maybe. Lots of things come through my store. Like I said."

"Okay. So I won't hold it against you if you lost track of something," I said. "I know you've always been helpful to us. And this is important."

"All right, all right," Lee muttered. He tapped the counter a few times nervously. "I knew it was too good to be true, anyway." He pushed aside the little bubbling fountain that had slowly filled with loose change over the year, revealing a little switch wired into the counter. He flicked it, and the entire counter rose to meet the ceiling. Replacing it was another counter, with Lee still behind it, but this one was all smoked glass and iron bindings, with just enough warping in the surface to keep an observer from getting a clear idea of what was inside. It emitted its own light, not from built-in electronics, but from the egg.

"Why would you keep something like that here?" I asked, holding my breath as he pulled on an oven mitt. Carefully, he retrieved it out from under the counter. The semi-translucent shell glowed with heat, and he produced an old metal lunch box padded with what looked like asbestos insulation.

"Would have moved it tonight after close," Lee said. "Had to make sure I wasn't being set up for robbery."

"Do you know how they got it in the first place?"

"Didn't say. Didn't ask. Not my business."

"You know who they stole it from?"

"Killed a dragon, didn't they?" Lee asked, now suddenly interested in the manner of somebody feeling the ice crack beneath their feet. Archades laughed.

"Killed a dragon? Who did they tell you they were, Sigurd? Have you ever seen a dragon's egg?"

"I've never even met somebody who's seen one. I assumed that some swamp dragon in Okefenokee had caused problems, and this bunch was just trying to make a little extra profit off their contract..." This sounded too much like the truth to just be a cover now. Lee was well known for asking no questions except "How much?" and "Paper or plastic?" Normally it wasn't as problematic as this. People who didn't deal straight with Lee tended to have problems. Well, a problem. The final kind.

"You keep thinking that," I said, gingerly shutting the lunch box and slowly swapping it with the bottle. "We'll just get this back where it belongs. No harm, no foul." I hope, I added silently. "Incidentally, they didn't happen to mention a wizard while they were here? Something about portals, or mephits?"

"Now you mention it," Lee said, scrubbing his chin and squinting off into the distance. "There was something about a meeting with Mr. Wizard?" I pulled out a small notepad from my back pocket and wrote this down. "They were talking amongst themselves, but for some reason, they seemed to assume that I only speak Chinese."

"And what would have given them that

impression?" I asked.

"Inexperience." He grinned like a piano at me. "Anyway, no wizard here. Not good customers anyway. Young wizards rack up too much credit, and old wizards spend all their money on the Ritual."

"Ritual?" I asked, cocking my head.

"*Sollemne Vitae*," Archades said, now holding a pair of brass spheres in one hand. He rotated them, seemingly without effort, so that they never touched each other. "The Ritual of Longevity."

"Well informed," Lee said, nodding. He flicked another switch on his countertop, and it sank slowly back out of sight. How he'd installed such a thing without drawing attention, I had no idea, but I suppose a contractor would keep his mouth shut for enough cash. "Putting off their appointment with death becomes more difficult as time passes."

"I've heard of it," I lied slowly. It never paid to seem behind the eight ball in these sorts of conversations. DIA was supposed to be better informed than almost everybody, except the three most experienced agents probably didn't know half of what Lee did in his ancient head. I jotted a note for later before putting my pad back in my back pocket.

"It becomes more difficult as they age, you know. I procure a number of rare and powerful ingredients, but eventually it becomes too difficult to maintain." Lee rubbed his leathery hands together in supplication. "Now, Miss Morris, is there any other way I can assist you? Or would you prefer to continue to interrupt my business?"

"Don't suppose you know where they were staying, do you?" I asked. Lee paused, then reached under the counter. I tensed immediately, hand twitching toward my holster as, for a moment, I believed that I would be putting dusty holes through this living mummy. Lee held his smile as he withdrew a slip of paper.

"As a matter of fact," he said, keeping his hand over it as he slid it halfway across the counter. "I gave them a deposit of security, as is custom for high-value items. Gold. I had it delivered to an address of their choosing." I reached out, and that hand slid away quickly. "Just a moment!"

"What?" I asked, trying not to let the irritation show.

"I feel like since I did not receive honest dealings from these gentlemen, I am entitled to a refund." I glanced at the hand-painted sign behind him. It read, in bold red letters:

ABSOLUTELY NO REFUNDS. NO EXCEPTIONS. NO EXCUSES.

"Fair enough," I said, frowning. "If the gold is still there when we arrive, I'll have it brought back to you. How much gold was it?"

"Standard deposit for items such as this. Your weight in gold." He gave a quick, bird-like chortle. "Luckily for me, their leading man was not a very large one, and it amounted for just shy of one hundred fifty-three pounds."

"Wow." Gold was a typical currency in these circles, partly because it could be spent literally anywhere, but mostly because it was classic. After all, an ingot of gold looks really nice, especially when surrounded by twenty others in your own personal safe aboard a yacht the size of a small city building.

Lee lifted his hand, and I took the paper and glanced at it.

"As easy as that?" I asked. He nodded.

"Their temporary headquarters, I'm sure," he said. I was already getting my phone out.

"Excuse me for one moment," I said, dialing the office. I must have reflex-dialed the wrong line, as I heard Rubin's tones of bewildering self-importance before I finally hung up. I went ahead and just called Yancy. After an excruciating conversation to convince her that I needed to be patched directly to LaFleur, I got through and told him what I'd found out.

"I'll have Agents Barlow and McIllwain check out the address," LaFleur said, taking a weight off my shoulders. I'd been afraid he would want me to go check it out myself. "Secure that package and return here, as quickly as you can."

"We're on our way," I said, ending our short phone call without any further discussion. I sighed with relief. The end was in sight. With any luck, the address would give us everything we needed to trace the source of the eggs, and they'd be tucked in nice and safe in a few hours.

"Can I interest you in anything else, so long as you're here?" His wrinkled face scrunched up into what was supposed to be a look of helpful contrition. "You know that I would do anything to assist the FBI in their investigations."

"Yeah, that's why there's a wall of bootleg movies behind you," I said. "Enjoy your Walker, Lee. You have my number if you can think of anything else." He shrugged one shoulder and turned his head back to the glowing screen. I jerked my head to the door, and

Archades sighed, set down a snow globe he'd been vigorously shaking, and followed me out.

"He seemed nice," Archades said cheerfully, falling into step beside me as we made our way back to the parking lot.

"Old grifter is so shady he doubles as a beach umbrella," I grumbled, drawing out my phone again. I texted LaFleur this time, simple code to let him know we were leaving. It was a chore, what with the shattered screen, courtesy of the high-speed wreck earlier in the day. Christ, had it only been that long? I rubbed the bridge of my nose, feeling the tension headache welling up. Get back to the office. Give LaFleur the last egg. Sleep for a week. Deal with everything else later.

I was so caught up in my phone that I walked full into Archades' back and nearly dropped the lunch box in surprise.

"Knock it off," I grumbled, glancing around to see what had him on pause. He wasn't even acknowledging me. He was staring off down one of the little alleyways between the old storage buildings. Since there weren't any stalls that opened down there, it wasn't lit, and I could just make out the lights of cars passing on the highway a couple hundred yards away.

"What is it?" I asked, pocketing my phone and shifting the lunch pail to my other hand. It freed my good hand to rest on the butt of my pistol.

"Not sure," Archades said, slowly. "But I'd like to know where everybody else went." I hadn't even noticed. When we'd arrived, it hadn't been exactly busy, but there'd been people still browsing the wares of the seedy salesmen that stayed open late. Shopkeepers had been tidying up their stalls or packing things up for the next day, but it hadn't been the ghost town it was now. I glanced back up the way we'd come. Lee Arnold's shop now had a heavy steel mesh pulled down over the entrance, and the lights were turned off. No doubt he had other wards and anomalous protections in place.

"Shit." I went to draw my gun. Before I'd cleared the holster, Archades turned and shoved me away, both hands on my chest hard enough to knock me straight off of my feet. The pistol went clattering into the darkness of the stalls, God only knows where. A blistering light erupted out of the alleyway, a focused beam of heat that crumpled the light steel walls of the stalls it passed before taking Archades full in the chest. His dark brown eyes shot wide open, his mouth made a little O of surprise and pain, and then all the liquids in his torso finished vaporizing, and he blew up like a potato in the microwave. His hips flew over me as I hit the ground with my ass and rolled, already getting on my feet and clutching the egg box to my chest like a football.

*Give me the egg, girl,* a now-familiar voice in my head demanded, and even as I pulled away from the alleyway, I could see the glow growing stronger as something came out of the dark. Part of that was the fire pouring out of the adjacent stalls, but I could see the flickering movement of the mephit just around the corner.

"Get your ass up!" I screamed, getting on my feet in a scramble of panic. I got to where the rest of Archades had landed, and glossy eyes stared up at me from his disembodied head. I grabbed it up, expecting to find it smirking or winking, but instead it simply did what most newly separated heads do and bled all over me. The jaw hung open, slack and empty, and I managed to turn my scream into one of frustration and not outright panic. The head fell from my suddenly nerveless fingers.

Of course. Lee Arnold had been happy to get rid of the egg. After all, he couldn't stay in his warded, protected shop for the rest of his life, and if he'd known there were creatures waiting outside for him, well, it was really just lucky that somebody came along to confiscate the thing.

"Don't move, lady," a voice said, just as I managed to shake myself loose and jump into the space between two of the converted storage units. I dug my fist into my pocket, fingers curling around a thick, heavy coin. Standing in front of me was a career goon, more a mass of tattoos and scars than an actual person. He had a short-barreled shotgun in one hand, which was somehow less intimidating than his turkey-sized fists.

"Drop the box," he said. He wasn't within arms' reach. Well, he wasn't within *my* arms' reach. I was certainly inside his. He could reach out and bounce my head off the wall without really stretching.

"FBI, get on the ground!" I yelled, for all the good it would do. This guy probably couldn't even spell it. He just smiled at me, with the kind of look that said he knew a good punchline. It was the kind that I was already in queue for.

I tossed him the lunch box in a high arc, clearly surprising him. Whatever his boss had told him about what I was carrying, he must have thought it was an explosive by the way he jumped to grab it before it hit the ground. He managed to catch the thing, triumphant in his moment of glory, just as a coin hit him on the forehead and stuck there. He had just enough time to raise his eyebrows in surprise and say something like, "Whuh?" Then he went blind, deaf, and dumb as the monkeys got hold of him.

They appeared on his back and shoulders, slapping their hands over his senses and digging in with all their little monkey might. The Sanzaru were always macaques, although where you got the amulet and when it was made always changed what specific type they were. Sometimes they appeared wearing fine ornamentation and others they were just dirty little monkeys straight out of the woods. They weren't real, not exactly. They certainly weren't real monkeys. They were conjured things, made out of magic, but they were very effective at their job, and nobody expected them.

Muscle Goon tried to scream, immediately dropping the steel box in his haste to try and rip the monkeys off his back, but the three of them were attached by arms, legs, and tails that might as well have been steel cable for all the good his efforts were doing. I grabbed up the box in one hand. In not one of my proudest moments, I kicked Muscle Goon as hard as possible right in the testicles. Right with the tip of my boot too. Even with the leathery hands clamping his mouth shut, the muffled scream was pretty gratifying, and he tumbled onto his face. The monkeys chittered and hooted at me, baring teeth and dancing on his back. They'd keep him like that for a few hours or more, depending on which coin I'd pulled out of the stack. Even if this one only lasted twenty minutes, it was all I needed. He'd see, hear, and speak no evil for the duration.

I crouched near the door and drew the belly gun

from my pocket. It was not an impressive revolver. Its only redeeming feature was that it fit into any pair of pants or even skinny jeans without being too obtrusive. It was as snub nosed as a pug and had about as much bite in a real fight, but like the name implied, if I could stick it into somebody's stomach, it would certainly work.

I took a few deep breaths, ignoring the scrabbling sound of Muscle Goon trying to pry three monkeys off his head. I twitched my head out into the open air, glancing in every direction at once, then dashed out toward the parking lot. I took a couple running steps before somebody with a nicer gun than mine opened fire, chewing a Morse code pattern into the corrugated steel wall behind me. I believe it was code for AAAAAAAAA!

"Shitshitshitshit," I retorted, sliding on the sandy concrete as I hurled myself into a blind alley. The gunfire stopped, punctuated by a shouting match between human voices, but I didn't stick around for details. I thought I heard the inferno-woosh of the mephit firing off again, but I didn't turn to ash, so it clearly wasn't aiming at me. Lunch box and gun in hands, I swung myself over a low chain-link fence and hauled across the vacant grass field in the center of the flea market. Behind me, there was a growing glow of spreading fire, as unit after unit succumbed to the heat and flame. I hoped fervently that Lee Arnold's shop was one of them. He could be inside it while it burned, for all I cared.

I could see the parking lot ahead, at the end of my mad dash for freedom. It was vacant, except for a few vans parked haphazardly and, near the farthest edge, my borrowed company car. It wasn't turned over or on fire. It looked so welcome and inviting.

The tackle hit me across the knees, taking me down in a confusing moment as part of my body tried to continue forward and the rest of me succumbed to the blow.

"I've got her!" a man's voice yelled out on top of me, hands scrambling to grab my head and arm. "Quick, before the elemental catches up!" I dropped the box with the egg to the grass and kicked out, trying to get my legs under him and force him away. He outweighed me by probably ninety pounds, at least, and he wasn't a stranger to a ground fight. One hand snaked around my neck and squeezed, while the other pinned my wrist to the ground with the gun pointed wildly to the side. I looked up into his face and let out a gurgle of a curse. He looked like somebody had taken a crowbar to a particularly large and lumpy radish, which was not what I had hoped to see right before I died.

I looked around for any help, and finding none as my vision began to turn gray, I swung my legs to the side and tried to essentially run away from him while on the ground. He chortled at me, shifting his weight to throw a leg to the other side and pin my knee to the ground. Now I could at least buck my hips up a little, which I did as I shoved my free hand behind my back. Too late, he pulled his hand off my neck and tried to pin my shoulder. I drew the belt knife from its sheath with a click and drove the length of it into his ribs, right into what I hoped was his lung. Maybe his liver. I didn't really have time to aim properly.

He shrieked, grabbing the arm with the knife and shoving it away. With both hands.

Even as the knife came free, I brought the other hand around and fired twice into his chest, muzzle pressed against his shirt hard enough to nearly push him back. Each shot was muffled by his body, quiet enough that I could hear each grunt he made as the impact tore him apart inside. He fell backward, freeing me, and I grabbed up the egg in its case.

Still staggering with each step, I loped toward the car, gasping for breath. He'd nearly crushed my throat in one hand, and I doubled over to cough raggedly as I reached the end of the fence.

"Don't let the bitch get away!" somebody yelled from within the flea market. I threw myself over the fence, got up, and made it to the car. I chucked the lunch box into the backseat, jammed the keys into the ignition, and nearly shit myself as Archades pulled himself into the passenger seat.

"We should go," he growled, his voice oscillating in tone between a normal man's and something unworldly. His eyes burned with actual blue fire, smoldering wisps of smoke curling to the dingy roof. Most of his body was formed from inky shadowstuff, writhing with every move of his body, and he reached over to jam a foot onto the gas pedal just as bullets began peppering the side of the car. Screaming in surprise and frustration, I managed to control the wheel enough to get us out of the parking lot and out of sight.

"Let go!" I shouted, shoving his hands off the wheel and kicking at his leg. It felt solid enough but looked like smoke swirling in a plastic cast. Archades put his hands up peacefully, withdrawing to his seat. The polished brass of his bracelets shone on his wispy arms, still indistinct in shape on his shoulders. In fact, the only thing that was definite about him was his head from the chin up. The rest was...well, maybe that was what he actually looked like. Shadowstuff inside a skin suit.

"What the fuck is going on?" I asked, ratcheting my fear down a couple notches and taking control of my tone a little better.

"You've got a little blood on you," he said. His voice had that eerie quality of echo to it that I'd heard at the Observatory. Almost like it had dropped into the wrong octave for human ears, almost too low to be real. Mixed in was the voice that he'd been talking with all day long. It was disconcerting.

"I'm fine," I croaked, coughing into my hand. I didn't even slow down at the first red light I encountered, bounding across the intersection without a care in the world. Let a local cop pull me over. See how he liked his world going to shit in a day. "What the fuck happened to you?"

"I hate to say it, but the mephit got the drop on me," Archades said, eyes narrowing to pinpoints of flickering blue. "I'm attempting to pull myself together."

"How'd you get back to the car?" I asked.

"Nobody stopped to check on me after you dropped my head," Archades said. "Manifested a body as quick as I could, circled around."

"How the fuck did they know we were there?"

"Good question," Archades said. I saw him raise a hand, little more than tendrils of shadow, and flex them purposefully. Pink and raw, five fingers formed out of the shadow and continued up his arm to the shoulder. He grunted, taking a few deep breaths.

"Are you okay?" I asked, swinging the car around the back of the closest fire station I knew and turning off the lights. The station was deserted, probably heading to the very fire we'd just left behind. Still, it was a very public place, and in the darkness of their back lot, we could take a second to regroup.

"I'm sorry?" Archades asked, taken aback.

"Are you all right?" I asked, reaching into the back seat and grabbing the egg box. I half expected it to have a smoking hole through it, or to open it and find the egg mysteriously vanished, but it was still there and wholly intact. It pulsed with life, glowing in the darkness of the car.

"Why yes, I am. Thank you for asking, Diane." Archades gave me a grin, showing his perfectly white teeth off. He flexed again, this time bringing the fleshiness back up his shoulders, manifesting a throat and half of his upper torso. When he spoke again, his voice sounded perfectly normal. No more strange undertones. "I'm surprised to hear you concerned."

"You pushed me out of the way back there," I said, breathing deeply as I tried to steady my hands. "Thank you."

"Oh, Diane, don't thank *me*," Archades said, with a dismissive wave of his hand. "If you died now, I'd be back in that stupid cell. Less than a day out, after forty years? I'd like to avoid that."

"Fair enough," I said. I pulled out my cell phone, wiping something sticky out of my eye, and stared at the smear of blood that came off on my arm. I set the phone down on the dash in front of me and took a few deep breaths.

"Like I said, a little blood," Archades said.

"It's in my eye," I said, each syllable almost its own sentence.

"And your hair. Oh, and the shirt too, if you haven't noticed." I was grinding my teeth. Grabbing the egg case, I opened the door and walked to the back of the fire station, where a hose reel for washing the trucks was idly dripping into the drain below.

"Where are you going?" Archades called, getting out of the car after me. Glancing back, I could see that he had manifested down to his hips. He was either unable or unwilling to manifest clothes.

"I'm fine. I'll just be a second. Go find some pants before you get real legs," I said, very carefully setting the egg where I could grab it at a moment's notice. I pulled off the polo shirt, once powder blue and now a deep crimson almost all over, and tossed it to the side.

Here I was, washing my hair with car soap and scrubbing my face with a hand cloth that probably saw use on greasy wheels. When you sign up to be a cop, this isn't what they tell you is going to happen. They warn you about a lot of things, like being shot at by criminals, or having to testify in court, or how boring paperwork was. What I wouldn't give to be bored at work. I'd climb a mountain of paperwork, every day a modern Sisyphus, if only I didn't have to know how congealed blood likes to stick to frizzy, fire-damaged hair.

Finally shaking most of the water from my head like a dog and sweeping my hair back as dignified as possible, I considered the shirt and finally just stuffed it to the bottom of the trash bin nearby. It wouldn't be the first time I'd been seen in my sports bra. They could just live with it.

"Here," Archades said, suddenly standing within arms' reach as I turned to go back to the car. I jumped involuntarily and gave a little suppressed curse that sounded like "Fu-gggnnn." He held out a fire department-issued cotton tee.

"Where'd you get this?" I asked, taking it and throwing it on without hesitation.

"Same place I got these pants," Archades said, gesturing to the basketball shorts he'd acquired. He wore a plain white undershirt with it and looked like somebody's grandfather who liked to sit out on the porch of his ratty old trailer and yell at the neighbor's kid for playing the drums. "Lockers inside are just wide open for the taking."

"Good grief," I muttered, shaking my head. I'd have to send these guys donuts or something. "I guess I'd better watch what I tell you to do."

"In the grand scheme of things, some petty theft isn't really *that* bad," Archades said, with all the innocence of a child caught with his hand in the cookie jar. I grunted something like a disagreement but picked up the egg regardless and headed back to the car. "I mean, it's not like I'm the one who killed somebody today." I could just hear the grin in his voice.

"Oh yeah?" I asked, suddenly feeling pretty heated. "You think that's funny?"

"Surprised you had it in you is all," Archades said. "Nice to see we have something in common." I turned before I reached the car and poked him in the chest with two fingers at once.

"We don't have *anything* in common, you, you..." Eternal symbol of evil? Overwhelmingly powerful being from another plane? Legendary enemy of mankind at the end of my short leash? All those stories I'd heard about what this thing had done over the years came flooding back to me, and I tempered my response. "You just keep any ideas like that to yourself. If I hadn't shot that man, he'd have done worse to me. Losing this, this here?" I waved the lunch box under his nose. "That'd be worse than him just killing me. I'd rather not see that over and over again when I try to sleep from now on, but at least it'll have to wait its turn with all the other shit I've had to do over the years." And now he was looking down at me, his frown tight and pinched, like a history teacher who'd just finished reviewing your test and decided that, no, there would be no curve after all.

"We might have something in common, after all," he said softly. I glared up into his face, preparing another mouthful of words I'd probably regret, except the roll-up doors at the back of the fire station suddenly and noisily began grinding up. I stepped away from Archades as the dull roar of a large diesel engine turned onto the back pad, headlights flooding across us. A fire engine pulled around, idling as it waited for the door to open all of the way. My first thought was that they must have put that fire out but quick.

"Let's go," I said, seeing the golden numbers on the side and feeling a perfectly mundane sinking sensation in my stomach. This particular fire engine was on the wrong side of town. They must have been sent to cover the district while the fire was being fought. What shift was it even? I tried to do a quick mental math, counting by threes, but had trouble focusing when I saw who was in the driver's seat.

"Shouldn't we at least say thanks for the clothes?"

Archades asked, as the fire engine pulled inside and parked. I heard some laughing voices from inside. The firefighters were heading out back to see who was loitering on city property.

"No, we ought to—"

"Diane? Is that you?" one of the firefighters, the one who'd been driving, called, close enough that I could see her face. Goddamn it. There are three shifts to choose from. Why couldn't it have been any other crew, any other day?

"Yep," I said, sidling toward the car. "Just borrowing the hose, you know." The other two firefighters, their common sense tingling, suddenly decided something more interesting was going on inside.

"What happened?" It was dark out, sure, but I could see well enough to see the details of her face. That meant she could see my wet, matted hair, pale face, and tired eyes, and couldn't overlook the shirt. I saw her eyes linger on the logo, and she crossed her arms and set her hips in a way I knew was the beginning of a line of questions I wasn't prepared to answer.

"Work," I said wearily, realizing that I had subconsciously hugged myself as soon as she approached, as if I needed to cover up. Well, it wasn't anything she hadn't seen before, so I forced myself to relax my arms and let them just dangle. People do that. Right?

"Work." Her gaze flickered to the car, counting bullet holes like somebody trying to connect the dots and see the cat. "Are you all right?"

"I'm fine." Keep it brusque. Don't start to talk,

since that might become The Talk, and nobody had time for that.

"It's good to see you, Diane." Her tone was a little softer now, and she took half a step toward me. "It's been a while. I thought you'd call."

"Sadie…" I said, looking busily off into the night as if something were more interesting across the street. Christ, couldn't the mephit track me down now? At least being vaporized would be quick.

"Good evening," Archades said, materializing out of the night beside me smoothly. In the moment, I'd forgotten he'd been there all along. "I'm Morty, Diane's new partner."

"Consultant," I said automatically as Sadie shook his hand.

"Sarah. Folks call me Sadie," she said. "Who do you work for?" Archades glanced at me, but any signal he was waiting for was too complicated to just blink at him. He smiled and smoothed back his hair before shrugging.

"Who even knows, these days? Now it's just private consultations, helping with numbers, or, when things are really interesting, acquisitions." Archades tapped the side of his head. "Making a killing on overtime tonight."

"Uh-huh," Sadie said. "And you don't have anything to do with the second alarm fire half a mile away?" I blinked at her innocently, or at least as innocently as I could for somebody who'd just finished rinsing congealing blood out of what little was left of her eyebrows.

"Not us," I said. "Quiet as church mice for us."

"I've heard that before," Sadie said. She sighed

visibly. "All right, Diane. Go ahead and go, if you're going. I guess I can forget about that phone call." She glanced at my chest again. "And you can keep my shirt too. I want my surfboard back, though."

"You'll get it back," I said, shuffling toward the door of the car. "I need to call the office. It was nice to see you again." That, at least, was sort of true. She gave a little huff of a laugh, full of sarcasm and venom, and walked back into the station. It was late enough now that the bunch of them would probably pile into armchairs and fall asleep until the normal crews got back. I watched her go with a little mixture of guilt and, let's face it, desire. She was still good looking, no matter what else was going on between us.

"I-nteresting," Archades said, drawing out the I until it almost screamed.

"Not now," I muttered, thumbing my phone until I got to my contacts list. It rang a few times, until the eternally congested voice of Yancy answered.

"Intangible Assets Southeast, how can I help you?" she asked, in tones that made it perfectly clear that you could help her by hanging up and never calling again. I slumped my head against the car in frustration, biting back the first words I had. What the hell was she doing there so late?

"Director LaFleur's office, please," I said, managing a professional, if curt, tone.

"And who may I ask is calling?"

"Special Agent Morris, Yancy. Again. Put me through, it's urgent," I said, a little bit snippier than I intended. I could hear her indignant huff, and then I got an earful of ringing phone again.

Then, about thirty seconds later, "I am Rubin. If I

am here, I am listening. Speak your business, and I shall fulfill my duty."

I hung up and redialed the office.

"Yeah, you sent me to Rubin's office instead," I said, cutting off her repeated greeting. I could just hear the little piggy grin through the line.

"Did I? My mistake. Please hold." This time, the line rang twice before an answer.

"LaFleur." Even on the phone, he sounded neatly pressed and bald.

"Morris here. Second asset is in hand. Had some issues with a tourist and a few locals. Probably need to fill out some tax liability forms when I get back. Lying low at..." I glanced at the building, squinting. "Local firehouse, the one nearest the fire, I think. Station Thirty-Five."

"What fire?" LaFleur asked.

"Seems there's a fire at the Pecan Park Flea Market," I said, conversationally. "What're the odds of getting this thing picked up from here? Company vehicle needs to be detailed." It wasn't exactly a difficult code to break, our shorthand on the phone. These days, a freedom of information request would return a mountain of forms, spreadsheets, and tax information that would smother even the most dedicated national inquirer. "Is there an update to the audit I requested? At the provided address?" I really wanted some good news.

"Initial reports show signs of forced entry. Some light asset activity in the apartment unit, likely involved. Some items removed. I'm told they think a wardrobe is missing, based on room layout." I didn't curse right into the phone, but he probably heard me anyway. "Sit tight indoors for now. I'll send a retrieval team." LaFleur paused thoughtfully. "How is Mortimer?" I glanced sideways at Archades, who was staring off into space while he absently rubbed his wrist under the bracelet.

"Cooperative," I admitted. "No shenanigans here, boss."

"Don't become complacent." Like I needed to be reminded.

"And one more thing," I said, pinching the bridge of my nose. "I lost my abacus in all the excitement." Abacus is, of course, a gun. It's the one thing I can always count on.

"Naturally…" LaFleur never sounded angry, just disappointed. "Get inside and stay put. Help is on the way." The line went dead.

I glared at the fire station, leaning on the car with one hand on the lunch box. Archades sidled up next to me, stretching his arms out.

"These newly regenerated bodies are always so stiff. Old man Nathaniel had terrible arthritis, and it takes me forever to get limber again," he said.

"DIA is sending somebody to pick us up," I said. "We're to stay put for now."

"Affirmative," he said, throwing a salute. "Shall I reconnoiter the building and see if I can make a modern coffee pot function?"

"Didn't you already do that when you stole these clothes?" I asked, tugging at the neckline of my shirt.

"Well, sure, that's how I know where the coffee maker is," Archades said. "Or are we afraid of hostile action in there?" I glowered at him. Who'd have thought the master manipulator, deceiver, and plague across the ages would care enough to pay attention to mortal drama.

"Hostile's a bit of a stretch," I said. "Sadie and I are, you know…" I trailed off in the most polite and firm way I could think of to say I didn't want to tug at this thread.

"I really don't," Archades said, grinning widely at me. "Miss Morris, I would never have thought she'd be your type!"

"What, another woman?" I said, hearing the notes of warning in my own tone even if he didn't.

"Not that, heavens no," Archades said, waving one hand as if shooing away the mere thought. "I simply expected you to chase the skirts of more delicate ladies. Maybe the bookish librarian down the street, or one sorority girl after another at the local club."

"I like Sadie. She's…not too complicated," I said. That was true enough. We'd met at the beginning of summer, when I'd decided that languishing in my house, talking to my cats, and having only one of them talk back wasn't how I wanted to spend my free time. So, with the beach only half an hour from the house, I'd taken up surfing. Even paid for an instructor for the first week. Sadie had been an impatient, almost reckless teacher, and I had two left feet when it came to keeping on a board, but we'd connected otherwise and been on a few dates. Well, more than a few.

"So a simple woman is your type, is it?" Archades asked.

"Simple people, yeah, maybe," I replied. "Why are you so interested?"

"Probably just looking for some vulnerable spot to exploit, when the time comes," Archades said. I stared at him and his stupid Cheshire grin. "What? I'm not reneging on the bargain. Straight as an arrow, that's me. No offense meant, of course."

"Sure," I muttered. "Whatever you say."

"What happened, anyway?" Archades asked.

"Hmm?"

"Between you and what's-her-name, Busty Betty in there?" Archades asked. "I ask only out of professional conniving instinct," he added.

"Well, you can *tell* somebody you work assisting the IRS doing tax audits all year long," I said, grimacing. "And then, when they come over to watch a movie and find a handgun on a magnet on the bottom of the bathroom sink instead of new toilet paper, that comes as a shock. Which leads to some questions that I didn't want to answer, which leads to an argument, which kind of turns into somebody finding another gun under the kitchen table when she goes to get her purse. Lather, rinse, repeat."

"This is America, isn't it?" Archades asked. "Can't somebody have as many guns as their paranoia requires strewn about the house?"

"That's sort of what I said, but Sadie isn't as stupid as most people," I said, frowning in the general direction of the building. She actually had a great sense of humor, and while she didn't like to read, she wasn't the troglodyte most firefighters made themselves out to be. She'd held her own in that shouting match of an argument we'd had only a few days before. Christ, was that all it had been? Felt like a month now.

"And the fact that she works for the fire department doesn't have anything to do with it?" Archades asked.

"I don't know many girls that wouldn't be into a

big, strong firefighter," I said. "But, at the end of the day, she'd keep on digging and digging until she got to some truth, and then she wouldn't be any better off."

"You could just tell her the truth."

"Pshhh," I scoffed. "Not only is that against SOP 201: Dissemination of Information, it also wouldn't do her any favors. I know it's hard for you to imagine being just a mere mortal, living a perfectly normal life, but almost everybody likes that. Hell, I liked it, when I had it."

"Normal is boring," Archades said cheerfully. "Take it from a guy who just spent forty years living the definition of normal."

"Wouldn't exactly call you 'a guy.' " He shrugged.

"I'm going to get a cup of coffee while we wait." He turned on a heel and strolled toward the open mouth of the bay. "You coming?" I sighed, looked over at the bullet-riddled car dripping green fluid from the engine area, and followed him in.

## Chapter Eight

Fire stations, if you've never been in one, are sort of a cross between a mechanic's shop and college dorm in terms of smell-scape. One of the two bays sat empty, and there remained the lingering scent of oil, diesel fumes, and a subtle, yet inescapable, body odor. One corner was dedicated to a bargain-bin assortment of workout equipment, and a shop table dominated the space between where vehicles had left puddled oil. They had their own laundry room, a compressor system to refill air bottles, the works. That wasn't even talking about living quarters. Some places have individual rooms for each firefighter, but old-school buildings like this one had one large cavernous room full of sagging mattresses on bare iron frames, walls painted poorly in dark tones, and windows covered in foil to keep out sunlight. Not that this was where we were going, mind you, it just always struck me as sort of interesting from when I'd seen Sadie's station.

She and the guys on her rig were sitting at the kitchen table, coffee near to hand, bullshitting about whatever public employees talked about when nobody else was around. As Archades was already pouring himself a cup when I came in, they clearly didn't care that a couple of feds were impinging on their space. I didn't recognize the other two, so in the spirit of good manners, I shook hands and introduced myself to

Lieutenant Rhames and Firefighter Benson.

"You two know each other?" Rhames asked, idly fiddling with his phone. He was reading emails through a pair of cheaters perched on his nose, in the manner of somebody who wasn't yet used to reading glasses. Or adjustable font sizes. Or fancy phones in general.

"Yeah, do we?" Sadie asked, smirking over the table at me. I sighed, set the lunch box on the heavily lacquered wood, and picked a coffee cup off the hanging rack next to the pot.

"Do you care if they know?" I asked as casually as I could.

"Me and Diane used to see each other off and on," Sadie said. Rhames just grunted an acknowledgement, but Benson gave a conspiratorial grin.

"Yeah? You mean with clothes off and on, right?" He looked like he was in his early twenties, but that didn't stop him from having a teenage personality. Sadie waggled her eyebrows at him as lewdly as possible.

"You know it. As *off*-ten as possible," she said, her emphasis leaving no room for even a single entendre. "You know, we'd sometimes go…eat out." I slopped coffee over the counter as I twitched, and Archades gave a real hearty laugh in response.

"Didn't think you'd like 'em so little," Benson said. "All your other girlfriends were a lot taller."

"It's not the size," I said, sitting down on one of the ancient, creaking wooden chairs, blowing on my coffee. "It's how you use it."

"It's what my wife says to make me feel better," Benson said, shrugging. "So what're two feds doing out on the west side, this time of night?"

"You know, it's actually a real interesting story," Archades said, relaxing with both feet on the table. "But if I told you, then I'd have to kill you. That sort of thing."

"Don't listen to him," I said quickly, heading off Sadie's suddenly interested expression. "He's trying to make looking at the income records of a large pest control company sound more interesting than it really is. There were a lot of irregularities, and our IRS guy ended up staying late, so we stayed late." I managed not to openly glare at Archades where they could see, but I tried to at least be mildly scathing.

"Those books were so cooked, I burned up in the heat and lost my head," Archades said with an exaggerated wink. I groaned wearily, but at least I had the coffee to start giving me a little life again. I winced as I swallowed, my throat still swollen from the throttling I'd received.

"Which pest control company?" Sadie asked.

"What?" I asked, coughing up something that was either phlegm or an important part of my trachea.

"You said you were auditing a pest control company. Which one?" She watched my face with her piercing green eyes, and she had a good view of me as I fumbled for a lie that would fit.

"Dyson and Sons Termite and Pest," Archades said smoothly. "Over off of Lane Avenue." I paused my cough long enough to look and see if he was playing a joke of some kind, but he had a pleasant, professional look on his face. He looked like somebody who was enjoying a relaxing break after a long, hard day of boring work.

"I know the place," Benson said, nodding. "My

brother worked there for a couple of years."

"Well, their books are a mess, let me tell you," Archades said. "Wouldn't know an income stream from an asset declaration if it shot them in the chest at close range." Sadie never took her eyes off my face.

"Must be tough working so late. I'm surprised they were even open." I gave her a tired shrug. I hated this cloak and dagger, beating around the bush stuff. Normally, I just ignored it and let people have whatever suspicions they liked. Almost always, whatever they were imagining was less crazy than what was actually happening. Sadie had never made any specific accusations, only saying that she knew I was hiding something.

"You guys been keeping busy?" I asked, trying to change the topic.

"They've been burning them up today," Sadie said. "This is the third big fire today. We had a warehouse fire down on the Southside just after we got on shift, and there's still a crew cooling off what's left of old Forrest High just a couple miles from here."

"Yeah, and that don't even count the second alarm they had last night. Well, early this morning, I guess. Big house on the river sent two to the hospital, one dead inside before we got there," Rhames said. He glanced up from his phone, lips pursed with thought. "Fire's funny like that. Sometimes you can go months without anything, and then the whole world's burnin' up."

"Any fatalities at the other two?" I asked.

"The one we had this morning? I don't really know. Bitch was burning through the roof before we got there. Investigator might know by now," Sadie said.

"Talked to a guy from Ladder 18," Benson said,

idly stirring his coffee. "They found a bum or somebody burned up in one of the classrooms of the old school. Probably started a fire and fell asleep." He gave a half shrug in my direction. "It happens, sometimes."

"It's too hot for a warming fire," I said, frowning. Benson shrugged, as if the motivations of hobos were beyond his understanding, but now I was wondering what the odds of there being exactly the same number of major fires, with fatalities, as my encounters with the mephits.

*I'm no wizard,* I thought, sipping coffee as I worked through it. *But if I were, and I needed something to power a summoning, a big roaring fire with a sacrifice has got to be a perfect way to bring a badass tourist back over and over again.* It was a well-known phenomenon that followed catastrophes of great elemental significance, like tsunamis, hurricanes, or volcanic eruptions. Any huge expenditure of power like that had a tendency to leave unwanted tourists in its wake. Most evaporated quickly, or at least minded their own business and therefore were ignored, but sometimes it caused trouble. Especially in events where human life was lost, where the occult rules aligned to allow more powerful tourists through the veil. More than one zephyr had been spawned by a tornado, only to wreak havoc for a few miles until it ran out of power. A wizard who had figured out how to harness this kind of power would be the occult version of Benjamin Franklin with a key on a kite string.

"We need to go," I said suddenly, standing so quickly I startled myself. Some deep instinct was poking me in the ribs.

"I thought we were waiting on a ride?" Archades

asked. I shook my head.

"No, we've got another appointment. I just remembered," I said.

"Right, sure," Sadie scoffed. "An appointment, almost at midnight." At the center of the table, the station phone warbled from an abused speaker, and Benson reached across the battered wood to answer it. Sadie had a frustrated, almost pouting frown, and goddamn if she didn't still look good.

"Guess I'll be taking this coffee to go," Archades said, slurping as he stood.

"Diane Morris?" Benson said louder than the hushed tones of somebody having a private conversation. He was looking at me with confusion and then handed me the phone. "Asking for you, ma'am."

"Probably the office," I said, taking the handset and holding it up to my ear. "Special Agent Morris speaking."

"Ms. Morris," an unfamiliar voice on the other end said, so silky smooth it could have gift wrapped a scarf. "You have something of mine. I want it back."

"May I ask who's calling?" I said, trying to keep my tone light.

"You can call me...Mr. Red." This son of a bitch was smirking. I could hear the smirk through the phone. "Ms. Morris, my patience was never very good, and now it is at its end. The contents of that little box you're keeping with you are extremely valuable to me, and unless you prefer to see everybody in that building dead, you'll leave it on the front doorstep."

"Oh? Are your hot-headed friends getting impatient?" I asked, stalling for time while trying to meaningfully make eye contact with Archades.

"They're hardly friends of mine. Be glad I caught up to you first. They would not give you this chance. Front doorstep. Now."

"I'd rather talk about this face-to-face, if you don't mind," I said, patting my pockets to see what I had left at my disposal. Luckily, my stall for time was perfect: I didn't need very long to see that I was shit out of options.

"You have ninety seconds," Mr. Red said, and the line clicked dead. I stared at the receiver dumbly, then set it down.

"Mortimer," I said, walking into the station's kitchen and pulling open drawers at random. Silverware. Stirring spoons. A whole drawer full of tongs. "We're about to have some company. Would you be kind enough to help your new friends to a safer place?" I snatched open a wide drawer full of knives. Real, heavy-duty knives that would have been at home in any butcher shop.

"What kind of company?" Sadie asked, as Archades pleasantly started trying to talk the lot of them to their feet and out of the kitchen. I selected the longest, least-battered knives from the drawer, tucking a pair into my belt.

"Anybody here have a gun?" I asked, abandoning pretenses as I became keenly aware of the trickle of time passing. The confused firefighters, still seated, looked at Archades as if he would explain the joke.

"How about some sleep?" Archades suggested cheerfully. "Ten percent should do it."

"No!" I said, vehemently as I came back around to Sadie. I looked her dead in those beautiful green eyes, serious as I could be. "Sadie, I promise you that if you don't take your guys and get out of here, you're all going to die. Go hide in the showers. Mortimer and I will draw them off." Just because Mr. Red had dismissed the idea of the mephits didn't mean they weren't out there right now, ready to render us into vapor. Hiding in the showers wouldn't do much good then. Still, it was the best chance anybody had at the moment.

"Will you tell me what's going on when this is over?" Sadie asked. I nodded fervently, anything to get her to start moving.

"If we live through this, sure, I'll tell you whatever you want to know."

Archades was peeking through the blinds out of the kitchen, looking out into the street in front of the station.

"Guests have arrived," Archades said and recoiled from the window at the cracking sound of glass. He stumbled back, clutching his shoulder as blood spurted wildly. Out came a laugh. "Oh, that's pretty cute! Give me twenty percent, Diane. I'll sort this lot out."

"Sort yourself out first!" I shouted, grabbing Benson and Sadie by the shoulders and hustling them out of the room, toward the center of the building. Rhames, who'd gone for cover at the explosion of glass, crawled after me as that whole side of the station erupted in a shower of breaking glass and brick facade. The polite coughs of suppressed weapons advanced across the street, but I didn't dare look for their sources as I hustled into the more defensible hallway. Archades, in the meantime, strolled across the kitchen, taking a handful of the blood from his shoulder and smearing it messily across his neck and face. He winked, stumbled toward me drunkenly, and collapsed against the nearby wall. He lolled his tongue out in a comically grotesque mask of death.

"What the fuck is going on?" Benson screamed over the sound of bullets smacking into the brick. I kicked a door open, revealing the bathroom, and hauled the pair of them into it.

"Don't come out here," I commanded, helping Rhames scramble into the room. "Lock this door, turn the lights off." I paused. "Sorry about this. It wasn't part of the plan."

I slapped the lights off in the hallway, retreating to what turned out to be sleeping quarters, which I quickly darkened as well. From the kitchen, the sound of gunfire ceased with precision. There came footsteps on broken glass as people climbed through the shattered windows. Whoever was running the show had decided to abandon any sort of subtlety. A fire at a flea market was one thing, but straight up attacking a public building was certain to get some kind of attention.

"Got a dead one here," somebody said from the other side of the door. "No sign of the egg yet."

"Keep looking. No witnesses." A second voice said. Were there just two? How many henchmen did Mr. Red have working for him? Where did these people even come from? The Venn diagram of people who knew enough to be useful and people dumb enough to get caught up in illegal anomalous activity didn't exactly overlap much. Believe it or not, most of the dirty workers in these deals never even know what they're really dealing with. These guys not only knew what the package was, they weren't slouches when it came to taking chances. The first man spoke into a radio, ordering a second team to sweep around back and make sure nobody was sneaking out.

Four. Maybe five. No sign of any tourists yet, but that didn't mean that Mr. Mephit wasn't out there waiting with his flame-throwing soprano. What I needed, more desperately than a drink and some paid time off, was my abacus. Sooner or later, one of them was going to come into the sleeping area, and I didn't like the idea of testing a dull kitchen knife against a pistol.

Archades had asked for twenty percent. This was the thought running through my brain as I retreated farther into the sleeping quarters, slipping my phone from my pocket as I did. What would be the harm of giving him that much leeway, for only a few minutes?

"Slippery slope, Diane," I muttered to myself, thumbing my way through my contacts list until I got what I wanted. Contract or no contract, there would be a point at which Archades was powerful enough to do whatever he wanted. Loosening the chain could quickly turn into completely unleashing him.

"This is dispatch," a tired, overworked woman on the line said, after a few short rings.

"Good afternoon," I whispered, crouching down beside a bed and staring at the door. "Would it be possible for you to send an alert to Fire Station Thirty-Five at my signal?" I could hear the confusion at the request.

"Are you asking for a test call?" the dispatcher asked. The sliver of light under the door darkened for a moment as feet approached it, and I slipped toward a bed to prepare my ambush. It was actually pretty inspired. All the lights in the station would

172

automatically turn back on, and I'd catch anybody in the dark bunk room completely off guard.

"Yes, but only on my signal," I hissed. "Just wait for—" The bullhorn mounted to the wall blared to life, kicking the lights on and jumpstarting my heart. A panel lit up at the far end of the room, showing in bold red letters: TEST PAGE. Immediately, the door through to the kitchen swung open. Instead of taking my attacker by surprise, I was suddenly in full view of the man whose face was a hash-brown platter of monkey-induced scratches.

"I found the bitch!" the man shouted and swung the short-barreled shotgun to his shoulder as he advanced. "Give me that case!"

"Come and get it!" was the best I could retort, staring down the barrel and wondering if I'd have enough time to see the flash before he took off the top of my skull.

Instead of a bang, though, there was a squelch. It was the same noise a bog makes as it pulls off your new shoe, just before you realize you're going to have to walk home barefoot. A messy sound. It was followed by a man shrieking at the top of his voice. My assailant, professional goon he might be, reacted with human instinct. The threat was behind him, and he turned his back on the poor, defenseless woman he'd been getting ready to aerate.

That damsel in distress took the opportunity to sink eight inches of steel into the shoulder holding the gun. That roar of pain was cut off as I wrapped myself around his neck like a boa. It's relatively difficult to crush somebody's windpipe, but almost no pressure at all will starve the brain of precious blood. Not that his brain was a powerhouse to begin with, but before he could realize what was really happening, he was folding like a cheap suit under my weight.

I slapped a set of zip-tie cuffs on him, hobbling ankles to wrist hurriedly, and rose with his gun in hand. Unfamiliar make, unfamiliar model, but needs must.

"Thanks for cutting to the chase," I said, grinning despite myself as I stepped over his skewered shoulder. Easing my way to the kitchen, I peeked through the door before moving forward, clearing corners as I went. Archades sat on the table, swinging his legs idly as he watched me cautiously make my way in. He'd picked up Benson's coffee and was drinking it leisurely.

"Where's the other guy?" I asked, making my way to the wall beside the window and pressing as flat as I could.

"What other guy?" Archades asked innocently as he pointedly glanced at a set of kitchen cabinets barely large enough to hold a stack of dish towels. Blood was steadily pouring out of the bottom seam of the door, and what looked like a finger was wedging an opening in the cabinet.

"Jesus," I hissed at him. "I told you no to the twenty percent!" Archades rolled his eyes.

"Please. Even shackled, I'm not *completely* helpless," Archades said. "Besides, does it help that he pretty much folded himself up?"

"It really doesn't," I said and chanced a look out into the darkened street. Nothing moved except the wind in the trees. "You know where the rest are?"

"Sadly, my trammeled vision can't see any others," Archades said. "Can I keep this?" He twirled a pistol on one finger, producing it like a parlor trick.

"Can you shoot?"

"Never really needed to," Archades said, tossing the pistol my way. I tucked it into my belt, gave one last look out the window, and ran at a crouch toward the hall. Archades strolled along after me, hands in his pockets.

"I see you left one alive," he said, poking his head through a door. "Boy, he looks pissed off."

"Hopefully, he'll still be here when backup arrives," I said. I knocked at the door to the bathroom. "Sadie? It's me, open up." A deadbolt clicked open, showing her pale face in the dark room beyond.

"Christ, Diane. What is happening?" Sadie asked, head poking out to look up and down the hall. The station had seen better days. Ceiling tiles hung in pieces where they hadn't been reduced to powder by the gunfire, and by now the only lights were from emergency exit signs mandated by law. The test page fiasco over, the lights were off again.

"No time, can't explain. It's time for you guys to pile into your engine and get the hell out of here."

"Don't gotta tell me twice," Benson said, pushing past me toward the bay. Archades reached out a casual hand, snagging him by the back of the shirt.

"Perhaps you should allow us to lead the way," he said cordially. "Who knows what's out there waiting for us?"

"What's the plan?" Sadie asked. "We called the cops. Should we just wait this out?"

"By the time cops get here, this place is going to be a crater," I said. "Lieutenant, you need to get your crew to safety. They won't be after you." Archades poked his head into the vehicle bay, then casually gestured for everybody to follow him out.

Glass crunched underfoot as somebody came in through the shattered window. A man appeared in the kitchen with a rifle held at the ready.

"Go, go, GO!" I said, shooting wildly down the hall as the man swung his weapon at us. His shots fired wide, peppering the doorframe rather than us, and he grunted as one of my rounds caught him in the shoulder. I fired until the shotgun clicked empty, walking backward as calmly as I could. Another attacker, halfway through the window, went diving for cover behind the table, and then I was through to the relative safety of the vehicle bay.

"Get your asses in!" Rhames roared at his people, hauling himself into the seat of the apparatus and snatching at the radio. He was barely contained panic made manifest, but he began articulating into the radio in short, clipped phrases.

"Come on, Diane!" Sadie implored, leaning out of the back door of the fire engine. Benson, who'd been ahead of her, had gotten in the driver's seat and was preparing to leave with all haste. Good survival instincts on that one.

"We'll be along shortly," I said, drawing the pistol from my belt and checking the chamber. I had some very difficult, rapid-fire decisions to make, and not much in the way of good options. What were my priorities? Well, getting out alive was pretty damn high on the list. Always was. Living to fight another day, discretion being the better part of valor, these were core tenets of the DIA. We could jump on the running board and hitch a ride to safety.

But.

Nobody was actually after me. They were after what I had, and as long as they believed the egg was in my possession, it was unlikely that we'd escape on a twenty-ton fire engine. They'd proven that public exposure wasn't a concern of theirs. Odds were great that this was part of the same outfit that had chased me through suburbia, guns ablaze. This wasn't dealing with an elemental emissary, who had their images to worry about, or the goddamned Fae kingdoms who were one overtly hostile act away from getting erased from existence. These were hired professionals. Highly motivated, they were just going to keep coming.

"Goddamn it!" I snarled, running up to Sadie. I opened the lunch box and pulled the egg out, the heat of the thing scorching my palm. "You need to take this. Right now. Take it with you, and don't let anybody even see it."

"What the fuck is it?" Sadie asked, hot-potatoing it between her hands until she wrapped it in some padding from her gear.

"Think of it as a nuclear bomb, and you'll probably be careful enough." I clicked the silly metal lunch box shut again, holding it tight in one fist. The odds weren't great for anybody in this scenario, but they were better for her this way. "Go to my house. Knock twice, tell Jericho to let you in. He'll know how to get help."

"Diane," Archades called out, heaving weights and workout equipment at the door as somebody tried to muscle their way through. A fifty-pound kettle-bell mashed someone's emerging hand into paste.

"What are you going to do?" Sadie asked, as I closed the door on her. I shrugged, trying to put on a brave face.

"I've got some auditing to do," I said. The growl of the engine starting drowned out everything else, and Sadie gave me one last, desperately anxious glance before opening the bay door.

"Come on, Morty!" I yelled, ducking out from under the rattling panel and taking off at a sprint, the lunch box as visible as possible in one pumping arm. It would be a few moments before the fire engine had clearance to pull out, and I needed all eyes on me. I fired the pistol once into the air, eyes scanning for movement.

Gunfire poured out of the street, tactically clad figures with automatic weapons stepping out from behind parked vehicles and trashcans, and I threw my hands up in one futile, blind-panicked motion, not feeling the bullets that would certainly end me on the spot. There's a reason they don't teach "Run blindly into the open against unknown enemy forces" at the academy. It's not even the most effective way to kill yourself.

Obscenely wet impacts slapped into Archades' body, drawing grunts as he grabbed me and began to run sideways.

"Twenty-nng-per-agh-cent!" he stuttered in time with bullets. I could barely hear him. The brick wall of the fire station was being chipped apart, but the cascading fire wasn't directed at the still-opening door. Something hot and impossibly fast zipped behind my leg, and it took me three steps to realize that I'd been hit. I'd almost made it to the next building over, where I might have been able to break a window and find cover, hold them off for a few seconds.

"No!" I screamed, even as my brain's terror-induced state tried to force acquiescence to his demands. Archades would be able to mow these goons down, bullets and all. I could live through this wild night. It would even keep Sadie safe, something that was suddenly very important to me as I crawled in the grass with one numb leg dragging behind me. The gunfire had stopped, and then there was a throaty roar that I mistook for a dragon waking up.

It was the fire engine, finally free from the bay, accelerating out of the station and onto the street with all its might and speed. Sadie's face was dark in the window as her wide eyes stared at my predicament with horror, but in a flash they were gone. I saw some gunmen half-turn, raising weapons, and I fired my pistol dry at them, hitting nothing but their attention. Another welter of lead slapped around me, but intervening was Archades again, being so filled with shot that he must have doubled in weight. Blood, thick and red, poured from his mouth as he grinned at me, hit-enhanced physiology and regeneration overwhelmed by the impacts to the point where his lips could barely move. I could make it out.

*Twenty.*

After a moment, the haphazard onslaught subsided, and I could hear the clatter of magazines being replaced and weapons being readied.

"A moment," somebody's commanding voice demanded, and I propped myself up on Archades' shredded body. In the light of the street, five or six gunmen stood, weapons held ready, yielding to a robed man at their center.

"Mr. Red, I presume," I managed, teeth gritted in pain as I rose to one knee. My left calf had a hole through the meatiest part, and since I wasn't dead yet, I took the opportunity to pull my belt off and tighten it over the wound.

The man spread his arms, the crimson of his extravagant robes shining under the streetlamp. A hooded cowl covered his face, but the thick beard that poured down his chest was tightly braided, studded with gold rings and other ornaments. Arcane symbols stitched across the robes moved eerily, not when you were looking at them, but between glances.

"Quite the effort, Ms. Morris," Mr. Red said, voice oily as old pizza boxes. He stepped forward, the difficult, rickety gait of age hobbling him. "But that's quite enough out of you, my dear."

"You'd think so, right?" I said, managing to get to my feet. Archades struggled to roll onto his back, the dozens of bleeding holes in his chest showing through to a murky, swirling darkness underneath. The holes were closing, but slowly. I raised the lunch box, pressing the gun against the side of it. "How about you go away, and we'll all call it a night."

Mr. Red stopped in the middle of the road, and even under the darkness of the hood, I could feel his eyes boring into me. Judging me. I had no idea if a bullet was a threat against a dragon's egg, and it didn't really matter. The gun was dry as an Amish county.

"You should want me to have it," Mr. Red said. "If the mephit rebels acquire it, the ensuing civil war will have disastrous effects here on the Material Plane. At least if I take it, humanity will be brought out of this primitive time we live in."

Surprise cut through the pain of my leg, but at least my face was too pinched for it to show there. Mr. Red really wasn't with the mephits? Did that not make him the wizard who had been working with the thieves?

"I don't suppose you'll tell me what you want to do with it," I said. "I mean, everybody else wants a taste. I may as well weigh my options." I tapped the lunch box with the barrel. "Tell me, do you think it'll blow up when shot?"

"You're not going to shoot it," Mr. Red said. "If *she* awakens, and there is a single egg missing from the clutch, *she* will bring such devastation to your city that hasn't been seen in a hundred years."

"If I give it to you, it's the same thing," I said. Thank sweet baby Jesus this guy liked to talk. I mean, it was clear I wasn't doing any more running for the foreseeable future, but still. He had to know help was on its way. There'd be a dozen agents showing up, not to mention cops, reporters, insurance adjusters, food trucks. "I've got to hand it to you, though. Masterminding this whole egg heist? It'll go down in history as the most ambitious plot in modern times."

Red shook with laughter, deep rumbling from far within the cowl. For a moment, it was like hearing distant explosions at the bottom of a mine shaft, and I could feel the ground rumble underfoot with power oozing from this man.

"I am simply seizing opportunity, Ms. Morris," Mr. Red said. "The Magpies had the skills to infiltrate the lair, get close enough to actually steal the clutch of eggs. The mephit rebels had information. They knew precisely where the dragon slept, where to find the eggs, and where a portal could be opened. The wizard? A myopic fool desperate to live forever but too cowardly to actually partake in the thieving. One portal in return for one egg. They were begging to be relieved of their prize."

"So what are you then? You're not with the Cabal. Cabal wizards wouldn't have goons with guns."

"They fear any change to their precious traditions. They write with quill and parchment because of *aesthetics*, not because it's necessary. An incantation may be capable of killing an enemy, but it's so much simpler to have them shot and save the arcane arts for truly powerful works." Mr. Red raised his hand, a beckoning gesture with gloved fingers encrusted in rings and other ornamentation. "Hand to me this egg, Ms. Morris, and I will see to it that you come to no more harm. The other, your organization may do with as it wishes. Perhaps, it will be enough to quell *her* wrath."

I grunted as I stepped forward, barely supporting any weight on my injured leg. Vision swimming, I wavered where I was.

"Come and get it, bathrobe," I slurred. Mr. Red raised a hand overhead, and the goons lined up alongside him, faces tight with professional concentration as they raised weapons. Nostalgic feelings of having my picture taken at school, and the anxiety of waiting for the blinding flash, took me in an absurd way, and I laughed out loud. Well, I thought, seven years is a long run for someone in my position. At least I wasn't being eaten alive by wulfen. Or worse.

The fire engine hit the line of goons going something like sixty in a thirty-five, its lights off and surprisingly quiet against the sound of the smoke alarm wailing from inside the fire station. A symphony of bloody smacks accompanied the screeching of brakes as the vehicle came to an abrupt stop. Such was the force of impact I was missed just barely by a flying body still clutching a shotgun in a death grip.

Sadie hopped out of the driver's seat, skin pale and slick with nervous sweat. She looked ready to throw up and took a moment to look at the bloody ruin that was now impregnated into the grill of the truck.

"Oh God," she said, and I hobbled over to her as quickly as I could.

"Sadie, what the fuck?" I managed, throwing my arms around her neck and holding her as I held myself up.

"I just killed those guys..." she said, voice numb and flat.

"It's okay, it's all right," I said uselessly, not sure where to begin in reassuring her that it had been the right thing to do. "You saved my life." I looked past her and realized the rest of the vehicle's occupants were nowhere to be seen. "Where's your crew?"

"I dropped them off a few blocks away. I circled back around. I had to see if you were okay," Sadie said, monotone and looking foggily at the middle distance. "Oh, God..." I touched her face, locking eyes.

"Sadie, you're going to have to get it together for just a little while. We're still in the game," I said, looking around. I didn't see a crumpled pile of scarlet fabric in the middle of the road, so Mr. Red had to be somewhere. Wizard, ghoul, vampire, whatever the fuck he was, it was going to take more than a mundane vehicular homicide to bring him down.

"Maybe I should check on these..." Sadie said, trailing off when she watched me roll one onto his back and pull a handgun from a holster. I checked the magazine, the chamber, and rolled the broken body back onto its face. I didn't need to see that shit.

"You've got to drive us to the office," I said. Hot blood was starting to pool in my shoe, but I'd deal with that on the way. "You're in this thing now, and we better see it through to the end."

"Your partner's dead, Diane," Sadie said, looking woodenly at his curled body, still where he'd fallen shielding me. I'd honestly expected him to be up already, but even he had limits. This was reassuring.

"He'll be fine," I said, stuffing the gun into my waistband and promising that when this was all over, I'd never leave the office again without five or six weapons. Maybe Logistics would issue me a bazooka. "Get him in the back."

With great effort, I hauled myself into the passenger seat, using bandages from the fire department's medical equipment to clean and dress my leg. It felt on fire for the most part, but at least my foot hadn't gone numb. I had concerns about long-term damage, but to be honest, so did the rest of my body if we didn't make it back to the office with the egg intact.

Sadie heaved Archades' body into the back seat, where he bled slowly onto the floor, and then she climbed back behind the wheel and started the engine again.

"Where's the thing I gave you?" I asked, looking around. She reached under the seat and produced the egg, still wrapped in the thick layer of flame-retardant cloth, and I gave it a quick inspection before placing it back in the relative safety of the lunch box.

"What the hell is that thing?" Sadie asked, throwing the truck into drive and speeding forward. A few body-sized speedbumps later, we were clear of the carnage and headed toward the highway.

"It's a dragon egg," I said.

"Like, real dragon? Big lizard, breathes fire, hoards gold?" Sadie asked, and nothing in her voice sounded incredulous or mocking.

"Yes," I said. "Except this egg comes from a big momma dragon, and if she wakes up to find it missing, she's going to go on a rampage that will probably erase Jacksonville from the map."

"Why Jacksonville?" Sadie asked. "What's it got against us?"

"We think her lair is somewhere nearby," I said. I fished my phone out of my pocket.

"Jesus, Diane, you *think*? Something that dangerous needs an eye kept on it," Sadie said. "So I guess this means you aren't actually an auditor?"

"Nothing gets past you," I said, with a little more sass than I meant. Now wasn't the time to have The Talk. I needed to call the office. Get an update. Keep ahead of the enemy.

"That's real nice, Diane," Sadie said. "I knew you were hiding something big. All of this hiding in plain sight stuff, you might fool a lot of people, but I could tell you weren't just some tax jockey."

"I don't hide in plain sight," I said. "It's a well-crafted series of alibis and covers. I had to learn all kinds of tax code things just to keep up with appearances, and even people who work in the same building as I don't know what I…really…do…" Little pieces of the puzzle clicked into place, and my thumb hovered over the dial button on the phone. "Oh. Oh no." With a jerk of my hand, I threw the phone out the window, leaving it somewhere on the side of the interstate.

"What?" Sadie asked, vacillating between keeping her eyes on the road and worrying at my expression.

"I'm a moron," I said, running a hand through my fire-baked hair. "He's been listening to all my calls. That's how the damned mephits are finding me."

"Who? The what?"

"The goddamned wizard!" I said, slamming my fist against the dashboard. "That slick shit, he's always putting up a front of not knowing how a phone works, but he's been there the whole time. Feeding me bad info."

"There are wizards?" Sadie asked, playing catch-up.

"I thought it was magical tracking, but I've told him every step of the way where I was going. Mr. Red had been following Tomas, but the mephit only intercepted me after the wizard summoned it from the house fire near where I live! I thought they were working together, but...oh shit." I felt sick. I had one egg with me, sure, but the other was back at headquarters. Where Rubin worked. Rubin the Pontiferous, doddering old wizard who was absent-minded and harmless. Of course it was him. He'd eavesdropped on my conversation with LaFleur, intercepted phone calls, and maybe even tracked me through my actual phone's GPS. Mr. Red's forces had simply kept tabs on me the old-fashioned way, but the mephits were being sent by their wizard friend to retrieve his egg for him.

"So what do we do?" Sadie asked.

"We?" I asked. "You're going to drop me off. I'll

figure it out from there."

"No," Sadie said. "You're half dead, light about a quart of blood, and barely able to walk. I'm already in this too far to just back out now. What are we doing?" She didn't look at me. She stared straight ahead, jaw set in that way I already knew meant she wasn't going to have a conversation.

"Every minute the eggs aren't back where they came from is bad. The dragon could open her eye to check on them at any time, and when that happens, it won't matter what else is going on. We need to get the other egg from headquarters, find out how they got into the lair in the first place, and return the eggs."

"Okay. So we need to go to headquarters," Sadie said. "Where's that?"

"You know the Brightway Center?" I asked.

"That's on the Southside, right?" Sadie asked. I nodded. "Yeah, I think so. That's where you work? The FBI headquarters is off of Gate."

"No, we get our own place. Out of the way." I drummed my fingers on the lunch box, thinking furiously. The odds that Ziraxariz would open an eye increased the closer we got to the summer solstice. There wasn't time for subtlety. Even if I could get LaFleur on the phone, I had no way of being sure that Rubin wouldn't be able to hear. For all I knew, he had all the rooms in the building under surveillance, mundane or magical.

"You have your phone?" I asked. I was surprised to see that my home number was still at the top of her contact list, with a cute picture the two of us had taken down at the beach at sunrise one morning. We'd surfed all day, had a fire at night, talked until dawn, and kissed just before the picture had been taken. In the picture, Sadie had that smile she always had right after she'd told a joke, and I was caught laughing without knowing the camera was on.

My home phone rang three times, and I hung up. I dialed again, let the phone ring twice, then hung up again. I repeated this, letting it ring five times, then four, then once. The sixth time I called, Jericho answered immediately.

"Where have you been? I can't get into the pantry, and the food bowl is almost empty," Jericho said. On the phone, even the most suspicious person wouldn't be able to tell he wasn't human, but a cat was a cat was a cat.

"Listen, Jericho, just listen. A wizard made a portal into a dragon's lair. How do I figure out where the portal entrance is?" I asked. Jericho gave a little exasperated meow.

"Ask the wizard nicely?" he suggested.

"We're well past that now," I said. "Is it even possible that the portal's still open?"

"The duration of a portal is always, always directly proportional to the power it was formed with. Something like that, creating a portal into the dwelling of an absurdly powerful dragon? It'd last weeks. Maybe even months."

"So I just need to find it?"

"Most likely spot is somewhere out of the way, locked up, or well guarded. Probably a combination of the three." Jericho paused. "Where are you? Are you on the way home?"

"No. Listen, you still know the phone number to my office?" I asked, leaning down to adjust the bandage so it wasn't cutting off what little circulation remained.

"Yeah?"

"I need you to call there. Extension is, uh." I dug into my wallet for a cheat sheet that turned out to be smeared with God-knows-what terrible liquid. "Try 0404, and then try 0909. One of those should get you to an answering machine. Rubin. Can you still do a decent impersonation of my voice?"

Jericho laughed, and then his voice melted. It was the auditory equivalent of squeezing gak between your toes at a muddy river bottom, and I cringed from the phone as he replied, in my own voice, "Of course. How else am I supposed to order the pizzas?"

"Tell him you've got the egg, and tell him that you need his help at the…" I paused. Where could I send a dangerous wizard that wouldn't put people at risk? "Riverside Park. Tell him the egg is cracked. I need a wizard to stabilize it for transport."

"It's not actually cracked, right?" Jericho asked, voice suddenly back to normal. He sounded a little concerned, which was roughly the equivalent of hysterics.

"No, fit as a fiddle, but I need *him* to be concerned. You won't get through to anybody, but leave him a message."

"You got it, Diane," Jericho said. "Afterward, though, I'm using your voice to order pizza." I sighed and spent a minute reading out my new credit card to him over the phone. I looked forward to seeing what new and interesting charges he'd rack up in the time it took for me to call and lock the account.

I handed Sadie back her phone and then settled back in the seat, resting my head against the coolness of the window, and watched the night-wreathed streets pour past us. No flashing red lights, no siren, but still it was at least sort of cool to ride in the powerful, reassuring diesel-thumping fire engine.

"I'm sorry about your partner," Sadie said gently, awkwardly, clearly unsure how she was going to keep the conversation going.

"Morty's fine," I said, without the energy to cast a glance back to confirm it.

"Were you close?" she asked, merging onto a ramp that would take us south, toward headquarters.

"We just met today," I said. My hands itched to do something, anything, in preparation for what was coming. When preparing to handle a coven of witches, you made hex-proofers and dreamcatchers, things to muddle their abilities and protect yourself. Poltergeists and other specters required iron shavings, containers of purified salts, and the latest holy literature the church could provide. There were protocols and procedures for a hundred different encounters, each written in the blood of agents who had come before me, some even more ancient than that. The real classics, the vampires and lycanthropes, were so detailed that there was no end to the preparations one could undertake. The only vampire I'd ever had to deal with had, quite literally, evaporated under my opening salvo of holy water, garlic, silver shavings, flowing water, spoken words of power, and, just to put the kill into overkill, a huge silver cross worn by Pope Pius III. This didn't have a nifty little guide. I was writing with my own blood this time.

In an ideal world, I wouldn't be going into this thing alone, but it was how most of these things went, as it turned out. Seven agents worked out of Jacksonville, including LaFleur, and at any given point there might be three of us in the city itself. The rest were investigating, or mitigating, problems as far west as Louisiana and as far north as Virginia. As many as possible would be recalled for something this big, and maybe we'd get help from one of the other regions, but they all had things going on they needed to deal with. You didn't just walk away from a peace negotiation between the merfolk and their mortal enemies, bayou Cajuns. A pissant necromancer in a Tennessee valley could suddenly become a little warlord of the undead, and it was a lot simpler to handle while he still had to dig up the bodies himself.

I was grateful to be able to vent some of these frustrations to Sadie, to finally have somebody I didn't work with who could at least nod and commiserate, even if every new detail shattered her worldview a little more. She was real interested in mephits, which, as a firefighter, made a lot of sense.

"So they're just, you know, smart, living fire?" she asked. "Mean, nasty?"

"These ones lately have been," I said. "They're rare out in the wild, or at least outside volcanoes. These ones, I think, have been summoned by this wizard. He burned down some houses with people still inside and used the power to summon the same one over and over again. Maybe a few of them at a time." I'd never even heard of someone doing this before.

"I could take one," Sadie said, her bold confidence starting to show through the shock of what she'd just endured.

"Well, they have heat beams that can vaporize

steel, and they can see in all directions because they're psychic, but sure, you could take one," I said. "You happen to keep a carbon dioxide extinguisher on this rig?"

"Uh, yeah," Sadie said, in a clear tone of *duh!* She pointed at the embroidered patch on the shoulder of her uniform shirt. Fire department. Duh.

At least I wasn't going in empty-handed.

Chapter Nine

Concealing twenty tons of rolling steel and rubber isn't the easiest thing, and sneaking up is virtually impossible. She'd pulled off a hat trick earlier, but this time I had Sadie pull into the parking lot with lights turned off, running as quiet as the diesel-guzzler was going to manage. We parked far from the building in the deep shadows of the sycamores that rained leaves and spine-studded seed pods on my car in the fall. Oh, right. I didn't have a car currently. Another thing to worry about if I survived the night.

"I should be in and out in twenty minutes," I said, unbuckling my seat belt. I had the extinguisher between my knees and had fashioned a sort of shoulder sling for the egg case. I needed both hands for the time being.

"You can barely walk," Sadie said, even as I flexed my swollen leg in a careful measure of my range. I might be able to stand on it.

"Arc—Morty is going to help me hobble around," I said. Sadie gave the tight-lipped frown of someone worried about opening fresh emotional wounds by being blunt and went to cast a significant look into the back seat where she expected to see the limp corpse still on the floor. Instead, she came face-to-face with Archades' mellow, smiling face. I hadn't seen him move, or I'd never have set her up like that. It was pretty funny to watch her punch him in the mouth as she shrieked and jumped away in her seat. Kind of a "fight and flight" response.

"Charming," Archades mumbled, nursing his swelling lip with one hand. "This is why I didn't join in earlier. Your girlfriend would have run us off the road."

"I thought you were a corpse!" Sadie said, staring at the holes in Archades' shirt, at the fully healed and unblemished skin beneath.

"Exaggerated," Archades said, waving a hand. I hefted the extinguisher into the back, turning painfully in my seat as a new set of sore muscles and injuries let me know I needed rest. "How's the leg?"

"Fine and dandy," I said, through gritted teeth. "Can you overpower a mephit?" He glanced at the extinguisher and then picked it up. It was a heavier, more robust version of the little one you might buy at any store. It was bigger even than the one I'd used to fight off the mephit above the sewage processing station.

"With this? If I get lucky. Depends on how much power it has left."

"Let's assume it used the fire at the flea market as a battery."

"Less than likely."

"All right." I sighed. If I were Rubin, I'd have turned the office into one big death trap of elemental soldiers. The moment I showed my face with either egg, I'd be lucky to be history. I'd probably end up more like abstract algebra—something people couldn't really remember. "Could *you* overpower a mephit?" Archades' smile widened, hunger touching the edges of his eyes in a way that made my skin crawl.

"Oh, you meant that way. Yes, of course. I could

overpower a hundred mephits," Archades said. "Just say the word."

"I'm not releasing you, bub," I said, suicidally jabbing a finger into his chest. "I'm talking bare minimum, nothing more than that. How much?" Archades narrowed his eyes a little, and I withdrew the offending digit.

"Against the big, bad one that popped me earlier?" Archades mused. "I'd need at least thirty percent. Forty would be better. At fifty, they wouldn't stand a chance."

"I'm going to give you fifteen," I said. Archades rolled his eyes.

"Diane, I am trying to be cooperative here. Yes, I would like you to fully release me. I would settle this thing in a few hours, and we could part ways amicable friends. But, barring that, my best advice is to release me to thirty percent, and I will be *useful*. Half of that barely lets me use anything."

"Well, tough tits," I said, opening the door and gingerly settling on my good leg. Archades joined me in the shadows, just barely visible as a darker outline. "I am giving you permission to release from the first fifteen percent of your restraints, from now until I give the word to return to normal."

Sadie was coming around the front of the engine, but she didn't have to endure what came next. Archades growled, deep baritone thunder reverberating in his chest as the shadows of the trees seemed to brighten. It wasn't that there was any more light in the area. Archades himself was deepening into the black void of something beyond natural. Azure fire crackled to life, running in little rivulets of dripping power until it collected in an aura around the bracelets. Two loud pops, like circuit breakers snapping shut, killed the light show just as Sadie came around.

My skin was slick with freezing sweat, and my mouth had turned sandy as I recoiled mentally from what had just happened. Up until that moment, I'd never been really sure if there was such a thing as a soul. After all, it's not anything measurable, quantifiable, or tangible. I had just felt the brush of something unctuous, not against my skin, or even against my mind, but against some core foundation so deep within that I had never known it was there. My soul was the only thing that directly felt this unnatural intrusion into our world, and it was like treading water in the ocean and feeling just the barest slither of some immeasurable behemoth out of sight.

"Fifteen it is," Archades said, this time with just a bare echo of inhumanity in his voice. "Would you like me to carry your luggage?"

"No." I came off too curt. Too obvious that his subtle change in power had affected me. To Sadie, who was hovering nearby with questions I didn't have time to answer, I gave a reassuring smile. In the dark, at least, I hoped it came off that way. "We'll be back in a minute. If we're not…just drive. Go to my house. Tell Jericho what happened. He'll help you get to safety."

"Jericho?" Sadie said with such surprise that I knew where her mind had gone.

"It's not like that," I said, hopping awkwardly to her. "He's just a friend." I had to reach up to touch her cheek, but she didn't flinch away. "You know, I wanted to call. I just didn't want to risk exposing you to this." Sadie took my hand and squeezed it.

"I'm not afraid of dangerous, Diane," she said. She was overwhelmed. A routine day of sick people and fires and car wrecks had been turned into a nightmare. Most firefighters, even more cops, would have been headed for the hills. "I'll be here when you get back." God, she was beautiful. I pulled myself up and kissed her, surprised and delighted that she was kissing me back like it was the first time all over again. Except that first time, at the beach, she hadn't needed to hold me up because of the bullet hole through my leg.

"Agent Morris." Archades coughed into his hand, trying to be tactful. "It might be time to go." Sadie set me down again, and Archades came to act as my crutches.

Well.

At least there was more to live for than more paperwork.

****

We controlled every single security camera in the building, so I didn't mind one bit about keeping my pistol out and ready as we came in through the front door. My keycard let us in without a problem, a little chirp and green light affirming I was allowed, and then we were in the elevator. Once there, I leaned against the faux-wood panel and pressed the button for our floor.

"Listen, Archades," I said, pressing my forehead to the wall just to enjoy the chill. The night was still hot, and I was suffering greatly from exhaustion at this point. "I appreciate you taking all those bullets for me."

"I live to serve," Archades said, flexing his fingers as if trying on a new pair of gloves. Dark, swirling marks, living tattoos, had made their way down the short sleeves of the T-shirt and were stopped at the brass manacles. "Can't have you dying now. It would spoil my vacation."

"Sure," I said, checking the chambered round in the pistol once again. It was a compulsive habit, born from paranoia and one instance where the bullet hadn't been there when I needed it. "Listen, if it comes down to letting me die or making sure the eggs get back safe and sound, promise me you'll do the right thing."

"Asking a demon to do the right thing is a little oxymoronic," Archades pointed out. I chuckled despite the moment. The elevator, an old and worn-out relic from the sixties, finally finished trundling to the top floor and dinged open.

I stepped out into the lobby with every ounce of mustered strength I had left, forcing my wobbling legs to support me with only a little weight on my companion, who still carried the extinguisher in his other hand. We must have caught Yancy in the middle of one of her donut-fueled naps because her head snapped up from where it had been resting against the desk.

"Who—Special Agent Morris!" Yancy said, suddenly red and flustered from embarrassment. Half a box of glazed, cold and sticky, sat open on the counter of her desk.

"I need to see LaFleur. Let him know I'm coming back," I said, in tones that made it certain I wasn't going to wait for visitor badges or snide comments. I strode, or limped confidently, toward the hall.

"He's not in!" Yancy said, not too tired to put a little wheedle into her tone. "You'll have to wait, just like everybody else."

"What do you mean he's not in?" I asked, rounding

on her so quickly Archades had to put a hand on my shoulder to keep me from falling down. "He's always in. He probably sleeps in his office most nights. Do you know what's happening out there tonight?" I gestured with a hand grimy by dirt, blood, and sweat. "Where the hell is he?" Yancy's piggy little face pinched, indignant and mean.

"Well!" One word, forty years of offended southern belle. "There's no need to get nasty with me, Miss Morris!"

"What she's trying to say," Archades interrupted before I could string together the words that would probably earn me a month of anger management once HR got hold of the transcripts, "is that Director LaFleur would certainly appreciate knowing that we are here and have much to tell him."

"Director LaFleur just left a few minutes ago," Yancy said, much more pleasant once she turned her attention on the suave older gentleman she perceived to have an actual right to address her. "He and Rubin ran out of here so quickly, I didn't get a chance to ask. I'm sure the director has his phone on him."

"Son of a bitch," I said, turning and rambling down the hall, bracing myself off the wall until I got to my office. I hadn't expected my little ruse to work so well. If LaFleur thought one of the eggs was cracking, of course he'd attend to it personally.

"What's the issue?" Archades asked, following me into the room and closing the door. He set the extinguisher down as I approached my chair and collapsed.

"The other egg is in his office," I said, running my hand through my frizzing hair.

"Are you sure?" Archades asked.

"It's the most warded room in the whole state, Archades, so yeah, I'm pretty sure. He could have left it on his desk, if he wanted, and it would be as safe as a bank vault. Safer, probably. You can portal into most bank vaults." I opened the desk and fished out some ibuprofen, dry-swallowing half a dozen tablets.

"So? Why don't you walk in there and get it?" Archades asked. "We can take them both, hide them wherever, and work on finding the nest." I laughed hoarsely.

"Walk in without an invitation?" I asked, shivering at the idea. "Those wards don't give a shit how noble my cause is. The only people who make it into that room are LaFleur and his invited guests. Fuck, even Yancy can't go in there. She has to leave his mail on the hall table."

"We were invited earlier," Archades said, genuinely puzzled. When I stared at him blankly, he seemed to realize something about my assumptions and laughed. This did nothing to endear him to me. "Diane, I know all the wards carved into that doorframe. Magic like that is powerful, but come on, it's hardly sentient. Once he's invited you into the room, you're his guest until dawn. Or dusk. One of the daily thresholds. That's how threshold wards work."

"Are you sure?" I asked, hauling myself to my feet.

"Positive," Archades said. He raised one hand, Scout's honor, and I tried not to look at the squirming shadow that appeared on his palm in the shape of a licking tongue. "I'll even step through first, if that will assuage your fears."

"You're not just using your powers to break in,

only to watch me evaporate, right?" I asked. I doubted he'd do that. Not because of altruism, but because it would violate the core tenet of our agreement.

"At fifteen percent, those wards would do the same to me as they would you. Worse, since this body would simply reform over and over again." Archades shrugged. "Let me show you."

It was all rather anticlimactic. Archades opened the door to LaFleur's office and walked through without hesitation. No lightning bolts struck. Holy fire did not spring from the wood and blind me as it incinerated his mortal coil. It didn't summon any angels with flaming swords or rebuking trumpets. One of the wood planks underfoot squeaked. I followed him through and set to hunting for the last egg like a desperate toddler on Easter morning.

"Would it be in this safe?" Archades asked, kneeling at the foot of a bookshelf. I hobbled over, sinking to an excruciated knee. I put a hand to the safe. It was one of those relatively nice home safes, probably bolted to the floor from the inside. It was fire rated for important documents, but this one was warm to the touch.

"Can you get it open?" I asked. Archades smiled, extending one finger and winking at me. His eyes flashed, pilot lights of the soul igniting into blue fire as the shadowstuff coalesced down his arm. This time, it encompassed each finger and then flowed together into a strangely shaped hook. It wasn't until he plunged it into the steel and began working it back and forth in a looping line that I realized it was modeled after a can opener.

The light from within illuminated his work

warmly, and once the door was cut away, revealing the second egg, we squatted there in a little bit of awe.

"So now we have two nukes." It probably wasn't strictly true, but taking the second egg out using the oven-mitt still in the safe was just as nerve-wracking as holding highly radioactive material.

The nice, metal briefcase that had safely harbored the egg was still beside LaFleur's desk, and I was glad to put both within its much-more-secure confines. I set the Hello Kitty lunch box into the safe with a note explaining and apologizing, hoping LaFleur would understand when he came back. I held the heavy case, burdened by its contents and its implications.

"All right, let's get out of here," I said. We headed down the hall, Archades supporting my limp again. "Let's go down to the basement. Rubin should be out of his laboratory. Maybe we'll find a clue about the portal's location down there."

"Are you sure that's a good idea?" Archades asked. "With both of them on you?"

"These babies aren't leaving my sight," I said. "Not until they're back home with their momma." In the lobby, I thumbed the elevator, leaning heavily against the wall. I wondered if I could get away with using the safe house to get a few hours of sleep. It seemed dangerous. I could very well wake up to the news of a rampaging dragon and the end of my career at the Department of Intangible Assets. I yawned, suddenly feeling the night's activities wash over me. Coffee. I could get a cup of coffee from my office before we left. Sleep was coming fast now.

When I turned to head back, I was surprised to see Yancy standing on her desk, one arm extended toward us, the other wrapped around a heavy book that she kept glancing at for reference as her mouth silently formed words. Through drooping lids and fogging thoughts, I gave a chuckle. What the hell was she doing, playing around like that? What did she think she was, a wizard?

Oh.

Moving one hand like it was made of lead, I got my fingers around the grip of the pistol and managed to get it out of my waistband. I had one eye entirely closed, the other struggling against the inevitable sleep. I could see the intensity on Yancy's face, and while part of me was puzzling and puzzling, my survival instincts squeezed with all the might I had, unable to bring the gun up to point at anything.

One round, fired straight into the shitty stained carpet of the lobby, was enough to break the enchantment's hold on me. It also helped that I peppered my leg with shards of the concrete floor. Yancy recoiled, and as I came to my senses, I brought the gun to bear with one hand, holding the case behind me as I fired.

The bullets sparked in the air, hammering a few feet away from where Yancy stood, still on the desk. I could see them flattened and motionless. Yancy, smirking as if she'd managed to snag the last bit of birthday cake, made a curt gesture that tore a gouge in the floor. Only a reflexive juke to the side, after seeing my bullets fail to have any effect, saved me from being bisected as the force slammed into the wall and destroyed the door to the elevator shaft. My nose filled with sulfur, a sure sign that magic was afoot. Another subtle clue.

"Stairs!" I called out, trying to hobble my way forward and away.

"Don't go yet, Special Agent Morris!" Yancy sang out, a taunting bully. I ran full-force into an invisible barrier, as real as a brick wall, and bounced off so hard I fell flat on my back. I rolled, or tried to, and found another invisible barrier the other way. Panic was setting in, and I kicked out with one leg, trying to get purchase, until something clamped that to the floor in a vise-like grip. "You're always wanting me to give you your messages. I have one for you now."

"Oh yeah?" I asked, pointing the gun at her uselessly. The air around my hand solidified, invisible bonds keeping me from even pulling the trigger.

"Yes. It's from me. It just says, 'die.' " She raised a hand in the casual way magic users preferred before unleashing hell. At least I would die doing what I loved: rolling my eyes.

Here's the part where Archades appears, showing what unleashed hell really is, and saves me yet again. Or at least, that's what was supposed to happen. Instead, it was his laughter that gave Yancy pause, turning the attention of her spell at the man who hadn't moved an inch since she began her assault. Magic buzzed throughout the room, the same kind of high-tension hum that really intense electrical transformers put off on a dry day.

"What's so funny?" Yancy hissed, obviously surprised that he was still there. A clear impact profile had hit the wall on either side of him, and almost cartoonishly there was an outline in the sheet rock where his body had blunted the assault.

"You were right under her nose the whole time,"

Archades said, making a show of brushing dust particles from his shoulder. "And of course, she was too stupid to figure it out." Yancy narrowed her eyes.

"Who were you again?" I could actually see the forces worming their way down her arm, powerful magic building as she redoubled the spell in order to vaporize this perceived threat. Obviously, Archades was trying to draw her attention from me. I strained, trying desperately to find a weakness in my restraints. It's hard enough against chains you can see. Nearly impossible against the invisible forces of arcane might.

This is not covered under any specific manual or procedure, but more or less an unwritten DIA protocol: do anything you must to survive.

"Well, I'm supposed to tell you my name is Mortimer Mussalem," Archades said, folding his arms. He sat back and would have fallen on his ass if not for the black throne that unfolded beneath him. Shadow made solid flowed out of his back, driving very real spines into the floor as a baroque fauteuil rose up around him. He wound up with one leg crossed over the other, hands gripping armrests carved to resemble lunging tigers. "But I think you might know me by another name."

Surprise, confusion, and then intrigue fought their way across Yancy's pinched face, and the hand held on to the spell for a little longer.

"Have we met?" she asked, cocking her head to the side.

"I don't believe we've had the pleasure." He extended a hand, and I recoiled as it stretched into an insectile multi-jointed appendage. "Archades. In the flesh." Yancy didn't share my horror. Her eyes widened with fascination. She looked like a schoolgirl who'd just met the star quarterback behind the bleachers.

"The Thirsting Hunger." She took his hand, and I was dismayed when Archades didn't pull her into his cleverly laid trap. Instead, he smiled graciously.

"Ah, I love the old names. Such proper respect," he said, his arm retracting in a series of clicks and snaps. "Not like what this one has been doing. Treating me like a servant."

"Has she, now?" Yancy asked, looking askance at me. There was real contempt in her eyes now, and she met my stare without flinching. "How is it she came to hold sway over you?"

"There's a key around her neck. It locks the prison they made for me and was given to her by my warden. Now, I am bound in this form, unable to unleash even a fraction of my power without her say."

I felt like I'd been plunged face first into a frozen lake. The air caught in my lungs, sharp and heavy, and I could barely hear through the blood pounding in my ears. I'd been betrayed. Shame blurred my thoughts, shame that this was coming as such a surprise. It was, after all, Archades. The boogeyman for those of us who had ways to deal with actual monsters. I had to stop him. I had to prevent this.

"Archades! I command you to go back to— mmmph!" Archades slung an arm toward me, and a gob of sticky black tar slapped against the lower half of my face, sealing my mouth shut and binding directly to my tongue.

"Don't interrupt," Archades said serenely. Yancy seemed surprised that he'd gotten through her barrier magic like it wasn't there, but it was the pleasant surprise of finding the perfect gift under the tree at Christmas. "Now, Yancy…is it still Yancy?"

"It is." She lowered her hand, finally lowering her guard. I was trying to flop around, trying to panic, but my shackles were as firm as ever. I could only stare at their little exchange, hyperventilating until things went gray, then slowing my breathing when it became clear I wasn't going to fall unconscious and get off easy.

"I'm looking for a little freedom," Archades said. "Maybe we could assist each other. Diane here would only let me have fifteen measly percent of my overall power. If you were to grant me total freedom, I would help you with your little egg problem."

"What makes you think I need any help?" Yancy asked and with a gesture pulled the case from my nerveless fingers. It swooped through the air and landed on the desk beside her. "I have all that I want."

"True, true," Archades said, lounging in his chair now with one leg over the armrest. The form of the thing seemed to be shifting at his whim, reinforcing here and there in a nauseating display of shadowy movement. "But how are the mephits going to react to the news that you're carrying both eggs?"

"I'll be handing theirs over after I finish my ritual," Yancy said, checking inside the case and smiling at the results. I started pulling myself together, trying to ignore the claustrophobic feeling I had despite being in the middle of a wide-open room. With any luck, LaFleur and Rubin would be back quickly. Or any of the other regional agents, checking in. Of course, with Archades going renegade on me and a rogue wizard throwing around magic like it was going out of style, they were as likely to wind up dead before they could react.

"Yes, well, they don't know that. When you start your ritual, whatever that is, they're liable to believe you've reneged on the deal. And you can't risk going to them first. They'll almost certainly try to make a play for both eggs themselves. Two dragons are, after all, better than one." Archades shrugged. "On the other hand, at full power, I am more than a match for any number of measly mephits. I tried to tell this one"—he jerked a thumb at me—"and you can see where she got by ignoring my advice."

Yancy looked back and forth between the two of us. Then she sashayed over to me and reached through her bindings, found the cord around my neck, and retrieved the key Braeburn had given me. I *mmm*'d her as hard as I could, trying my level best to invoke latent powers that would melt her into a puddle, but since I'm as mundane a human as they could possibly make, all I did was strain a muscle in my neck.

"Seems a paltry thing to me," Yancy said, inspecting the key in the light. It really wasn't much special. It probably had been copied at a hardware store.

"If every powerful artifact were studded gold, it would be easy to pick out what was important," Archades said.

"And with this, I can command you?" Yancy asked, turning to Archades suddenly, clutching the necklace in hand like a talisman. Archades laughed.

"No, of course not," he said, turning her hopeful smile into a suddenly violent frown. "She couldn't *command* me. She could simply entice me with the lure of release from this prison of mine. If you would oblige me, I would voluntarily assist you. As a professional courtesy." Archades raised his arms, showing his brass cuffs off.

"Let's say we start with a little show of good faith," Yancy said. "If you cooperate, I will see to it you're fully released from the prison they've kept for you. If you don't…" She swung the key on its loop of cord, smiling cruelly. "Well, after my ritual, I'll have the power to make things very unpleasant."

"Cooperation is my middle name," Archades said and lifted from the chair effortlessly back to his feet. The black shadowstuff retracted into his body, suffusing the air with a deep baritone thrum as it did. "However, I will give you some advice, in the spirit of cooperation. First, allow me the use of at least thirty percent. The mephit leader is powerful enough to give even you a run for your money, but I would be able to hold him off at that level." Yancy nodded, obviously well aware of what she'd been summoning into the world over and over again. "Second, allow me to eat this one."

"Mmmmph!" I protested, even as he pushed through the barriers holding me with no apparent effort. Shadowstuff poured up his neck, overtaking his face until it was a mask of angular, harsh features. The mouth widened, a formless void surrounded by long, needlelike teeth, and I screamed against the gak covering my mouth as he leaned down and began to engulf me, starting with my outstretched arm.

Revulsion nearly outweighed the horror as my arm turned to static to the wrist. He didn't bite down but shoved farther until he had me up the elbow, cold blue eyes aflame as they stared into mine with hungry intensity. Pins and needles were all I could feel in the consumed limb, not pain, but the sudden absence of sensation that newly amputated victims must have felt.

"Stop," Yancy commanded, earning her a sudden surge of gratitude from my poor, confused heart. Archades paused in his advance, inches from my shoulder and then my head. We were nearly nose to nose. I had a feeling that mouth was only going to stretch into a maw that would accommodate the entirety of me. "Leave her be." Archades, features furious, withdrew from my arm and rounded on her.

"After what she's put me through, I deserve this at least!" Archades intoned, voice going all wonky as he lost his temper. For my part, I was too busy staring at my intact arm with a newfound appreciation for having five fingers to notice the ensuing argument between the two of them. Nothing seemed to be missing, or corrupted, or otherwise changed in any way. The gun was no longer in my hand, but compared to the wonderful news of being able to arm wrestle with my good hand, I considered it acceptable losses.

"After. She has information I may require, after I complete my ritual."

"This soul is what I want to consume the most!" Archades snapped. Yancy held the key up, swinging it gently. All of the fangirl adoration from before was gone, instead replaced by a more familiar, imperious expression. It was the same look she'd always had on her face when she told people to go make their own copies. She wasn't their personal secretary. Of course, the copier was behind her desk, so you had to endure her smug little grin as she watched you struggle with the relic.

"Come now, Archades. Let's not bicker. You'll get what you desire, after I get what's coming to me." I really hoped she had cancer coming.

"Very well," Archades said, a tad petulantly. Shadowstuff drained back into the covered parts of his skin, and he stood with arms crossed, looking for all the world a slightly aggravated grandfather. "Shall we get on with the ritual here?"

"We need to return to my sanctum," Yancy said. Of course she called it a sanctum. Wizards always had to find the most impressive way to say things. Not that I was sure she even qualified for wizard. Hard to grow the requisite beard/ear hair as a woman. I mean, not impossible, but difficult. The Cabal wouldn't hear of a member without a Y chromosome. After all, you can't spell wizardry without it.

Archades picked me up like luggage. Free of the magical bindings, I finally had the ability to kick and squirm until he took my own handcuffs and applied them with gusto.

"Let me blindfold her," Archades said, eliciting Yancy's piggish laughter.

"What for? She's not going to be in any condition to tell anyone," Yancy said. "Come on then, let's get a move on before any more of these idiots return." She laughed again. "Here I had been worrying about how I'd get past Flower Power's defenses, and she just did all the work for me."

"It's only juicier when you learn that it was my idea to go in and get the other egg and not wait for Jermaine to get back," Archades said, trotting me down the three floors and out into the parking lot. I shot a desperate look around, hoping to see help arriving, but there was no sign of anyone. In the deep shadow of the tree line, I couldn't even tell if Sadie was still there. How long had it been? Even if she saw me, she wouldn't know how to call for help. For what it was worth, I tried to make enough noise to count as a cry for help, but muffled as it was, I only brought out cruel snickers from Archades, so I stopped.

I wound up in the trunk of Yancy's piece of shit sedan, alongside a couple bags of dirty laundry that might have been used to soak up dog vomit by the smell of them. I mulled my options. Unfortunately, with Archades' gag in my mouth, I couldn't even bite through my tongue and get myself out of the game. I had no way of stopping what was coming, and unless Yancy turned out to be a sloppy gloater, I wasn't likely to get a good shot at escape again. Another option was to have a nice, cathartic cry, reflect on all my misdeeds, and pick a religion out of a hat at the last minute in hopes of getting lucky with a sympathetic deity.

Too angry to cry, and too cynical to ask for divine intervention, I tried to eavesdrop through the cushion on the short, bumpy ride. I also worked loose my boot knife, silver and brittle though it was, in the hopes that Archades actually fell into a category of tourist that was vulnerable to such things.

Archades opened the trunk and frowned at me with mild surprise when I sprang out and sank three inches of blessed metal into one of his thighs. He hoisted me from the trunk with one hand, pulling the knife free with the other, and I watched with vomit waiting to come up as his palm split apart and a tiny human mouth swallowed the blade.

"This girl doesn't know when to quit," he said,

hauling me under one shoulder like a sack of potatoes. I had a good view of the river, lights of the city twinkling on the opposite shore, before we went into a derelict warehouse pressed up against the spans of a bridge high above. The intermittent roar of big trucks on their late-night runs drowned out their talking, but Yancy gave a pleasant giggle at something Archades said, and then we were through a heavy steel door.

"She has all kinds of access to things that would be useful. I'm sure once they figure out she's gone, they'll lock her out of the system, but think of the useful things she must know. Artifacts, books of power, trinkets, and beings. The DIA hoards the arcane. Someone just has to come along and have the courage to use it." Yancy was speaking breezily, as she went around throwing switches and pulling on chains to move heavy objects around. The middle of the warehouse was actually blocked off on all sides by machinery and boxes, but a few minutes of work cleared a path to a space large enough to have a stone altar, bookshelf, desk, and what must have been at one time a fine antique wardrobe.

"If it's knowledge you want, I can help you get it without killing her," Archades said, plopping me down unceremoniously beside the ceremonial altar. Yancy turned, suspicion plain on her face.

"Minutes ago, you wanted to eat her. Now you want to save her?" Yancy asked. Archades shrugged.

"It occurs to me that once you free me, I'll be able to leave this old man's mortal form. Finally. I've been stuck in it for forty years." Archades shivered as if the mere thought of another minute disgusted him. "However, I'll be in the market for a new host. One without inflammation in all his joints."

"You want to possess her?" Yancy asked, pausing at the desk to riffle through some notes, and retrieved a diagram of complicated runes.

"It is, unfortunately, the only way for me to remain in this world," Archades said, proffering a piece of chalk. Yancy started on the altar, white lines starting at the base and working their way up with the complicated interlaced lettering endemic to all magic. I would have paid more attention to it, except my mind was trying to find some way to get me out of my predicament before I wound up sharing a skull with the fiend of the month.

"I like the plan," Yancy said. "If you play the role well, nobody will even know she's been replaced."

Archades looked over at me and gave another toothy smile, this time showing more teeth in his head than a crocodile. "I think we'll make for good allies," Yancy mused.

"It does pay to have friends," Archades said and sniffed the air. "If I'm not mistaken, Yancy, your mephit associates appear to be on their way. If I were you, I'd go ahead and release me from my bonds. I'll keep them entertained until you finish the ritual."

"I'll not do anything so stupid," Yancy said, pulling both of the eggs from the case and considering them. "I will, however, partially release you, as discussed. You asked for, what? Thirty percent?" She touched the key hanging around her neck with one finger. "I grant you that much."

Archades reacted immediately, arms raising dramatically to the ceiling as steam poured from his pores. His form slightly obscured, I could see shadows writhing and dancing as he was cloaked in a meshwork of shadowstuff. He looked like he was wearing chainmail. The brass cuffs glowed red hot, standing out with shimmering heat as they struggled to contain what was happening, and unless my eyes were deceiving me, I could see hairline fractures forming across the metal surface. Yancy looked on hungrily, holding the key with delight across her lips. After a minute of this display, Archades swept one arm through the air and produced a scythe-like blade in place of one hand.

"Ah," he said, and the timbre of his voice was now unearthly in its entirety. "This is more like it." Blue fire in his eyes had taken over his features, and now his jaw stretched to his chest in an open gape lined with blanched, jagged teeth. From his back, a spider-leg tendril, jointed and bristling with barbed hairs, extended and hoisted me from where I was hunkered. I recoiled, kicking and trying to scream, but it simply lifted me like a child being abducted from a playground. Archades laughed at my struggle, cruel and without any humane qualities that I'd imagined him to possess.

"What about you, girl?" he asked. "How easily can you pick this? To fight until the end or submit to the will of others?" That struck me as a little odd. I'd pegged Yancy as someone who would take the opportunity to gloat, but not Archades. Everything I'd ever heard from him indicated that cruel efficiency was more his calling card. Here he was mocking me, and then there was even a *wink*. One flaming eye blinked out for a moment and then reappeared. The nerve of this guy! If he could read my mind, he was certainly getting a full description of the ways he could go fuck himself.

He tossed me. It happened so quickly and carelessly that I didn't have time to tuck or roll, and I hit the desk hard enough to knock it over and send various implements flying. I landed on a stack of papers, arms pinned clumsily, and I struggled like a turtle to right myself.

"Enough!" Yancy shouted, not annoyed by the mess but by the break in her concentration. Contrary to popular opinion, female spellcasters rarely work naked. I guess it's a lot like cooking. Except, instead of bacon splattering hot grease everywhere, the arcane manipulation of reality tends to splatter eldritch madness on anything nearby, and warded robes are a must for anyone who doesn't want to grow a second, malformed head out of their chest. Yancy's robes were thick leather, studded with bits of bone that were more likely human than animal. "Go ensure that I am not disturbed by the elementals!"

"You got it," Archades said and stalked out of the sanctum on the extra limbs he was growing from random places on his body. He moved with arachnid grace, simply climbing obstacles on his way out of the secluded alcove of junk. That just left me, Yancy, and her ritual.

The eggs had been placed on the altar. Both of them. At some point, Yancy had decided that her deal with the mephits wasn't worth the extra power she'd siphon out of these mythical creatures. One was probably worth immortality. A second? It might be enough for a full-blown apotheosis. Godhood, or at least close enough for mortal purposes.

This wasn't right, I thought, still a little breathless as I got myself sitting upright. I could get my legs under me, charge her, and probably end up vaporized by the magics being wrought. Already, the altar was aglow with chalk lines that had burned their way into the stone, making little channels of molten rock held in place by raw power. Yancy was obviously gifted with fire. It explained her alliance and why she thought she could draw out the strength of two dragons without killing herself.

As much as I would have liked to sit there and watch the ritual go off without a hitch, and later end up host to a powerful demon and lose all autonomy, I found myself in a position to actual do something useful. That position was on my ass, handcuffed and gagged, but to my surprise, with a bunch of paperwork nearby. Paperwork, it so happened, held together by a paperclip.

Now, it's not exactly *easy* to pick the lock of standard-issue handcuffs. There's a knack for it some people have, and it still takes some practice. Spend as much time as I have sitting at stakeouts, bored out of your mind, and see if you don't learn a thing or two.

Yancy was engrossed in her magic, with all the throaty chanting and hand waving one normally associates with such things. Too focused, it turned out, to notice me rise unfettered, holding a piece of steel that I'd picked up from a pile of machinery junk. I still couldn't get the gunk off my face, like hardened resin now, but now I could at least die on my feet like a professional.

The air filled with the stench of ozone. The ambient temperature inside the warehouse rose by twenty degrees in a matter of seconds. Nearby, there came the exact same snap a bug zapper makes when a moth flies too close, and a roiling column of fire belched toward the ceiling as a barrel of something flammable ignited. I lunged forward, swinging the pipe wildly, just hoping to connect, but Yancy's head was already turning to look at the source of the heat. The knobbly end of the pipe came within inches of connecting, and I'd have taken her nose off in one satisfying swipe. With a firm gesture, she caught me in one of those invisible barriers. She couldn't tear her full concentration from the ritual, not without losing something in the process, but she didn't have to. Another twitch of her hand sent me flying back, hitting the machinery with agonizing results. My leg was on fire from my rushed lunge. I was bleeding freely again, except now that pain competed with what might have been a fresh concussion and a twisted shoulder.

Damn it! I was frustrated but back on my feet and fighting through the pain. What I wouldn't have given at that moment for a single Sanzaru Amulet. A Zephyr Wind Stone. A Glock. Whatever it took to get through her defenses. Now she had one wary eye on me, unable to actually crush me like a bug, but keeping something between the two of us that shimmered in the heat of the air and moved as I tried to circle.

"Mmmph!" I called to her, inaudible above the rising chaotic din from the rest of the warehouse. The steaming air was only thickening with heat, and sweat poured from me faster than the blood from my wounds. Nearby, a large hook for moving heavy equipment hung from a chain, suspended from the ceiling. I heaved it back. Took aim. Chucked it with all the strength I had left.

She deflected it to the side with ease, laughing as she did so, and worked a little more magic until I hucked the pipe at her head. It rebounded off the barrier, earning me a withering stare from her as she once again turned her eyes from the altar to me. It was just in time for the heavy hook to finish its swing and start on its way back, picking up speed as it came.

The plan had actually been pretty good. The hook was supposed to come back, hit her hard enough to knock her down, and then I'd cuff her and rescue the eggs. I could deal with the others as I went. Instead, the hook slammed into the stone altar, and the combination of the impact and stored magics blew it apart in a geyser of flame and molten stone. I shrieked right alongside Yancy as both eggs were lobbed free by the force, tethered together like bolos with the mesh of magic that had been about to crack them for their essential energy. Yancy had been thrown free of the ritual, her voice full of rage instead of pain, but the eggs were coming my way.

Thank God my father had signed me up for softball for so many years. It had gotten me my scholarship, and now I was using my protesting legs to run backward, arms overhead, praying that I would take both eggs without harming them.

Their burning weight hit me in the stomach, heavy and safe, and I clutched them tight even as my legs gave out and I fell backward. I hit something wooden and yielding, the front of the wardrobe, and the doors swung open without protest as I tumbled through. I was too concerned with shielding the eggs using my body, bruises and scrapes a fine price to pay.

I didn't hit the back of a wardrobe. I didn't wind up tangled in old coats, and I didn't smell mothballs. Instead, there was sulfur. Not, like, the sulfur associated with brimstone Hellfire, which is so strong it'll burn out your nose hairs and cause vomiting. This was like…fresh well water. Rotten eggs, but gently.

I was standing in a tunnel of limestone, suddenly very aware that the temperature had cooled substantially. In one direction, the wood panels of the wardrobe were sealed again, but the other way snaked down at a steep enough incline that I had slid quite a ways before coming to a stop.

Damn portals. I clambered to my feet. I was forced to pull my shirt off and use it as a makeshift oven-mitt, holding the eggs carefully. My first thought was that Yancy had her lair connected to an escape route, in case things got too hairy. A lot of wizards were paranoid like that, and all the famous ones kept a last-resort refuge to hole up in when circumstances got bad. I set off down the tunnel, knowing only that going back meant dealing with Yancy, Archades, and any mephits that had shown up.

The tunnel made a dozen switchbacks, like kinks in a hose. Before long I was panting and wishing my leg wasn't in such poor shape. By the time I came out into a wider cavern, dimly lit by some kind of fire at its center, I was ready for a rest. I didn't immediately see any other exits, but there was some kind of shale or rock pile nearby, so I sat there and caught my breath. The pile made a peculiarly metallic clink when I sat, and I picked up one of the flat, smooth stones from the pile to inspect it.

It gleamed gold even in the dim light.

This is a common quality of golden doubloons. Especially ones that have been polished to be a part of a hoard.

The dim light of the cavern brightened slightly. An

eye had opened, the light that had been mostly obscured suddenly rising like a sun, and suddenly there was Ziraxariz. All around me. Encircling the cavern and its mountains of gold.

Sigurd, it's said, killed full-grown dragons as a matter of course. Like, as a profession. Sigurd had all kinds of gear to help, like magic swords and such, which was a lot more than I was sporting when the Matriarch of the Black Dragonbrood opened an eye to find me holding both of her eggs. An eye which was taller than my entire body.

Ziraxariz raised her head out of the hillock of sparkling gems it had been half-buried within, long features studded with clinging diamonds and rubies stark against ebony scales. The head, as large as a school bus, swiveled toward me on a long, sinuous neck that gave her the ability to bite anything in her cavern without moving the rest of her body. It was hard to tell where the cavern ended and she began. All sense of scale was difficult, but judging by what I could see, and the fact that her tail was beginning to lift up right behind me, she had to be hundreds of feet long. Maybe even a full thousand. Sigurd's documents indicated some of the oldest dragons never stopped growing. If that was the case, then Ziraxariz could very well have been the oldest native creature in the world.

At least I'd die in a way nobody else in the DIA ever had. Dragons were incredibly rare. They'd probably teach a whole class about how I went out. *New Tactics in Appeasing Dragons*. Step one: Don't look like someone who's been caught stealing eggs.

Chapter Ten

There was a lot of beauty in the dragon, in how its red eyes flickered and moved like wildfire, and how the scales absorbed just enough light to make it appear fluid, but every single bit of this was lost on me as I sank deeper into my bed of coin.

The instinct to hold the eggs tightly against my chest, hoping to protect myself, nearly got me killed. The rational part of me, the part that had read the histories and knew something about dragons, was all too aware that the eggs weren't in any danger of being burned. Big momma dragon could fill the chamber with fire, turn her hoard to liquid gold, and the eggs would probably be healthier as a result. It was probably only sheer outrage that was holding back the fires of this dragon, and I pushed my way to my feet. The scaled, horned head of the dragon reared back, tracking my movement as I hobbled toward it. In the center of the cavern was the nest, built out of the finest parts of the dragon's hoard. Who even knows why the dragons love valuables so much? A lot of the smaller dragons, the ones that were more active in the modern world, were often found with televisions, computers, and stock certificates in their lairs. Ziraxariz was more old-school than that. The sheer amount of wealth around me would have driven the value of gold to an all-time low if it was dumped on the streets of Manhattan. The nest reflected that wealth, and it was on a cushion of millions that I set the two eggs. Ziraxariz hissed as I did so, but I stepped back with hands up, not turning my back to the dragon. In a way, this had worked out extremely lucky for the citizens of Jacksonville. With the eggs in place, and only one person to blame, I'd done my job almost perfectly. LaFleur would be unhappy that I wouldn't be around to file paperwork, but they'd figure out the details in good time.

I would have tried explaining myself, if my lips hadn't been sealed with Archades' handiwork. I *mmmph*'d a little, salaaming away as I tried backing toward the tunnel, but I bumped into the end of the tail instead. It was unnerving how quietly it had moved into position, and it was like having a wall made of scales thrown down in the night. Entirely defenseless, with no avenue to retreat, I was at the mercy of a dragon.

Tenderly, Ziraxariz lowered its chin until it nuzzled first one egg, then the other. Those furnace-like eyes drooped, half-lidded, and a contented rumbling filled the cavern like a mild earthquake. It took a moment to realize that the dragon was, against all logic, purring. She sounded like the engine room of a battleship at idle.

The dragon spoke. She did not debase herself with English, any more than a man would try to speak the language of ants. And I, the ant, held myself upright in a sheer act of will to avoid cowering as each dread syllable collided with me. She was looking right at me again, burning a hole in my mind with those terrible eyes. There was majesty, yes, of course—how could there not be—but my brain could only hearken back to a primitive fear of monsters in dark caves. There was a pause. An expectant one. She was waiting for me to respond, although I had no clue what the question was. I grabbed at the gunk on my mouth, sensing her growing impatience, and when I didn't make any progress, she reached out with her forelimb for me. Not quickly. I might have flinched if she'd swung it at me with any speed, my reflex to survive overpowering the logic that I stood no chance. Instead, it came out from under a pile of gold like a surfacing whale, one of the four digits a mere stump at its base, the others wreathed in priceless jewelry custom fit to her huge frame. A claw approached, and I froze in place as it grazed my face, somehow catching against the shadowstuff gag and peeling it painfully from my skin. It clung to the black-iron of the bone like a drop of pitch and slowly evaporated. The dragon watched it closely as it left and then rested on her leg as she leaned in again to regard me. The cavern quaked with draconic voice again, almost certainly a repeated question from before.

I didn't cough in her face. That would have been rude in any culture. My mouth tasted like it had been a dumping ground for ash, and I would have sold a dragon egg for a drink of dirty water from a ditch, but I didn't even smack my lips. Instead, I did what Sigurd would have done. Not the dragonslaying part. The getting out alive bit.

"I am Special Agent Diane Morris, Department of Intangible Assets," I said, drawing out my badge and presenting it as if she were any other person of interest. "I've come to return your stolen eggs, and to see if there's anything else that might be done to make amends."

Ziraxariz spoke again, slowly and carefully in the universal way one does when they know they aren't being understood but want to still have some kind of conversation. I could only guess. Supposedly, dragons understand all manner of human speech, but maybe that was just Sigurd thinking they spoke Norse *and* Danish.

"I do not speak Draconic," I said, also employing my slightly louder, slightly slower tourist voice. "If you would like, I can arrange to have a translator brought here, so we may discuss your wishes." Maybe Jericho could do some translating. I had, after all, gotten all my information about dragons from him. He had a fairly impressive library of original manuscripts, although God knows where he kept finding them.

"Intruders." The word boomed throughout the cavern, and Ziraxariz looked furious at being forced to resort to such a common language.

"The intruders who stole your children are all dead," I said. The dragon lifted her tail and gestured with her claw at the tunnel, where I'd come from. It was a small hole in the wall compared to the chamber itself, but it obviously disturbed her to see it. "The portal to your nest will be closed. I'll see to it myself." Bold talk for an exhausted, half-crippled human who'd already lost a lot of blood. I had to say something, though. The dragon looked pretty awake to me now, and if she decided that she wanted to come out of her lair to wreak havoc on the petty humans who had dared to make such an attempt, there wasn't much I could do about it. Frankly, I was still a little surprised to be alive. It was time for a dragon's favorite pastime: flattery.

"Great Ziraxariz," I said, loudly and with the sort of humble pride expected of top-notch servants. "Don't trouble yourself with the workings of idiots. While they are nothing beneath your wings"—and there were wings, each an acre of folded leather, bone, and sinewy muscle—"it is my responsibility to bring them to justice and to hold them accountable. Allow me to serve you, and you'll find that I am worthy of that responsibility." Don't, I thought, come out of this ground like a natural disaster and go on a rampage. Dragons were mighty, and it would be a long time before she could be stopped, but eventually she'd be brought down, and that would be the end of it. Probably.

Ziraxariz's claw lifted from the ground again, ponderous and deliberate, and she touched me on the forehead. It was gentle, just the barest caress, right where I'd split my scalp open in the sewers the night before. A shiver ran down my spine, my mouth flooded with acrid bile, and my eyes rolled back into my head at the moment of contact. It lasted briefly, or it lasted for hours, but when she withdrew the claw, nothing had changed. No magic had been bestowed, no mysticism or draconic shenanigans. It had simply been a gesture of acceptance, a rare and almost unthinkable acknowledgement of trust from one of the mightiest living creatures to a lowly human. My reaction had just been that of prey under the claw of a descending raptor. She was going to let me handle this. There would, after all, be time to rampage later if I failed.

The dragon watched with interest as I addressed the wound on my leg. Now it was mostly clotted. The bleeding had slowed considerably, although I think part of that was probably because my calf was so swollen I could barely get my pant leg up over it. Dragons weren't known for their skills at healing, and Standard Operating Procedure 218: Sanctioned Use of Personal Magic requires that any attempts at anomalous medical care be undertaken with the supervision of another member of the DIA. So pretty much, all I could do was wrap my shirt over the wound in the hopes that it was a little cleaner having been heat-treated by the eggs. I resisted the urge to banter a little with the dragon, who had curled back into the hoard with one clawed limb settling lightly over the nested eggs. She was watching, yes, but the less attention she paid to me the more likely it was that I was going to make it out alive.

No weapons. Literally on my last leg. One foot in the grave. There was a chance that I'd come back through the portal in the wardrobe only to find the warehouse fully on fire, or that Yancy and Archades were waiting to ambush me. The longer I waited, the more likely one side had won, and the less likely it was that I'd be able to just slip out in the confusion.

"Well…" I said, heaving myself to my feet as I tested my leg out. I nearly collapsed under my own weight. I caught myself on Ziraxariz's tail and then recoiled with the fear that such an act would be my last. I spun, expecting open jaws and the first spark of dragonfire, but the old girl was just smirking at my trepidation. She flicked the tail slightly, scraping it forcefully against the rough wall of the cavern, moving it up and down against the scales until one worked loose and fell almost at my feet. I stepped back from it, confused, until the dragon chirped politely and nudged the scale toward me with her tail.

Okay. So. *Technically* dragon scales are magical. SOP 218 *probably* covers them under subsection C: Employees shall not accept gifts of an anomalous nature from any source, and any such materials shall be immediately reported to Logistics for characterization and classification prior to personal use. But it would have been rude to decline such a queenly gift. Especially since, as Ziraxariz seemed to know, it was exactly what I needed.

I carefully picked the scale up, the warmth of it in my hands as pleasant as fresh laundry in wintertime. This wasn't dragonhide, cut from the corpse of a slain creature, fit only to be worked like any other leather. This was a still-living part of the dragon, and it knew what I needed.

The scale split in two, curled and warped and melded into itself. It moved like it had its own mind, but really, it was the dragon choosing what form the scale took. In a few short moments, I was holding a pair of boots in my hands. Boots which turned out to be just my size.

It was painful slipping my leg in, but once I squeezed the calf down into the leather and hitched it up to my knee, the pressure lessened, and the leather supported my weight. With both of them on, I stood for the first time without pain since being shot. Another upshot was that the boots made me at least two inches taller.

"Thank you," I said, bowing in the polite way dragons always love to see mortals do. Ziraxariz inclined her great and mighty head and then gestured toward the tunnel now that her tail was out of the way. I gave a few experimental strides with the boots, still feeling the injury down there but no longer crippled by the pain of the thing. Now, at least, I could make a run for it.

I left the nest the same way I got in, but with a little more hope and dignity. I'd survived the worst the day had to offer, and now I was in the home stretch.

Imagine my disappointment when I came through the wardrobe to find Archades standing there, a smug look on his shadowy face, Yancy at his side.

"Goddamn it." I couldn't even make a break for the side exit. Apparently, in my absence, Yancy had settled her differences with her elemental allies. The lead mephit, bandoleer of gold marking his station, was floating to the right of the wardrobe, far enough away that I wouldn't be able to spit on him but close enough that he'd vaporize me before I could move. Another mephit was to my left. The heat of them was intense, and while signs of battle were clear in the warehouse around me in the form of molten metal spitting from machinery, they were done fighting each other.

"I wanted those eggs," Yancy said, face oddly serene for how angry she sounded.

"You'll have to take that up with big momma Z," I said, astounded at my own familiarity. I looked at a fire that had sprung up at the other end of the warehouse, working its way down a line of crates. "You know, it's too bad this place doesn't have a sprinkler system. I'm going to have to call OSHA on you when I get out of here."

"I think we all know that's not going to happen," Yancy said. She snapped her fingers, and Archades stepped forward. He wasn't a multi-limbed horror any longer, simply shaped into a man with a seething aura of darkness. Every footstep left behind an inky imprint, a long trail of shadow that disappeared out past the rubble-strewn sanctum. "You are going to help us in other ways, Diane. Your department holds many tools that I, and my friends here, can make use of."

"Archades is going to betray you, just as he betrayed me," I said, determined to hold my ground as long as possible. I might have been able to get back into the wardrobe, but what then? Hang out with a dragon for the rest of my life?

"Not so long as I have this, he won't," Yancy said, holding the key in one hand triumphantly. Archades grinned. His blazing eyes flared, crackling wildly in his face as the lower part split into a crescent moon of dead, bleached teeth.

"What can I say, Diane?" he asked. "You've got to take your shot when you can."

*Restrain your pet, sorceress,* the mephit boss intoned, its greasy thoughts injected directly into my skull.

"This dog's got teeth, Crockpot," Archades said, casting a sidelong glance with a deranged, lopsided smile. "Remember that you came in with three more of your buddies."

*You are depleted,* the mephit drawled, wafting one withered limb contemptuously. While they were occupied with each other, I edged back, the confines of the dragon's lair no longer looking too terrible. Maybe Ziraxariz had a guest room.

Archades lashed out, grabbing me by the neck with one powerful hand, hauling me off the ground. The shadowstuff that had engulfed his body tingled painfully against my bare skin.

"Not so fast, Diane," he said, still watching the mephit. I fought his grasp, slapping at his arm until I had no choice but to hold myself up or choke to death. He didn't feel solid, exactly, but there was enough substance there to keep me steady in place.

"That's enough, Archades. We need her alive," Yancy said, but sounding amused. She put a hand on his shoulder, standing with her chin nearly on his shoulder. "Not that she'll enjoy the experience."

"Fuck you," I wheezed, trying to spit in her face but only managing a dribble. Something about her stupid smug face drove me crazy with anger, and I lashed out, hitting Archades in the chest, hoping to get him to drop me. If I could just bite off her nose or something, leave a lasting impression before it was all over.

My fist sank wrist-deep into the barrier of shadow covering Archades' torso. That static, buzzing sensation of confused nerve endings engulfed my fingers, but not before they collided with something hard and cold. Archades' smile widened, no longer sinister and menacing but conspiratorial. The same smile an uncle might give to a favorite niece just before sneaking out for ice cream. I recoiled, but Archades pulled me closer, shoving my arm up to the elbow, forcing my palm against a plastic and metal shape that I couldn't see, but certainly felt familiar.

As my fingers wrapped around the grip of a pistol, the shadowstuff burying my trapped hand rippled and flexed. Archades did me a favor and lowered me slightly, now holding me eye level with the sudden tunnel through his chest. I could see Yancy's stupid pink cardigan, visible between the edges of her magic-infused robes. It was probably the only vulnerable spot anybody could hope to attack, and here it was served up on a silver platter. So I did what had come naturally the first time I'd gotten my hand up Elizabeth Baker's shirt in the backseat of her Honda Civic: squeezed for all I was worth before my luck changed.

The gun only had the one shot left, but it took Yancy through the chest and blew a hole out her back roughly the size of a pomegranate. Her confused screech was a punctuated agony, cutting off as blood filled one lung and the other struggled to compensate. Archades, dropping me entirely and spinning to face the mephit leader, swung his hands in an effort to protect himself from the opening maw of flame.

*Burn.* The mephits acted in unison, seemingly unfazed by the Reverse Jimmy-Jam that Archades had orchestrated. I grabbed the sides of the wardrobe, heaving it down as a temporary barrier, just as the first tongues of fire leaped across the warehouse. Yancy, on her back and struggling to make any purposeful movements, managed to pull her robes and hood over her exposed body, and I cowered behind the meager protection of the magically reinforced wooden box. Archades, however, stood strong against the leader of the mephits, the shadowstuff umbrella being projected as quickly as the heat could scour it away.

"Do you have this?" I shouted over the freight train roar of power. Archades shook with laughter, and I watched as he actually began to shrink in size while the heat overwhelmed him.

"I have no idea!" Archades called out, voice strained and hollow, but still laughing his ass off. The skin on my face was beginning to burn, and I had to hunker my head into my arms as firepower scorched around and under the box. The portal inside was protected by all kinds of magic, but even that had a limit. I couldn't even take a hot breath to try and give Archades more power. Not that I would have. At this point, dying in the line of duty wasn't the worst thing that could happen.

Steam blasted the warehouse, and the mephit attacking me was abruptly gone. Swirls of obscuring mist billowed around me, superheated and burning exposed skin as it came. Heat-addled and on the verge of fainting, I pulled myself up against the charred ruin of wood, throwing caution to the wind in an attempt to see what was happening.

A golden knight was advancing through the warehouse, a lance tucked under one arm. The lance was at least a hundred feet long, coiling back through an open door into the night, and I wiped away fat droplets of condensation as the knight stepped over the smoking, bloated corpse that had been a mephit. This didn't seem right. Historically, knights in armor rode down dragons, not mephits. Someone was mixing their mythologies.

"Get down, Diane!" The knight's voice was muffled through her faceplate. I rubbed my eyes, exhaustion joining pain and hyperthermia to turn my brain into a muddy pile of confusion. It wasn't a lance. It was a hose, thick with charged water, and the knight was nothing more amazing than Sadie in all her firefighting equipment, air bottle and facemask connected to shield her from the worst of the heat. That was amazing enough.

Sadie planted her feet, leaning forward to brace herself, and opened the nozzle back up again. Later, when I had time to ask questions, I found out that this particular nozzle would throw nearly three hundred gallons of water a minute. That's more than a *ton* of water, every single minute. In terms of elemental power, this was like opening a flamethrower up directly into the enemy trenches.

Archades and his barrier dissolved just as Sadie opened her nozzle, the heat of the mephit too much to hold against, but the jet of water slammed visibly into the power of the elemental, throwing out hissing geysers of steam in all directions.

*NO!* the mephit shrieked into our minds. Most mortal humans, lacking preparation for a telepathic scream, would have thrown their hands onto their head and been vaporized. Sadie leaned farther into the hose, holding it firmly with both hands, and actually took a step forward.

"Yes!" I croaked, watching as best I could from where I was shielding myself in the leeward side of my barrier. The mephit was raw power incarnate, born from a place where churning magma was as common as babbling brooks. It had feasted on the power of several fires, human sacrifices, and the magic of its human ally. It probably thought, right until the end, that a mere human had no chance to defeat it.

The mephit faltered. It had been pouring its power out for over a minute, longer than I thought possible for its kind without evaporating. The visible heatwave buckled, compressing like an accordion against the stream of water, and before the mephit could regain its concentration, it was overwhelmed. Its tiny, shriveled body took the brunt of the water, red-hot skin charring and turning black as soon as the water contacted it. It swelled like a sponge. With a gasp, someone suddenly up to their waist in ice water, it flailed and was overtaken entirely. The body swelled so rapidly, it burst the golden bandoleer into pieces, scattering etched metal across the floor. The mephit hit the ground with a soggy squish, the hose stream shoving it violently backward until it banged against some machinery and could go no farther.

There were sirens in the distance. How long they'd been coming, I couldn't say, because I was only just now beginning to hear anything that wasn't a high-pitched whine in my ears. I wasn't sure how I'd gotten outside. Probably, a big, strong firefighter had carried me and set me on the only patch of grass in ten blocks. The warehouse wasn't on fire, but smoke wafted out of every opening as I stared at the middle distance in a sort of daze.

"Water?" Sadie asked, having shed her firefighting gear down to the waist. She had a bottle in each hand, beads of sweat clinging to the cold plastic. I took one gratefully, fumbling with the cap with stiff hands. Sadie looked like she was in better shape. I liked the way the suspenders looked on her as she drained her bottle in one draught.

"You okay?" I croaked, my throat scorched from breathing hot gas and my lips blistered to high heaven.

"I told you I could take one," Sadie said. "I've got help on the way." I turned my gaze at the fire engine, parked next to a nearby hydrant, the hose she'd slain the mephits with still where she'd left it. "You need a hospital."

"I've got great insurance," I muttered. "Where's Arc...Morty?"

"Haven't seen him," Sadie said, looking around. "I thought I saw him inside, but then I couldn't see much through the steam. How badly are you burned?"

"I'll live," I said. The fact that my whole body

stung was actually a good thing. It meant all my nerve endings weren't seared off, and I wasn't going into shock yet. "I told you to get out of here if I didn't come back."

"Well, I saw them shove you into the trunk of a car, so I figured I may as well see where that was going," Sadie said. "Who was the chick with you?"

"Receptionist. Wizard. Sort of. Was going to use the dragon eggs to cheat death and live forever." I poured the remainder of the cold water down the back of my neck, shivering violently at the delicious sensation of cold. "Would have gotten away with it too if Morty hadn't changed his mind about betraying me."

"Why, Diane!" Archades said, slipping out of the shadows of the parking lot nearby, barely surprising me and totally panicking Sadie. "You wound me. I never betrayed you!" He was back to being just a normal-looking older man. His clothes had holes burned through them, like he had a habit of falling asleep with a lit cigarette in one hand while drinking heavily.

"You sold me out," I growled. "Told her about the key. Why'd you let me kill her? Get her out of your way?"

"Oh, I thought you'd figured it out," Archades said, flicking some ash off his sleeve as he sat cross-legged on the asphalt in front of me. "I just told her what she wanted to hear. She never had any control over me."

"She released your bonds, Morty," I said, eyes narrowing. Archades clutched his heart as if shot. "Hey, no, you can't just play this off like it was all part of some grand scheme. I know what I saw!"

"Saw? What you saw was…well, it was some very convincing theatrics, but theatrics nonetheless,"

Archades said. He held one arm up, and in a moment was recreating the transition I'd seen inside the warehouse. The patterning of shadowstuff on his arms. The crackling binding. Only this time, since I was looking for it, I could see that this wasn't actually what was happening. It was just an image over the top of the brass cuff, sound effects and all, but nothing was actually touching them. "Yancy the 'wizard' was so sure that by taking the key from you, she had control over me. Your reaction? The hate, the fear, the fury? It completely convinced her. But a key is just a key." Archades produced the string, twirling the key on one finger before tossing it to me. "That one was three dollars for five copies at a locksmith in Reno. The mantle of responsibility has to be given. It cannot be taken." Archades shrugged. "When you refused to let me have more power, I had to improvise. Luckily for us, even at fifteen percent, I have quite a bit of leeway when it comes to making illusions."

I stared at the key in my hand for a long time. Questions formed in my head but never made it to my mouth. I was too tired.

"What about the eggs?" Sadie asked as the sirens worked their way through the industrial park to where we were. I pulled out my badge holder and had it ready for the inevitable, awkward conversation with the locals.

"They're back home, safe and sound," I said. "I'm glad their mother saw reason." Archades clapped me on the back, earning him a glare that would have been withering if my eyelids weren't starting to droop with fatigue.

"Good work, boss," Archades said cheerfully.

"Now, before you head into the land of Nod, don't you want to throttle me back a bit?"

"Oh. Right." An embarrassed flush took me. "Please. Revert to one percent." Archades inclined his head, and while nothing changed overtly, I could feel the subtle pull of power being locked away again. Awful cordial of him to remind me. I just had to stay awake long enough now to explain things. Then—

## Chapter Eleven

I woke up in the hospital a couple days later. At least, that's the one I remember. The other times I started to come around, I got a swift dose of sedatives to go on top of the antibiotics and pain management, which were dealing with the infection from my forehead wound and the burns across my body. My gunshot wound to the leg was actually one of the simpler injuries to heal. Thank God I was unconscious when they debrided my seared flesh. If you don't know what that is, imagine that you accidentally burned the chicken on the grill, and the way you chose to take the char off was to use a cheese grater until you got to fresh meat.

There's no private ward in the hospital for DIA agents injured in the line of duty. I was lucky, in a way. There aren't a lot of agents that wind up in hospital beds. Most DIA agents who run into that much trouble disappear without a trace or end up in a cheap pine box in a forgotten cemetery.

When I woke up, Sadie was sitting at my bedside. Part of me would have liked it if she had been holding my hand, worrying without a break about my well-being. The rest of me was relieved to find her reading a magazine and making faces at the stupid articles. That's how I knew I was through the worst of it. If she'd been the other thing, it would have been a sure sign that they'd taken the leg.

"Feels like I got chewed up and spit out," I groaned, sitting up in the bed. I felt weak, the genuine post-injury fatigue that only comes when your body has been spending some honest effort in mending the fences.

"You're looking better," Sadie said, folding the edge of the magazine to look over at me. "Are you actually up this time?"

"Ugh…" I groaned, rubbing my face. A thick bandage had been applied to my forehead, and my arms had swathes of wrappings over the cleaned and dressed burns. "Looks that way. Was I talking in my sleep?"

"Not really," Sadie said. "You woke up a few times and spouted off some nonsense."

"Hell's bells, I hope I wasn't blabbing classified information." We weren't even supposed to go under anesthetic without another agent in the room. Some of the things we knew weren't safe for anybody to hear.

"Not unless the classified information was about what a good idea peanut butter and jelly pizza is." She smiled at my tired, bewildered look. "You were very insistent." Then she actually did take my hand and gave it a squeeze. "Good to see you made it through."

"Me? Believe it or not, this turned out better than expected." I looked around the hospital room and was actually surprised to see a handful of vases, flowers and all, on the windowsill. "How much trouble are you in at work?"

"Me?" Sadie laughed. "None. The guys don't seem to remember anything about what happened. The engine I drove through those guys was reported stolen that night and found at the bottom of the river. Station

Thirty-Five is closed as they investigate the drive-by shooting that damaged it so badly."

"That's the Public Relations people taking care of business," I said. It was a lot of effort, but I managed to sit up in bed, legs dangling over the edge. "Anybody talk to you yet?"

"Oh, sure," Sadie said. "Plenty. Couple of suits, real G-man type of people. None of them could believe I acted on my own with the hose line."

"Shocked they didn't try to amnesthetize you too," I said. I looked around the room, trying to spot a pair of pants. I was still hooked up to some kind of medication drip, but I'd see about getting it to go. I wanted to be home.

"Well, they were going to, but some guy in charge is holding them off," Sadie said and held her hand up to indicate someone tall. "Big black guy, shiny bald head?"

"LaFleur." Made sense. He'd want my take on it. Sadie now had enough exposure to the anomalous side of things to be considered an independent asset. Like the paramedics who patch up our agents in the field without asking questions, or the dozens of other working stiffs who provide peripheral support, it always paid to have people who could handle the truth out there.

"Would you rather not remember?" I asked and immediately regretted it. Sadie looked like I'd just shit on her front porch and lit the pile on fire.

"Would *you?*" she asked, scoffing. I gave a half-formed smile, wobbling to my feet. My injured leg supported the weight, tremors of effort shaking me, but I eased myself into it.

"No," I admitted. "I'd rather know what's out there." She held out an arm, and I took it to steady myself, a few experimental steps proving to my brain that I could still get around.

"Me too," she said.

"Where'd Morty end up?" I asked.

"On a coffee run," Sadie said. "Mostly he sleeps in here. He's a nice guy. Is he some kind of monster too?"

"Did the whole 'not dying in a hail of gunfire' thing tip you off?" I asked.

"I did notice something like that, yeah," Sadie said. I smiled, patting her on the shoulder.

"Morty's a special-case thing. I really can't tell you anything else about him. Sorry about this. I know it's just more secrets."

"Secrets are fine, Diane," Sadie said. "It's the lies that I didn't like."

"Well, you did save my ass. I guess the least I could do is tell you the truth from now on," I said.

"Well, it is an ass worth saving." Sadie laughed, giving me a playful smack. With the open-back gown, this was a very saucy move, and it left me red in the face and eying the door like someone still afraid of being caught.

"Get a room, girls," Archades said from the hall, holding a pair of cups in one hand and a bag of chips in the other. Unlike my mortal, weak body, his showed no signs of fatigue, damage, or even stress. He looked exactly like he had the first time I'd laid eyes on him in his prison. His mustache was evenly trimmed, and he'd acquired khakis and floral shirt. He looked like a tourist. No, he looked like a tourist's grandfather.

"This is a room, old man," Sadie said, taking her

cup. She took a sip and looked surprised. "Cream, no sugar? How'd you know?" Archades winked at me.

"Oh, it's written all over your face," he said, sipping on his. "Feeling good, Diane?"

"Never better," I said. "You just been hanging out here?"

"Well, I tried leaving the hospital, but some gentlemen from your offices persuaded me to stay nearby."

"I'm surprised they haven't already sent you back to Nevada," I said. Archades' smile widened.

"Well, interesting thing about that..." He sprawled into a chair by the door, one leg over the other. "Our agreement is still in effect." I furrowed my brow, visibly confused. "You never stipulated that I would return directly after the eggs were recovered. In fact, by the letter of our agreement, I don't return unless I break faith or otherwise violate my end of the terms."

"But you..." I stopped. No, he hadn't. Foggy as my mind was, the agreement remained pretty clear. It didn't matter that my intent had been for him to assist only as long as necessary. We'd quibbled over some other details. I hadn't been very specific. If I forced him back now, then I would be the one to break the agreement. That was the sort of thing that could be catastrophic. I managed to smile thinly. "Well, all right then. It's not like you didn't pull your weight on this one."

"I like to think of myself as the charm, and you're the brains," Archades said.

"What does that make me?" Sadie asked.

"I'm not sure. What would you like to be?"

"The muscle?"

"That works," Archades said. I sighed, already

regretting having woken up. It was probably too late to get another sedative and sleep away a few more days.

"Has anybody gone by my house and fed my cats?"

"I took care of it," Sadie said. "You left your TV on, by the way." Yeah, that followed. Jericho was probably pissed off at me. My credit card statement was probably an astronomical figure by this point. It was a small price to pay for my own repository of insight into the affairs of the bizarre and the anomalous.

****

Director LaFleur was kind enough to not fire me for stealing a dragon egg out of his office. He didn't even dock my pay for the safe we destroyed in the process, though Rubin was sure to give me an earful on putting the elevators out of commission. The wizard could have probably found another way to travel from his basement lair to our offices, but I think he enjoyed complaining about it more than he disliked the exercise.

It took me a week to finish the report. The official one, I mean. For anybody other than Director LaFleur or one of his superiors, that report ended up being essentially ten pages of blacked-out redactions with a few articles and nouns littered around. We chased up a few leads regarding Mr. Red, our mystery guest at the fire station, but as far as aliases went, that was a thin thread to follow. None of his goons had survived long enough to give up information, and even the one I'd hoped to keep for questioning had been found suffocated. He'd swallowed his own tongue. I don't think it had been his idea to do that.

"All things considered," LaFleur said, setting down my report and preparing to make some notes of his own, "good work."

"Lot of sloppy stuff here, boss," I said. "Still no idea about Mr. Red, Yancy was killed rather than taken for interrogation, and we never got the name of the mephit boss."

" 'As our circle of knowledge expands,' " LaFleur began, prompting me to finish.

" 'So does the circumference of darkness surrounding it.' Yeah, thanks a lot, Einstein." It's hard to say that without sounding sarcastic, but in this case, it was appropriate. "They ought to put that on our badges. I came *this* close to flubbing it with those eggs time and time again."

"Ever the self-critical cynic," LaFleur replied, not looking up. "There aren't ten agents I can name who could have gotten the better of a wizard operating in our midst like that. Maybe five people in the world can claim they've been face-to-face with a dragon of that status and power."

"Yancy would have gotten the better of me if it hadn't been for...you know."

"The cooperation of Archades is a dangerous, tenuous thing," LaFleur said. "But"—and here was a man who would have rather swallowed *his* tongue than say what followed—"he has proven that he'll honor his word and provided some value to your efforts. I'm proud that you didn't give him free rein, and that you are wary. Please don't forget what you're dealing with."

"I won't," I assured him. He nodded, coming close to looking relaxed. He even leaned back in his chair, studying my face. The stitches had come out of my forehead, but the thin white scar was probably going to be a longtime feature. I'd left it without real good care for too long.

"Why don't you take another week?" he said. "Come back well rested. I'll have some basic investigations for you to follow up on, nothing too demanding."

"I appreciate the offer," I said, standing stiffly. I'd be limping around for at least another month, but I was too stubborn for a cane and too stupid to stay off the leg entirely. "I'll be back at work tomorrow. I just wanted you to have this as soon as possible."

"Thank you, Special Agent Morris," LaFleur said, standing to shake my hand. I turned to limp away. "Oh, and Diane?" I glanced back at him, hand on the door handle.

"Yes, sir?" I asked.

"Nice boots."

"Thank you, sir. They're bespoke."

## A word about the author...

Robert Gainey is a born and raised Floridian, despite his best efforts. He lives and works in Northeast Florida, where he spends as much time as possible writing.